Praise for *The Finders*

"It's a good tale, both warm and tense, with

—*Star Tribune*

"I enjoyed every minute of this serious thriller interspersed with humor. It's got dogs, the fascinating world of scent detection, and a mystery with lots of twists and turns. What more could a dog lover want?"

—*Dogster*

"Burton keeps *The Finders* on a short leash as he melds solid suspense with a strong look at how service dogs work and enhance investigations."

—*South Florida Sun Sentinel*

"*The Finders* gets its hooks into you and doesn't let go."

—Spencer Quinn, author of the *New York Times* bestselling Chet and Bernie series

"If you're a dog lover, you'll love *The Finders*. If you love a thriller with a particularly nasty villain, you'll love *The Finders*. And if you love both dogs and thrillers, well, have I got a book for you."

—F. Paul Wilson, *New York Times* bestselling author of the Repairman Jack series

"*The Finders* is an irresistible, expertly woven thriller about a canine savant, her loving master, and the insidious killer after them both. Compelling and suspenseful . . . I loved it!"

—Christopher Golden, *New York Times* bestselling author of *Ararat* and *Snowblind*

"*The Finders* boasts a compelling roller-coaster ride of a plot, but ultimately the star of the show is Vira, a fierce beauty of a canine that dog lovers will find impossible to resist."

—Paula Munier, *USA Today* bestselling author of *A Borrowing of Bones*

"I was hooked on *The Finders* before finishing the first paragraph. Burton's novel is steeped in authenticity, entertainment, and education at the forefront of this twisty thriller. Unforgettable!"

—K. J. Howe, international bestselling author of *Skyjack*

"Unique voice and compelling characters, both human and canine, make *The Finders* a terrific thriller."

—Margaret Mizushima, author of the award-winning *Burning Ridge: A Timber Creek K-9 Mystery*

ALSO BY JEFFREY B. BURTON

The Eulogist
The Lynchpin
The Chessman

THE FINDERS

A MACE REID K-9 MYSTERY

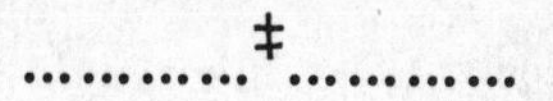

JEFFREY B. BURTON

MINOTAUR BOOKS
NEW YORK

To Barrel—
tug-of-war champion, Frisbee aficionado, literal chowhound, and the best first dog a kid could ever have asked for

Published in the United States by Minotaur Books, an imprint of St. Martin's Publishing Group

 Printed in the United States of America. For information, address St. Martin's Publishing Group, 120 Broadway, New York, NY 10271.

www.minotaurbooks.com

The Library of Congress has cataloged the hardcover edition as follows:

Names: Burton, Jeffrey B., author.
Title: The finders : a Mace Reid K-9 mystery / Jeffrey B. Burton.
Other titles: The finders : a Mace Reid canine mystery
Description: First edition. | New York, NY : Minotaur Books, 2020. | Series: A Mace Reid K-9 mystery
Identifiers: LCCN 2020001295 | ISBN 9781250244536 (hardcover) | ISBN 9781250244543 (ebook)
Subjects: GSAFD: Mystery fiction.
Classification: LCC PS3602.U76977 F56 2020 | DDC 813/.6—dc23
LC record available at https://lccn.loc.gov/2020001295

ISBN 978-1-250-79671-4 (trade paperback)

First Minotaur Books Trade Paperback Edition: 2021

10 9 8 7 6 5 4 3 2 1

ACKNOWLEDGMENTS

English-mastiff-sized kudos to my agent, Jill Marr at the Sandra Dijkstra Literary Agency, who worked like a dog to find a proper home for this puppy. And a Great Dane–sized debt of gratitude to Daniela Rapp, senior editor at St. Martin's Press, who ran the manuscript through multiple dog parks in order to make it leaner, meaner, faster, and more fun. Other editors that teethed away at the novel include Jill Marr and Derek McFadden at Sandra Dijkstra, copy editor Sarajane Herman at St. Martin's Press, and, as always—my father—Bruce W. Burton. A heartfelt thanks to all of you. You made my tail wag.

A dog has the soul of a philosopher.

—Plato

PART ONE

THE PITCH

Dogs love their friends and bite their enemies, quite unlike people, who are incapable of pure love and always have to mix love and hate.

—Sigmund Freud

CHAPTER 1

Christine Dack was hung over.

It had been a crazy Chicago wedding weekend all right. How could it not be with her old sorority mates? Sure, even though she and Sierra had been besties from back in their AOII days at dear old Ski-U-Mah, Christine hadn't been selected as one of Sierra's bridesmaids. And everyone knew the reason why. After all, Christine had dated Brad for nearly half of college—their sophomore and junior years—and she knew Sierra remained a bit touchy on the subject. Evidently, when it came to marriage, it's not necessarily sisters before misters or whatever the female equivalent of bros before hoes was these days.

But it didn't matter. Being left out of the bridesmaid parade gave Christine more time to visit with old friends, get caught up on their lives, and, especially, to drink champagne . . . and, more especially, to dance the night away.

Christine now found herself on her early-Sunday-morning trek back to Minneapolis, cruising at seventy miles per hour down I-90 in her white pearl Miata—she had a training seminar to present with her boss and her boss's boss first thing Monday—when the nausea washed over her. Christine jerked the Miata into the right lane, thanking God there was no traffic, no one to piss off. She'd just missed the exit ramp for Egg River and figured she needed to get to the shoulder—publically puking on I-90, not the greatest of ways to start the day—but then spotted the blue sign signaling wayside rest and goosed the Miata. She was able to glide the ragtop into the first parking spot in front of the facility.

In retrospect, Christine should have caught more z's last night, but she wanted to get home with a chunk of her Sunday afternoon to spare. Christine had prep work for Monday's dog and pony show—a final review of the slide deck—plus laundry to do. Then she wanted to spend the remainder of the day vegged out in front of the TV, eating ice cream, and resting up from the crazy-festive Windy City weekend.

Christine never slept well when she'd been drinking . . . and Christine had certainly been drinking.

Toward the end of the evening, the champagne had gone down like water.

Thank God it was early and no other cars were at the rest stop. Christine didn't need the added humiliation of fellow drivers bearing witness if she couldn't make the restroom in time.

Champagne going down looks far more attractive than when it comes up.

Christine made herself throw up in the women's room. Actually, she only had to picture herself putting a finger down her throat when her mostly liquid wedding feast came gushing up like an uncapped oil well. Afterward, when Christine was done washing her hands and face and neck, she forced herself to take a long drink from the fountain to hydrate and get her body fluids back in whack.

She hoped the H2O would stay down.

Oh God, Christine thought, am I still drunk?

Could I get a DUI even after six hours of choppy sleep?

Christine bought a 7UP out of the vending machine, twisted the cap off, and sipped as much as she could handle, which was maybe a quarter of a cup. Perhaps she could burp her way back to sobriety. She went outside and noticed a black van that had pulled in next to her Miata was now backing up to depart. Christine figured she must have been *indisposed* for quite awhile if the black van guy had arrived after her, done his business, and was now exiting the facility.

The driver caught sight of Christine standing in front of the entrance and waved a hand.

Sometimes she got that from guys, but today Christine felt anything but attractive.

Then she spotted a tow truck parked at the far end of the lot. A lone figure sat behind the wheel. Christine couldn't make out the driver's features at this distance, but could tell he was staring at his smartphone, probably trying to pinpoint exactly where some stranded motorist was calling in from.

She took another hit off the 7UP and watched as an old-time station wagon pulled into the spot just vacated by black van guy. Four doors opened and a family popped out—a young couple and two kids that screamed early grade school.

Christine stepped off to the side of the walkway—out of smelling distance, although she hoped the 7UP had altered the aroma and fragrance of her breath. She also hoped the air had cleared in the women's restroom.

She'd been fortunate that there'd been no other vehicles, especially cars full of females, when she'd pulled into the Egg River rest stop. And that none had arrived right on her heels. Christine knew that for a fact as when she'd knelt in her stall before the toilet—between long bouts of disposing of what appeared to be everything she'd ever drunk in her life—she'd peeked under the stall.

No other feet.

Thank God.

Christine, a minor hiking enthusiast, noticed a sign boasting of a half-mile nature walk that encircled the facility. Perfect. She could sip the rest of the twenty-ounce 7UP, breathe in some fresh air—if the air off I-90 could be considered fresh—and belch like a prize sow. No one would hear her and, if her unsettled stomach went into round two, she could always add her biodegradable two-cents to the foliage and shrubbery of this particular area of Illinois. This strolling detour might also help Christine sober up, keep her from being pulled over, and keep her from having to call in from some northern Illinois detox center, absenting herself from her Monday-morning presentation.

Christine bypassed the sidewalk, cut across the lawn to where the trail began, when the memory of what happened at the end of last night struck her with the impact of a freight train.

Oh Christ. Oh Christ. Oh Christ.

Christine cringed. Her heart caught in her throat. She almost threw up again, more from her recollection than from nausea. Christine remembered sneaking out of the Ritz-Carlton banquet room in order to use the ladies' restroom down one of the hotel's hallways. On her way out, she'd caught Brad's eye.

They both smiled as though in on a shared secret.

And when she came out of the ladies' room, there stood Brad, waiting for her.

"I've missed you," he said.

Without saying a word Christine walked over, placed fingertips on his cheek, leaned up, and kissed him on the lips. Their tongues touched. She felt his breath in her mouth.

After several seconds of quiet intimacy Christine had left Brad standing there, stuttering in her wake, and headed back down the Ritz-Carlton hallway—at the end of which stood her old sorority bestie . . . Sierra . . . dressed in white, hands on hips, tears in her eyes.

She had walked past her old friend without so much as blinking or any other hint of recognition, as though Sierra wasn't even there, and strode quickly toward the elevator atrium, and on up to her room.

Christine felt sick in more ways than one as she began her nature hike. So horrified at the remembrance she didn't look back, and she didn't notice the driver step out from the tow truck and follow in a direct line behind her.

Had she, Christine may have noticed a few simple details.

The man was Caucasian. Middle-aged. Five-foot-nine or -ten. Maybe a hundred and sixty or seventy pounds. Brown hair, receding hairline. A minor paunch if any.

Generic-looking.

Forgettable.

Average in every aspect of the word, Christine may have observed.

Hell, Christine may have said, *as far as I know, he could be everyman.*

Christine Dack never made her training presentation Monday morning in Minneapolis.

Two weeks later her Mazda Miata showed up in Milwaukee.

CHAPTER 2

Dispatch called out a suicide.

Technically, Officer Kippy Gimm and her partner, Officer Dave Wabiszewski, were being sent to a townhome in Forest Glen to conduct a welfare check, but Gimm read between the lines as the police dispatcher relayed additional information from the 911 caller. The owner of the townhome in question was one Scott Granger—Caucasian male, age forty-two, five-foot-eleven, a hundred and eighty pounds—and, Gimm noted, Granger had two DUIs on his record, the latest one recently put to rest. Drunk driving aside, Officer Gimm knew the stats on suicides—how the rate among men is nearly four times that of women and that, in recent years, middle-aged males had raced ahead of their younger counterparts to rack up the highest rates.

But it wasn't statistics or a potential drinking problem or Granger not answering his landline that tilted it away from being a straightforward welfare check, from her and Wabs checking in on some forlorn chap sipping pinot noir at midnight—pondering the one that got away, brooding about the roads not traveled—and firing off texts on shedding mortal coils to the handful of friends he'd yet to alienate.

No, what tilted the scale toward Officers Gimm and Wabiszewski dealing with the genuine article was what Granger's next-door neighbor, Mencken, phoned in. An insomniac in the adjoining town house, Mencken had gotten up to raid his icebox and click through late-night TV when he'd heard some kind of humming-vibration sound coming from what he believed to be his garage. Thinking he'd been dim enough to leave his car idling when he'd hustled his bag of burgers in for dinner—so excited to eat that he'd left his car running—Mencken had rushed out to verify, but it wasn't Mencken's Regal Sportback that'd been left running. He'd not been such a dipshit after all. Nevertheless, the humming-vibration din was louder now and most definitely coming from the townhome unit next door. Mencken hit the button to slide up his garage door and jogged outside. He had stepped onto Granger's driveway and placed an ear against Granger's garage door.

Yup, a vehicle was running inside, and it had been for God knows how long.

And that meant combustion fumes. Carbon monoxide.

Unable to lift Granger's garage door—it wouldn't budge—and after banging on Granger's front door a short eternity, Mencken had run back to his town house and dialed 911.

It was the last day of Officer Kippy Gimm's rookie year with CPD—the Chicago Police Department—so of course she'd been looking forward to a minor celebration at shift's end; perhaps a couple of cheap beers at Gamblers to get in the mood. Maybe she'd even con Wabs into tossing some darts. Gimm and Wabiszewski worked out of the 17th District—Albany Park—on North Pulaski, so when the call came in with a nearby address, she and Wabs hit the lightbar and sped toward the Forest Glen location.

When their squad car stopped at the townhome address, a round man in gray sweats and flip-flops was out front, frantically waving with one hand, his other pointing at Granger's garage door. After a brief huddle with the man in the flip-flops, Wabs rushed to the front door while Gimm slipped around the squad car to grab the Halligan bar from the trunk.

"I'm worried about the woman and boy who live there," Mencken said.

Gimm froze. "Granger was married?"

"I don't know—girlfriend or something. Her and her son have been staying there the last month or so." Mencken pointed at the single vehicle in the double-car driveway. "That's Granger's Mercedes CLA, so I think he's got an old Chevy C/K running in the garage, which explains the loud idle. Them older trucks with no catalytic converters make the carbon monoxide poison more deadly."

Gimm figured neighbor Mencken to be some kind of gearhead hobbyist like her father. "What's the girlfriend drive?"

"A blue Ford Fiesta," Mencken replied. "And I hope to God it's not in the garage with the C/K."

By the time Gimm ran the forcible-entry tool to the front door, it had become obsolete. Officer Wabiszewski had gone macho man and breached the town house with two kicks to the doorframe.

Inside, both cops jogged a half-circle around the family room, past the steps leading to the upper floor, and into an empty kitchen. A nearly drained fifth of Jack Daniel's sat atop the center island. The sink was an elephant's graveyard where spent Corona bottles went to die. It turned out the kitchen wasn't empty, as once they passed the island they discovered the owner—Scott Granger—spread-eagled on the floor, next to an overturned stool.

"I've got the garage," Gimm said, thinking about the woman and her son. She stepped over Granger while Wabs squatted to check on the prone figure.

Gimm yanked open the door, banged her fingertips against the garage door opener, flipped up light switches, and dashed toward the running pickup truck—fortunately the Chevy C/K was the solitary vehicle in the garage. It was then Gimm spotted the golden retriever puppy lying atop a bundle of old blankets against the near wall, not moving, with what she took to be vomit on the garage floor near the pup's open mouth.

Gimm turned away, kept her focus on the pickup as the garage door wound upward. She jerked open the door to the

Chevy, reached in, and twisted the keys, shutting down the engine. A quick glance told her the vehicle was empty. It was then she turned around and stood over the cream-and-gold-colored puppy, looped and intertwined with the blanket, as though clinging to it for deliverance.

Asleep . . . like a limp towel.

Motionless.

Heartbreaking.

In Gimm's 365 days on the force, she'd witnessed the aftermath of drive-by shootings—this was Chicago, after all—and had once applied a tourniquet to the arm of a five-year-old girl whose only mistake had been sitting in the backseat of a car at a red light just as some gangbangers pulled up in the next lane. Gimm had also seen a man burn to death inside the cab of his own crashed auto when the heat became too intense for the firefighters to bring the Jaws of Life into play. And that time when Gimm and Wabs had once been dispatched to a retirement complex where a peculiar odor emanating from one of the units had seeped into the hallway and become impossible for immediate neighbors to ignore, and was thus brought to the manager's attention. It was the apartment unit of an elderly woman, a widow who'd not been seen in at least a week and wasn't answering her door, obviously, nor her phone, and all of the aged residents involved, the manager included, understood what that signaled.

But Kippy Gimm had been a dog lover from way back, since her father let her name the bulldog puppy—she'd gone with Rocko—he'd brought home for Kippy and her older sister one Christmas Eve. A cop's hours made it tough on pets, but Gimm figured, in the off-chance that she'd have a family someday, then there'd be one or two four-leggers as part of the clan. And Gimm loved taking care of Zsa Zsa and Eva, her sister's twin Pomeranians, whenever their family went on vacation.

If she and Wabs made it to Gamblers in time for last call, Gimm would be in need of something a bit stronger than beer.

Gimm returned to the house, stepped around Wabs as he

continued CPR on Granger, and then jogged through the remaining rooms in the split-level, turning the search into an exercise—a cardio workout—to shake free what she'd seen in the garage. She cleared the two bedrooms—master and guest—bathrooms plus the basement family room and laundry in under a minute. No one else was in the house—no woman, no son. The townhome appeared generally tidy, well kept, except for broken glass and hundreds of pennies that littered the hardwood floor of Granger's home office.

Gimm figured something had occurred in there.

She bypassed the kitchen, exited the town house through the busted front entrance, stepped down the driveway, and headed toward the concerned neighbor. "Did you know they had a dog?"

"The kid came by to show off a puppy the other evening," Mencken said. "I think they'd just gotten it."

Gimm thanked him for his efforts, gave him the bad news about the golden retriever, and told him an ambulance was on its way for Granger.

Mencken nodded and began speaking about how Granger was an odd duck—quiet, standoffish, and, as far as he could tell from various post-sunset encounters, a nighttime lush. Mencken prattled on about bad vibes, and how Granger always seemed to have something percolating beneath the surface.

Gimm half listened to Mencken's ramblings as she scanned about the yard, the driveway, the street, looking everywhere but toward Granger's open garage. After Mencken paused for a breath, Gimm turned toward him, thanked him again for his help, and warned the man against glancing into Granger's garage on his way back inside, as it was a most unpleasant scene—a horrible scene—and one that he would not soon forget.

Mencken stood a moment longer; his navel peeking out below his sweatshirt like a bashful groundhog checking for its shadow. He looked a bit gloomy, realizing he'd just been dismissed by the female cop. But Mencken heeded her warning and shuffled back into his unit without a single glimpse.

Gimm hadn't meant to be curt with Good Samaritan Mencken. He'd been very helpful, but she couldn't stand to hear another word about Scott Granger.

A minute later, Wabs was at her side. "He's dead. Nothing I could do. I think Granger was gassing the dog for whatever fucked-up reason, but the carbon monoxide seeped into the kitchen and did him in as well."

"Fine by me," Gimm said. "Poetic justice."

Officer Wabiszewski said nothing.

Gimm turned around and looked back toward Granger's garage, back toward the motionless mound of blankets and fur. She could now hear the ambulance off in the distance, dopplering closer. She ran a sleeve across her eyes and . . . *oh my God* . . . there was movement.

"Wabs," she said, grabbing her partner's shoulder.

Wabiszewski spun around, spotted what his partner was seeing. "What the hell?"

She thought it could have been a trick of light and shadows at first. The makeshift bed itself appeared to squirm and jostle, and then the scene became clear as the lone puppy wiggled out from the pile of blankets and pillows, tumbled down the side, and meandered erratically toward the driveway, walking on four wobbly legs, heading toward the two police officers.

Gimm's jaw dropped.

Unbelievable.

She took quick steps toward the garage and then squatted down as the puppy approached her.

"It's okay, Honey Bear," Officer Gimm said, holding out a hand. The little dog licked at the police officer's finger. Gimm took the puppy into her arms. "It's okay, Honey Bear," she said again, scratching behind the dog's ears. "It's going to be okay."

A moment later, the ambulance arrived.

CHAPTER 3

"The lady cop keeps calling back, Mace." Paul Lewis was the executive director of CACC—Chicago Animal Care and Control. "Says she works long hours but wants us to know she'll take the golden retriever if no one else will."

I nodded.

"I told her the dog-whisperer was stopping by today."

"Oh God, Paul," I said, cringing, "don't call me that." I'd known Paul for several years. We moved about in the same canine community. I own a dog training school, and maybe half my income comes from doing work for the city.

"It gives you an air of mystique."

"It makes me sound like a dick."

"There is that."

"So what the hell happened?" I asked, having only received the nutshell version about the maltreated golden retriever puppy over the phone.

Paul handed me a photocopy of his typed notes. "I got this mostly from the woman that had been staying at the townhome and, of course, from the police report."

Half a dozen bullet-pointed paragraphs took up the bulk of Paul's sheet. I've witnessed him give PowerPoint presentations and am aware of his fondness for emphasizing words and phrases or, if he gets really excited, bold-facing and italicizing and underlining entire sentences—sometimes even complete paragraphs. And, if Paul's had his two cups of morning coffee, he'll toss in those arrow bullets and make each of them the size of Mount St. Helens. Today's composition employed a copious amount of bold text with only a smattering of underlined nouns.

I wanted to ask why he felt the need to short-sheet italics but instead followed along in Paul's handout as he walked me through the highlights.

"The puppy's previous owners—for all of a week—were a single mother and her six-year-old son. The woman was a secretary at the same company where this jackass Granger had worked. Her and her boy had been living in a small condo with her sister—evidently, not much fun. She and her son had a two-month wait on an upcoming rental home and should never have moved in with the jackass, but the woman and Granger had hit it off at work. They'd been dating. Once she and her son moved in, everything went to hell. Turned out Granger was a classic Jekyll and Hyde—reserved and pleasant during the workday or on dinner or movie dates, but he drank to inebriation when at home. And the more he drank, the more bent out of shape he seemed to get with them . . . with the world . . . the universe. Toys left on the family room floor spelled a nightlong harangue, a bottle of face cream on the bathroom countertop turned into an endless tirade."

"The guy had them living on eggshells."

"And pins and needles." Paul continued, "But the puppy was the final straw. Early last week the woman and her son had brought home—with Granger's approval for crying out loud—this golden retriever puppy. The woman's sister worked at a veterinary clinic, so the two of them had come up with the grand scheme of breeding the pup's mother with a stud dog in order to sell the puppies off, bank some much-needed cash, as well as keep one for her son. You know how puppies are born with their eyes shut and ear canals closed—basically blind and deaf during those first weeks of life. And Illinois law stipulates a puppy shall not be separated from its mother until the pup has attained the age of eight weeks. Therefore, at exactly the eighth week mark, the woman and her son brought a little golden-furred package to Granger's townhome, setting the puppy up in Granger's previously pristine, debris-free garage. According to her, you'd have thought they had burned his place to the ground."

"She should have moved back in with her sister."

"She'd already made up her mind to run out the clock until her rental unit commenced and then get the hell away from the guy. Her observations over the course of the past month had evolved from," Paul glanced down and quoted directly from his notes, "*You sure do drink a lot* to *You really ought to ease up a bit* to *I think you have a problem* to, finally . . . *You can be a mean drunk*. As you can imagine, everything came to a head the other night, culminating in Granger kicking at her son."

"What a gem."

"Anyway, that was all she wrote," Paul said. "The woman bundled up the boy, stuffed him and a suitcase into her car, and made it clear to Granger they were finito. Though she'd packed in a hurry, it'd been implied that she'd be back for the rest of their gear as well as the puppy first thing in the morning . . . after the jackass had sobered up."

"Which clearly never happened."

"You know the rest," Paul said, "but the woman shared some dime-store psychiatry with me. Granger never talked about his past, but she believes he'd suffered some emotional or physical abuse as a child . . . and it warped his psyche. Instead of seeking therapy, Granger self-medicated—he drowned his hurt in alcohol," Paul concluded, dropping his notes on his desk. "I guess after they'd vamoosed, Granger got it in his inebriated skull that he'd show her a *mean drunk* she'd never forget."

While Paul brought me up to date on the golden retriever puppy I'd come to visit, I sat in his guest chair and steamed, like veggies in a pot. I didn't give a damn about Granger's childhood. In my book, cruelty to animals merits the death penalty. If I had my druthers, we'd hang the Grangers of this world in the village square like Christmas ornaments. And if this particular jackass hadn't managed to punch his own ticket—had not Darwined himself out of existence—I'd have driven to Forest Glen and popped him in the mouth.

"So what about the woman and her kid?" I asked. "Why aren't they taking the golden?"

"She feels awful about that night, said it was her fault leaving the puppy alone with the lunatic, but they were heading to a hotel. Never thought he'd do anything like that and—well, the woman and her son have been through a difficult situation, are currently in-between homes, and therefore no doggie."

"Can't blame her, I guess."

"I got the sense she hadn't told her son what really happened. They'd been through a bad enough ordeal, and she probably doesn't want to heap more trauma on the poor kid." Paul shrugged. "Said she would get another puppy from the original litter when they move into more permanent housing, probably let the kid believe it's the same dog. I suspect she's afraid, after what occurred, that the dog has special needs or is brain damaged or something."

We left Paul's corner office and headed toward the south side of the building, where the kennels were kept. Chicago Animal Care and Control was a fifty-four-thousand-square-foot facility on South Western Avenue. CACC acts as a shelter and can house over five hundred animals in separate kennels at any given time. It's also the command center for Paul's squadron of animal control officers, with a fleet of nearly twenty CACC trucks and an extended van equipped for off-site adoptions and vaccination clinics.

I have a handful of friends I consider close, of which Paul is front and center. He likes dogs and, as far as I can tell, there are only two kinds of people in this crazy world of ours—those who like dogs . . . and assholes. Paul has about ten years on me; he's pushing forty, is a good Catholic boy, and has either four or five kids—forgive my mental block, but I'm a guy—that are in either grade school or junior high. Paul's wife, Sharla, is one hell of a cook as Paul's expanding waistline can attest. As head of CACC, he always sports a suit and a tie, whereas you'll never catch me out of a pair of jeans, hiking boots, and, usually, a fresh T-shirt. Paul is what you'd call well-groomed, never a five o'clock shadow and every hair on his salon-cut head perfectly in place. On the other hand, I'm lucky if I remember to break out the Gillette twice a week or finger comb my thatch of brown after a morning shower.

"So you're going to make the pitch," Paul said as he held open a metal door leading into one of the facility's numerous corridors that were lined with kennels. Chicago Animal Care and Control housed predominantly dogs and puppies, cats and kittens, but the occasional coyote or raccoon would also be listed among its alumni.

"I'm going to make the pitch," I replied.

The kennel rooms contained five-foot-high cages on both sides of a lengthy hallway that smelled of fur, dog food, piss, and cleansers. Each cage was a four-by-four-foot square with four inches of tiled concrete on each side and a cement wall running along the back—there had never been a prison breakout. A rectangular slot at the bottom allowed food and water dishes to be slipped inside. In front of the cages ran a narrow trough, all of three inches deep, that emptied into drains and made hosing out the kennels an easier task.

I'd once made an offhand comment regarding the jail-like look of CACC's kennel rooms that had sent Paul into a huff, and I wound up on the receiving end of a ten-minute lecture on annual budgets and the dire need for volunteers. Today, I spotted a volunteer at the far end of the corridor, checking on the animals and filling bowls from a tin watering can. A dinged and dented mop bucket awaited use at a faucet station at the halfway mark in the kennel passageway—it was just a matter of time before it became a sought-after item.

The corridor was alive with the sounds of snarls, growls, and barks mixed with whines, yaps, and periodic yelps—an off-tune Von Trapp family gone canine. It wasn't as shrill as it was on other days when I'd visited the facility, perhaps a notch more boisterous than some. Whenever Paul guilts me into pulling a volunteer shift, I have the ability to tune out the noise, or, more often than not, I crank some Lynyrd Skynyrd on my earbuds.

Dogs evolved from wolves tens of thousands of years ago. In fact, the domestication of wolves set the whole shebang in motion, but somewhere along the way canine linguistics hit a fork in the road—with dogs barking while wolves continued to howl or keep quiet. Sure, wolf cubs bark, but mature wolves know that if danger is present, they should just shut the hell up and stay hidden until the threat has passed. Whereas man's best friend tends to bark at threats until they go away.

I once caught a show on TV where they mumbled something about being able to interpret six different emotions per the sound of a dog's bark—you know, anger, fear, happiness, whatnot—but I suspect there are many more.

CACC's newest arrival was located in the second kennel on the right, the first dog nearest the door, likely per Paul's instructions. Plastic sheaths were affixed to the center of each cage at gut level. These clear casings made it easy for Paul's crew to slide in a slip of paper containing vital statistics on the guest du jour—name, age, weight, sex, shots, temperament, you name it. The vitals on today's visitor referenced the puppy's age at nine weeks and a few days, but none of the other fields had been filled in.

I unzipped my duffel bag, removed a yoga mat, and unrolled it in front of the kennel cage, making exceedingly certain it dippeth not in the runoff trough, as I knew firsthand what nasty biological waste flowed down that tainted river. Working with dogs can get painful on the knees, so gear like yoga mats and a set of carpenter kneepads are my tricks of the trade. I spread out on my stomach in front of the cage, eye level with the kennel's newest resident, while Paul crossed his arms, leaned against the metal door, and watched.

I stared at the golden retriever. Despite the sound and fury of the corridor—signifying territorial disputes, greetings, alarm or fear, boredom or unhappiness—the newest resident lay silent and motionless. The poor thing was in a fetal position at the far end of the kennel. Her food and water bowls appeared untouched. Her head lay on front paws, one eye peeking out in my direction. Poor kid—taken from her mother and siblings, then a turbulent acclimation into a new family, quickly culminating in some nutcase trying to asphyxiate her.

We studied each other for a time.

"Hi, little girl," I said after a minute. "My name is Mason Reid, but my friends call me Mace. Paul told me all about you, about what happened, which is heartbreaking—a damned shame—and you look like you could use a best friend."

I took a jar of peanut butter out of my duffel and grabbed one of the numerous Milk-Bone treats that floated freely in the bag. I popped the lid, dipped the small snack in peanut butter, and shoved it into the kennel. I'd done this routine at least a thousand times. It was idiotproof, after all, who could refuse peanut butter plus Milk-Bone?

The puppy didn't move a muscle.

"I'll just let that sit there for whenever you feel the need," I said. "I wish a Scooby snack could heal all wounds, but, sadly, it doesn't work that way." I shook my head. "Anyway, it was nice of Paul to give me a call. Paul's a good guy, even if he plays blackjack like a four-year-old. You won't believe this, but he once split a pair of tens—a winning hand—even the freaking dealer tried to talk him out of it."

Still no response and I finished the story about the director of CACC's defeat at the blackjack table to fill the void.

Paul shrugged and said, "I felt lucky that night."

"I felt embarrassed sitting next to some guy who would do something like that. Anyway, Paul called because he knows I need a new best friend. You see, I had an English springer named Amie."

"Pure Prairie League?" Paul asked.

"Yup."

"But they're not country."

"American country rock," I said. "I don't only go country. You remember Jude, my Australian shepherd?"

"Great country band, them there Beatles."

"Paul's a good guy," I said again, "but what he knows about country music you could stick in a bug's nose." I refocused on the frightened puppy eyeing me from the back of the cage. "Now, Amie was a Mensa-level spaniel, a brilliant sniffer dog, but recently she got sick, renal failure—you know, the kidneys. Amie was only nine. And . . . well, now I need a new best friend."

The retriever's head had slowly risen by this point, and her two eyes now stared into mine.

"You have eyes that look like heaven," I said and stared another long second. "Elvira."

"Statler Brothers?" Paul asked.

"The Oak Ridge Boys made it famous, but it was written by a country gent named Dallas Frazier." I slipped a forefinger into the cage and pushed the peanut butter treat an inch or two in the golden pup's direction. "You come home with me and we'll call you Elvira. You're a beautiful little girl, and anyone would be blessed to adopt you. You'd score a walk now and again, maybe chase a Frisbee every night. Maybe one of the kids would even sneak you real food, but I suspect you'd also spend a great deal of time in a kennel like this one. Sure, there's nothing better than dropping a load in the yard and watching your master step in it, but that gag gets old pretty quick."

The puppy stood up and gave her head a couple quick shakes, as if to blow away the cobwebs.

"However, if you *adopted* me, Elvira, life would be different. Us two would play a lot of games, lots and lots of games—*training games*—and I'd toss treats your way every time you learned something new. And we'd master that beautiful-dazzling snout of yours."

The puppy took a few steps toward me, leaned forward, and licked at the peanut butter treat.

"You'd live with me and a few other friends. You'll get a kick out of Sue, who thinks he's King Kong, and I've a couple of short-haired farm collies—sister collies, actually—named Delta Dawn and Maggie May. They'll mother you to death. And guess what else will happen? After our training games, you'll become an HRD—a human remains detection dog. And you know what we do for a living?"

I slipped my forefinger back into the kennel. She stared up at me for another second, and then she gave my finger a quick lick.

"We find dead bodies."

PART TWO

TRAINING DAYS

Every dog must have his day.

—Jonathan Swift

CHAPTER 4

TEN MONTHS LATER

I thought she was having a seizure. She stood atop the heap of busted cement, tumbled bricks, and other rubble, her body quivering. Her eyes squeezed shut, and the trembling intensified. She shook as though caught in the clutch of a nightmare.

"Vira?" I said, taking a knee and stroking her brow, which felt both warm and damp.

Trance broken, her head jerked sideways toward me. Her eyes flashed open, and then she sat down—like I'd taught her to do whenever a discovery is made—and commenced to paw at the broken concrete beneath her feet.

Though formally christened Elvira, I'd informally shortened her name to Vira to make it easier for me to issue commands. Cream-yellow fur and round, inquisitive eyes that missed nothing—Vira was now nearly two feet tall at the shoulders and almost sixty pounds of untiring enthusiasm.

Dogs, in general, live in a world of scent and hearing, and cadaver dogs are trained to detect human remains via the scent of compounds—unique odors—given off by decomposing bodies. Decomposing human remains release nearly five hundred different chemical compounds. Scientists are still trying to decipher which of the numerous compounds really matter to human remains detection dogs, but whatever the chemical signature, it's present in fresh corpses from shortly after death to several-years-old skeletons. It's also present in a variety of tissue, such as fat, blood, and bone.

Vira has been trained to find and follow the scent of decomposing human flesh that rises up from the soil. She's been trained as both a trailing dog that can follow a scent that has fallen on the ground as well as an air-scenting dog, which can pick the scent of decomposition out of a breeze and track it to its point of origin. A good cadaver dog can find human remains in the ruins of an earthquake or a fire, as well as inside a shallow grave. They can sniff out a complex and elusive scent, such as dry bone, to, well, let's just say more moist substances.

Vira, like most golden retrievers, is as smart as Einstein. She took to finding smells not unlike my ex took to remarrying—with passion and speed. But today was Vira's first hunt—her maiden voyage in search of the departed. Some would say I started Vira too young, but she's had extensive training, and has proved to be a prize pupil in chasing down the unusual scents, no matter where I've placed them, aboveground or below.

"What have you found, kiddo?" I said, pulling on my leather gloves.

Vira continued patting her paw against a chunk of concrete.

"Yes, I'm coming."

I spray a protective film on all of my dogs' feet in order to protect and toughen their pads. I like to think the damned stuff works. In the places we frequent, I'm always concerned with any debris or wreckage—sharp, ragged, or scorching—that my dogs might step on.

I bent down and rolled the broken piece of concrete forward, like a snowball in winter . . . and that's when I saw the woman's ankle.

They call him the Velvet Choker Killer because he kidnaps young women, keeps them captive—having his way with them for months—until, inevitably, they displease him in some way, shape, or form. Then he strangles them with a thin piece of rope or laundry cord, places a black velvet choker necklace over the asphyxiation marks, and leaves their bodies for us to find as part of his warped game.

I'm not sure if I should include "us" in reference to the Chicago Police Department as my cadaver crew and I inhabit the private sector, not government, and we assist CPD upon request. Now and again—I wish more often because the pay is good—I get a gig at the CPD's Canine Training Center in Des Plaines. At the center, I spend most days training their German shepherds on the art of locating missing persons or tracking suspects who've fled the scene of their crimes. When it comes to the CPD's K-9 units, the dogs can accompany officers on patrol or are used to sniff out drugs or explosives. They can also be utilized to assist SWAT units.

Cadaver dogs, however, are a wholly different species. They're trained to smell death. And unlike the more common patrol dogs, cadaver dogs are not in daily use. Vira and I only come into play in cases of tragedy, such as today.

I call my pack of human remains detection dogs *The Finders*, and would order T-shirts emblazoned with that were we to compete in softball tournaments or get invited to a company picnic.

My canine curriculum starts out as a game. In fact, I refer to my training regimen as *cadaver games,* and whenever the kids hear me mumble those words aloud, tails wag as they race out to jump into the pickup while I grab the gear. I teach my dogs to associate the scent of death—decaying human flesh, blood, and bone—with one of their tennis balls or other favorite toy. To accomplish this, I utilize artificial scent tubes in a variety of odors: the recently dead, the decomposed, and the drowned. I also use my own blood, but, before you start thinking I'm weird or twisted and ghoul-like, it's not as though I slash my wrist, squirt a quarter cup onto the ground, and then kick a rock over it. A nurse at the local clinic helps me siphon the occasional vial—I hardly feel a thing. Many dog handlers use their own blood in order to make the hunt as authentic as possible, how it'll play out in the real world. At this point the dogs and I essentially play hide-and-seek with their scented toys on different terrains, in the light of day or dark of night, in sunlight or under a driving rain. And I teach my dogs to pat gently with a paw or sit down whenever they locate a scent's origin.

In this line of work, jumping up and down or digging can destroy evidence . . . plus, there's really no need to spike the ball in the end zone.

An old sausage shop a half dozen blocks north of Polish Village was demolished earlier in the week, taken down for a hair salon whose grand opening was scheduled for next spring. The lot had been fenced off by the construction crew so that neighborhood kids wouldn't get injured playing in the wreckage or thieves wouldn't misappropriate the crew's equipment. When the site foreman arrived at work this morning, he noticed two items that had not been present when he'd departed the evening before.

The less startling of the two items the foreman discovered was that somebody had cut through the chain-link fence in back, the secluded side of the site, shrouded by woods and a steep ravine. The more startling item was that a summer dress—blue chiffon and lace—had been tied to the front gate and left for all to see.

For those following the news about the Velvet Choker Killer, which included most Chicagoans, a blue summer dress was the last thing Kari Jo Brockman was seen wearing on the day of her disappearance, the day of her abduction fourteen weeks earlier. And, to make matters worse, a sixteen-year-old by the name of Becky Grohl had gone shopping for makeup after school this past Monday and never returned home. Her parents' rusted Saturn, which Becky had driven that afternoon, was found abandoned in the mall's parking lot. The physical description of Becky Grohl fit the Velvet Choker

Killer's M.O., which did not bode well for the missing Kari Jo Brockman.

The foreman had immediately called Chicago PD. An hour later, CPD called me, and Vira and I came running.

We sat on the curb beside my pickup, an eight-year-old Ford F-150 with a supercab for the dogs as well as four-wheel drive to get us in and out of some of the crazier spots we've been asked to search. I gave Vira a playful yank on the tail and, when she looked my way, I scratched behind her ears and kept repeating, "Good girl. Vira is a good girl."

Quite frankly, I'd been bowled over by my young dog's performance. Vira had all but run to the spot where Kari Jo's body was concealed and then, outside of that initial quaking episode—probably when she realized the odor didn't stem from a tennis ball this time round—Vira began speaking to me, sitting and patting the ground, letting me know that this was most definitely the spot. We sat curbside and waited in case the investigators wanted what would be the world's briefest statement on how my brand-new cadaver dog had discovered her first body in an astonishing two minutes—record time.

I shouldn't have been so surprised. A week or two after bringing Vira home, I had a newbie class in Schaumburg and took her along with the rest of the gang. I switched between Maggie May and Delta Dawn as we walked through some basic commands that dog owners should know. Sue stood nearby and stared into the auditorium of people and pets as though he was with the Secret Service—all he needed was a pair of sunglasses. As Maggie and Delta demonstrated a handful of commands—come, sit, lie down, drop it, wait—a string of chuckles drifted across the room. Instinctively, I ran a sleeve across my nose in case I had anything repugnant hanging there, but as Maggie demonstrated how to roll over, the amusement grew louder. I glanced about and, sure enough, there was Vira rolling over.

Evidently, and behind my back, she'd been mimicking the exact commands Maggie and Delta had been performing.

"Looks like we've got us a show-off," I said to the class, but bent down next to Vira, gave her a small snack, and scratched under her chin. "That's amazing, Vira." At that point I'd not even begun working with her; I was still giving her time to acclimate to her new family. "Pretty darned amazing."

Vira gave a half bark.

"Hush, Vi," I said, scratching at her neck, lost in thought. I was teaching an obedience training class in Buffalo Grove in the early afternoon, and I didn't have the roster of who'd already paid versus who'd registered to attend and hadn't yet paid. Business matters like that were forgotten in our haste—Vira and I had jumped into my pickup as soon as I'd gotten off the phone with CPD—so now we'd need to haul ass back to my home in the small village of Lansing before heading out to the Buffalo Grove location. I was doing mental gymnastics over the quickest route to take.

Vira began growling. I snapped out of my internal deliberations and looked up. There were five police cars, a couple of unmarked ones in the mix, and an ambulance. I suspected they would shortly be bringing Kari Jo Brockman out in a body bag. Across the street, a crowd had formed, restrained by a police line, and it was the crowd that appeared to be the focus of Vira's mounting discontent.

"What's up, girl?" I asked, unsure exactly what was happening. I looked about the faces across the street, their attention now leveled back our way.

Her growl evolved into a series of snarls.

"What am I missing, Vira?"

She stared question marks at me a long second, then flipped her attention back to the crowd of gawkers. She lifted herself up from the curb, full height, her body taut, the fur on her back rising, now barking continuously at the gathered horde.

I looked again at the throng of people, searching for movement, wondering what the hell had set her off. Then, as though shot from a cannon, Vira flew across the street, tearing her leash from my hand. The crowd split in half, a Red Sea of pedestrians parting and running from the crazed dog coming for them. But Vira's attention was centered on one particular man, a guy in dark jeans and a blue denim shirt, a guy who tripped backward over his own feet and brought up an arm as Vira leapt for his throat.

"Stop, Vira! Stop!" I screamed, racing across the street. I latched onto her leash with one hand, her collar in my other, and stumbled backward myself, using all my strength to pull her from the carnage. Paramedics spilled out from the fenced lot and rushed toward me, past me, to render first aid to the young man writhing on the pavement in a deepening puddle of his own blood.

I had my dog in a bear hug and began backing toward my pickup truck, trying to digest the horror I'd just witnessed.

My golden retriever had torn a man's eye from his socket.

CHAPTER 5

"I got the kill order."

"Get me a day, Paul," I said. "One day."

"If an ambulance wasn't already on the scene, Mace, that guy could have died."

"She's not an attack dog, you know that. No aggressive temperament, no predatory instincts, no territorial bullshit. She's up to date on rabies." I shook my head. "Something's going on here, Paul. She saw something."

He stared across his desk at me. "You and I both know about her past."

I tossed up a hand. "She was only nine weeks old back then."

"But she mauled the living shit out of that guy today."

"Just give me twenty-four hours," I pleaded.

Vira and I had been inseparable since that first day at Paul's CACC kennels. In retrospect, that's probably why he initially contacted me about Vira. Paul knew what I was going through back then; he knew I needed a new project to distract me. Vira not only helped me get through Amie's premature death, a devastating blow, but, you see, earlier that very week I'd finally given in, called the whole thing quits, signed the divorce papers and returned them to my wife. My ex, Mickie, had pushed for a separation and—after a few months of floating that trial balloon—decided it might be best to separate on a more permanent basis. I felt like a fish who'd been filleted alive and tossed in the gut bucket—still breathing, but not really—and suddenly there was this poor little kid that desperately needed my help.

As it turned out, I needed hers, too.

Together we climbed out of a dark spot.

And now the poor kid was back in a cage.

"Look, Paul, if I can't figure this out, I'll come back and . . ." My voice broke. "I'll come back and put her down myself."

"You know these freaks like to stand in the crowd and watch their work," I said. "That's like Serial Killer 101."

I was at Chicago PD on South Michigan talking to the lead homicide investigator on the Velvet Choker case, a black detective named Hanson.

"We already looked into him. No record. The kid drives a school bus and delivers pizza part-time while saving for college." Hanson looked haggard, likely catching hell from all sides on Homicide's lack of progress in the Velvet Choker case. "We've got video of the looky-loos from each of the other crime scenes and the kid's not in them. We've been hoping for repeats in the different crowds, but no such luck."

"But that's just the immediate crowd. At the other scenes, this guy could have been sitting at a bus stop half a block away or in a parked car using binoculars."

"Your time would be better spent contacting your insurance company." The investigator shook his head. "Your dog maimed that kid for life and, as the owner, you're liable for the kid's injuries. What with medical bills, rehab, mental anguish, and all that other lawyery bullshit, that kid's going to own your ass."

It was obvious Detective Hanson didn't enjoy the dog handler telling him how to do his job. I looked at the detective a long instant, taking in the round face on the thin body, and would have bet two bits it was the result of recent dieting. Hanson leaned forward, expecting a response, likely hoping that, like the average Joe, this would be the time where I'd thank him for his time and head toward the exit.

"If he delivers pizza and drives a school bus, what business did he have hanging out at the construction site, especially at that time of the morning?" I said. "That's way the hell off his beaten path."

Detective Hanson leaned back in his chair and turned a frustrated sigh into a Broadway production.

"Are you checking his clothes for any DNA?"

"Clothes? You mean the clothes drenched in his own blood?"

"Then how about his car?" I asked. "Did you check the trunk?"

"Right, top of my list," Hanson replied. "Hey, kid, I know you're missing one of your peepers and the use of an arm, but we need to validate your parking."

"Why do you keep calling him 'kid'? The guy looks like he's pushing thirty."

"That *kid*," Hanson said, in a tone that didn't bode well for me, "has had a hell of a tough life. His parents died in a car crash when he was four, and he's lived with his grandmother ever since. He's got a sister—two years younger—who we've been trying to contact. Quite frankly, it looks like she took off after high school and just kept going."

"What about his grandmother?"

"We've left a message, but haven't heard back."

"No one's at the house?"

"We sent a car there and no one answered. Granny's seventy, so she's probably out and about shopping or visiting friends, or at church or on one of those bus expeditions for seniors. Hell," Hanson said, waving a hand in the air, "maybe she still works, but we don't know that because the poor bastard keeps going in and out of it at Mercy Hospital on account of your goddamned dog chewing his eye out."

"Did you go inside and check the house?"

"No." Hanson looked as though he'd bitten into a lemon.

"Why not?"

"Why not? You want to know why my men didn't B and E after granny didn't come to the door?" Hanson now looked as though he'd been beaned in the face with a bag of lemons. "Because fuck you—that's why not."

I sat in silence, fully aware of incoming glances from Hanson's colleagues. My eyes settled on the detective's desk. In the mishmash of Velvet Choker case files sat a single photograph of him and two kids at what appeared to be a theme park. There was no corresponding wife hovering about in the picture and Hanson wore no wedding ring.

Probably divorced, like me.

"Look, Reid," Hanson shifted to a more conciliatory tone, "I understand the squeeze you're in, and I've granted you all of this time—done you a solid—because of all the good work you've done for us in the past. Okay?"

I gazed at his desktop and nodded.

"But you need to take a hard look in the mirror instead of wasting my time," the detective continued. "The kid's attorney will go after your homeowners' insurance or umbrella coverage or whatever canine liability policy you've got and then, after that, he's going to sue you personally. You can lawyer up and fight it, but the jury—especially in a civil case—they're going to find for the poor bastard with the missing eyeball." Hanson stared at me. "That's what you need to be focusing on . . . not dicking around here."

CHAPTER 6

The kid's name was Nicky Champine and, sure enough, the "kid" was a youngish-looking thirty-two-year-old. He lived with his grandmother in a single-story rambler in Bridgeport, up near Bubbly Creek. Night had long since fallen as I drove to his home address. Hopefully the darkness would cover what I planned on doing. Otherwise I'd be mourning Vira's death in a jail cell. Luckily for my plan, the lane twisted and dead-ended at the Champine property, with an acre or so of crabgrass and weeds between him and the next nearest house.

Finally, something had spun my way.

Make that two somethings. The moon was a lightless splinter. I parked across the road from the Champine house and sat thinking about Vira. How Vira had kept me jumping, kept me occupied, and helped fill an empty spot in my heart these past ten months. And I remembered that first night as though it were yesterday. I'd set a bed up for her in the corner of what passed for my trailer home's master bedroom. I'd been sound asleep—passed out, actually; cheap beer—when a soft whining raised me from my stupor. I stumbled about, somehow managed to pick her up, and tripped backward onto the bed. When the dust settled, I had an arm around Vira and scratched at the back of her neck with my free hand.

"We'll get through this," I remember saying as I scratched her neck. "We'll get through this, girl."

During Mickie's reign, dogs had not been allowed on the bed, but after that first night, Vira claimed squatter's rights over Mickie's side of the bed. My collies, often Maggie and sometimes Delta, would join her. Sue could be counted on to march in, voice his displeasure at the breakdown in protocol, before retreating to his throne upon the living room couch.

My ex says I'm an introvert, believes me to be detached and distant from contact with my fellow homo sapiens. Mickie had pointed out on more than one occasion that I got along better bonding with those of a four-legged variety.

And I can't argue with that.

While Detective Hanson read me the riot act on South Michigan Street, I kept my head down and nodded at what seemed to be the appropriate moments, but my true focus lay on his desktop. Papers were splattered across the surface—case files—in a manner only the detective could decipher. However, as I sat down on Hanson's single visitor chair I noticed a single slip of paper off to the side and away from what I assumed were the most recent Kari Jo Brockman reports. It was a driver's license enlargement of the man Vira had attacked this morning. So as I nodded along with the detective, I focused on the driver's license. It was difficult reading it from the reverse side of Hanson's desk, but I made do.

And I burned Champine's name and address into my memory.

I'd brought Sue along with me, my black and tan German shepherd . . . my male German shepherd. I wish to this day I'd not named him Sue after the Johnny Cash song. Anyone who checked under Sue's hood came away with the inevitable question—*hey, wanker, why'd you give your dog a girl's name?* Even after hearing my Johnny Cash dissertation, they'd still stare at me as though I weren't right in the head.

Maybe they had a point.

Not unlike the protagonist in Johnny's song, Sue was

our pack's alpha male. He strutted about my trailer, chest out, exerting his dominance over the other members of the household—all of us lesser betas—as well as presenting his Old Testament–like editorials on passing cars, squirrels and rabbits, mailmen, the doorbell, and the sound of toast popping up. Quite frankly, Sue wasn't that much of a human remains detection dog, but he scared the living piss out of any marketers that happened to stop by my trailer.

In short, Sue was perfect for tonight's task.

My gut told me Vira didn't attack Nicky Champine without cause—no way, not in this universe. I tapped Champine's home phone number into my cell and let it ring. No answer. No flipping over to voicemail. No lights came on. No movement. Nothing. Sue and I slipped out of my F-150. Gingerly, I picked up the sledgehammer from the bed of my pickup. The two of us darted across the yard and leaned under the front window. Sue looked up at me as though I'd lost my mind, but fortunately he kept quiet.

I called the number again. This time I could hear the ringing coming from inside the Champine house. After a dozen rings, I clicked off.

I'd already peeked in the mailbox—junk mail from, ironically, a pizza place as well as a pre-approved credit card for Eunice Champine. And speaking of the old Champine woman, where in hell was she? It was too late for church and I doubted she worked an overnight shift. Had she finally received the news and rushed to the hospital to be by her grandson's side? Or was she still oblivious and away somewhere? On an excursion?

My parents were strict—definitely never-spare-the-rod-and-spoil-the-child types—but the running joke in the family was how much my siblings and I loved being palmed off to be spoiled by the grandparents. Didn't matter which side, because both sides let us get away with murder.

Would Grandma Champine let Nicky get away with murder?

Detective Hanson was correct. I faced financial ruin, but Vira's fate was much more imminent and I didn't believe—not for a nanosecond—that she'd picked Nicky Champine at random out of the crowd and accosted him for no reason whatsoever.

Moreover, the Velvet Choker Killer's latest victim, Becky Grohl, was still missing.

I quietly stepped up onto the stoop, rang the doorbell, and listened. Sue sat a few feet back, following the night's proceedings like an owl scanning for mice. I rang it again, and then again, and again. Then I propped open the screen door with an elbow and rapped hard on the front door with my knuckles. I repeated this several times before I began hammering on the door with my fist. I continued pounding for a half minute and, though there was about eighty yards between the rambler and the next nearest house, at this time of night I began to fear that some of Champine's up-the-block neighbors might come outside to check on the ruckus.

I leaned an ear against the door. I heard no movement from inside.

The house was dead.

CHAPTER 7

Time for the heavy work.

I picked up the sledgehammer and stood before the front door like Babe Ruth in the batter's box—at the point of no return. I needed to get inside Champine's house with as few strikes as humanly possible, lest neighbors spill outside or cut to the chase and call the police. I took a swing—hard as I could—hitting the deadbolt full on. The door shook and swayed, but stayed in its frame. Christ, it had been loud. I wanted to grab Sue, flee for my pickup, and get the hell out of here, but instead I stood still for several minutes, staring across the property lot at Champine's neighbor's house, watching for any lights to pop on, for any sign of movement.

After granting potential light sleepers a few more moments to drift back into unconsciousness, I used the hammer like a battering ram—shorter distance, less sound; more thump than thunder—smashing hard into the space between the deadbolt and the doorknob. On the second punch, the door shattered inward. I paused a long second, listened for sirens, glanced about the street for any curious passersby.

I gripped the sledgehammer with white knuckles and, sweating from exertion mixed with fear, softly stepped into Nicky Champine's home.

Penlight in mouth, I carefully shut what remained of the front door—so nothing would look questionable from the street—located a nearby light switch, and flipped it on. The living room looked as though I'd traveled back to the 1970s, orange chairs with shag carpeting and brown paneling on the walls. My German shepherd swept in ahead of me, keying off my mood, growling lightly.

Sue was ready to kick ass and take names.

He tested the air—air scenting they call it—something dogs do as much as sniffing the ground. Fry up some bacon for breakfast any morning and you'll catch your dog doing more than a fair amount of air scenting. When dogs sniff, they inhale scent particles into their nasal cavities, and their vast number of scent receptors enables them to identify thousands of different smells. At that point, not unlike running a computer program, those odors are processed by their sensory cells—by their hundreds of millions of olfactory receptors as well as by that completely amazing sense of smell receptor known as the Jacobson's organ, an olfactory chamber that allows dogs to both smell and taste at the same time.

And when a dog like Sue follows a specific scent, his nose secretes a shallow layer of mucus that helps him capture the scent particles and, as a result, he can smell better. By licking the mucus off his nose, Sue absorbs the scent particles through his mouth. In essence, licking their nose helps dogs maximize their sense of smell. But licking also helps them clean their nose from previous smells, like humans cleansing their palate with crackers between drinks at a wine-tasting party.

But tonight was no wine-tasting party.

I marched across the shag, twisted past a folding table in the undersized dining room, and entered the kitchen. The cupboards held nothing of interest—plastic dishes, bowls, and cups. The fridge contained bottles of Orange Crush, the remains of a store-bought blueberry pie, and an empty bottle of mustard. The freezer was stuffed with dozens and dozens of chicken potpies and nothing else. Not even a frozen pizza. A pantry the size of a phone booth had one shelf stocked chockfull of blueberry Pop-Tarts and cans of Dinty Moore stew.

Evidently, the Champine family wasn't into variety. It didn't appear the most nourishing of diets a grandmother would provide for her brood. My dogs eat healthier.

The bathroom was green tile, both floor and walls. A lonely towel hung on a green bar. A single toothbrush sat beside the green sink, next to a tube of Colgate that looked to have been hit by a steamroller.

The master bedroom—Grandmother Champine's room?—was in tidy condition, that is if you discounted the thick layer of dust on the dresser top and bedside table. The dust was so thick you could write notes in it. Aside from that, the bed was neatly made, curtains pressed shut, nothing on the floor. The room didn't look lived in, not for a long, long time, which went a long way toward explaining why the police were having such difficulty locating Eunice Champine.

The guest bedroom was a different ball of wax, with damp towels and blankets strewn about the floor. The room contained a bunk bed and threadbare carpet—a couple more years of wear and it'd be down to the hardwood. It appeared that Champine preferred the bottom bunk. I peeked under the bed and into his closet. A jumble of T-shirts, some jeans, but nothing of interest. Same thing when I peeked into the single-car garage, sitting empty as whatever car Champine drove that day was gone. Probably abandoned at a parking lot in Avondale—walking distance from where Kari Jo Brockman had been found—when the ambulance rushed him to Mercy Hospital and Medical Center.

That left me with what I'd been consciously avoiding . . . the basement.

Sue and I headed down the hallway, back toward the kitchen. Framed photographs had been hung on both sides of the home's thermostat and I spotted a younger-looking Nicky Champine from what appeared to be a picture taken of him for the high school yearbook. I figured Grandma Champine had been responsible for setting up this shrine. I started to look at the other pictures, but something caught my eye. There were multiple dimples—slight depressions—peppered about the Sheetrock at eye level. I turned and noticed similar bumps on the opposing wall.

What the hell?

Did Nicky Champine punch at the drywall on his way to and from the bathroom and bedrooms? I'm not the neatest of freaks, and none of the dents were terribly deep, but there were enough of them that I'd have picked up spackling paste at the hardware store and filled them in.

The basement door was off the kitchen. Sue and I crept down the wooden steps; the light from overhead was dim. Even after uncounted decades, Champine's basement remained unfinished. The odor hung thick in the air. It smelled of mold, dank and clammy, certainly in need of a dehumidifier. The main floor had been burglary-like terrifying—as in get-caught-and-do-prison terrifying—but descending the steps into the basement, feeling the drop in temperature wash over me, changed all of that. It became haunted house terrifying. I looked down at Sue. He stared back with wide eyes and a low snarl. He was not pleased to be there.

Neither was I, but Vira's life hung in the balance.

I began my recon in the laundry room. A pile of clothes lay on the floor in front of a Westinghouse washer older than I am. A couple of brown and blue T-shirts hung on a makeshift clothesline. I kicked through the dirty laundry, but it looked to be only men's underwear and jeans.

The walkout back door contained two deadbolts—interesting—as well as a motion-detector light that kicked on when I stepped outside. It seemed out of place with the way the rest of the Champine household screamed indifference. Perhaps the light was used to scare away any neighborhood kids.

I glanced about the backyard, but saw no storage shed or other structure.

I shut and relocked the back door, walked over to the steps and began my ascent. Halfway up I stopped. There was something odd about the basement, but I couldn't put my finger on it. Hell, there was something odd about the house in general . . . and something even odder about me having broken in.

Then I began to second-guess myself. What if I was wrong? What if Nicky Champine's only offense was that of being an unkempt bachelor, not unlike me, just trying to eke out a living delivering pizzas and driving a bus for some local schools? What if Nicky Champine just happened to be in the wrong place at the wrong time and my dog, for whatever insane reason, took serious umbrage at the mere sight of him? What if Detective Hanson was right? Right that I'd best forget investigating and gird my loins for the coming legal onslaught?

Sue and I should have gotten the hell out right then, jumped in the pickup and floored it out of Bridgeport, but I decided to tempt the fates a few seconds longer. There was something I hadn't finished and we returned to the hallway with the photographs and dimpled Sheetrock. Sure enough, there were four pictures on the left side of the thermostat that captured Nicky Champine in what must have been his freshman through senior years in high school. On the opposite side of the thermostat were four photographs of Champine's sister, also capturing her progression through the high school years. I got a glimpse of broad, bland features and dark brown hair, but that wasn't what caught my eye.

What caught my eye and nearly sent me into cardiac arrest was what covered Champine's sister's neck in all four photographs . . . a black velvet choker necklace—thick and wide—exactly like the one I'd seen earlier in the day, when the policemen had pushed aside enough of the rubble to make out the figure beneath. A choker like this had been left about Kari Jo Brockman's neck.

It had covered her strangulation marks.

My heart raced and I backed into the wall behind me. Then a second thing dawned on me and I lurched back toward the kitchen with Sue hot on my heels. If the basement was unfinished, why was there a wall beneath the staircase shrouded with brown paneling? Not that Champine had all that much to shove into it, but wasn't this where you'd traditionally place a closet or create some kind of storage space?

I took the steps down two at a time, hit the concrete floor, cut around to the side of the stairs, and rapped my knuckles along the partition of paneling, enough to realize it wasn't adhered to anything solid, not to beams or cement. I rapped again and placed my ear against the dividing wall. I thought I heard a nearly subliminal droning, perhaps a low moan, but at this point my imagination was two exits past Panic Town.

I stepped back, took a long breath, and swung the sledgehammer. Smashed paneling dropped to the concrete floor like eggshells; dust from thick drywall blew back on me. Several swings later I broke through, and then, like I'd done with Champine's front door, I used the hammer as a battering ram to widen the hole. I set down the hammer and stuck in my penlight.

The opposite wall was papered with Polaroid photographs. My blood froze. I found it impossible to catch my breath. I'd discovered the Velvet Choker Killer's hidey-hole. Turned out my hearing wasn't faulty. I swung my light down toward the moaning sound. Atop a cot, a solitary figure, head-leaning-upright, a girl doing her best to fight off the effects of some kind of drug.

"Heeelp meee . . ."

I recognized her from pictures that had appeared in the newspaper and on TV. It was the missing girl.

It was Becky Grohl.

CHAPTER 8

My T-shirt was quickly drenched in sweat as I worked the sledgehammer like a modern-day John Henry, smashing a hole in the wall large enough for me to squeeze through. On the inside I noticed hinges along the far corner. Champine must have rigged up some kind of hidden half-doorway to grant himself easy access. And, to make matters worse, Champine had a metal collar around Becky's neck, which, via a half-dozen feet of chain, was tethered to a plate in the wall.

I squeezed her forearm. "You're safe now, Becky. Champine's not here and he's not going to hurt you anymore."

Grohl's eyes were dull with whatever sedative he'd been using on her. She kept shaking her head as though to prove this wasn't a dream or that her nightmare had, in fact, come to an end.

I didn't have bolt cutters on me so I attacked the wall plate with the hammer. This cost more time as I didn't have much room to maneuver in this makeshift prison cell beneath the staircase. I was hunched over, didn't have a good arc for swinging, and had to be careful not to injure the girl—not more than the hell she'd already been through—but eventually I was able to bust the metal plate free from the wall. I gripped Becky under the arms and pulled her dead weight up from the cot, into as much of a standing position as the overhead steps allowed.

I held Becky until her unsteady swaying stopped and she was able to stand on her own two feet.

"He can't hurt you anymore," I kept saying, over and over again. "You're safe now, Becky."

Sue had followed me into the hidden room. He'd sat out of my way as I'd swung at the plate, emitting the periodic snarls, but now as we'd managed to free Becky, he began to growl. For all of Sue's machismo, I suspected the situation freaked him out as much as it did me.

Grohl's chest shuddered, her face a streak of dirt and tears. Her eyes struggled for focus in the murkiness of the closet room, finally settling on mine.

"You get the other one?"

"*The other one?*" I said.

Sue began to bark as I turned around.

A flash of shadow rushed at me; in the penlight, I saw something shiny in the dark figure's hand before Sue leapt between us. I stumbled backward as both *the other one* and my dog smashed into me. I heard Sue yelp, and we all went down like bowling pins, my penlight bouncing across the cement floor. Sue gave a final squeal as he rolled off me and I came face-to-face with the other one. Greasy hair in an unwashed mullet, a torn sweatshirt and underwear. I shot a left arm up in defense as what looked like something Jim Bowie had used at the Alamo plunged toward my neck. It went sloppy, sliced open my forearm, but I managed to get a grasp on his wrist.

In the haze of the penlight, I could make out my attacker as he began to win the battle against my feeble grip on his forearm. The tip of the knife edged downward, now an inch from my throat. I could smell his foul breath, like meat left too long in the sun, and memorized the look of hate and determination frozen on his face. And I knew I was about to be killed by someone who couldn't be more than twelve years old. They say that, pound for pound, a chimpanzee has twice the strength of a human being. And that's exactly what this preteen attacker felt like. As the blade began cutting into my neck, I realized I was being murdered by some savage feral-boy, some crazed juvenile delinquent from south of hell.

Becky Grohl had squirreled around us because suddenly she was behind and above him, dropping the chain that had tethered her to the wall about his neck and yanking backward. The feral-boy screamed, his arms and legs fluttering as though they were helicopter blades. I pushed myself up. Feral-boy still clutched the massive blade, and I knew where he was going with it. Feral-boy was going to stab behind himself at Becky's torso. I dived forward, grabbed his knife-wrist with both hands, and kept him from stabbing at the girl. A knee came from nowhere, pounding me in the groin, and a heel from his foot caught me in the eye. I lost hold of the wild boy, stumbling backward and down again, and Becky lost her grip.

A second later, we were back where it all began. I shot both arms upward as the feral-boy leapt upon me. I clasped a piece of his sweatshirt and possibly skin with my right fist and kept jabbing at him with my left, trying to keep his knife at bay. Then something from the darkness was on my chest, and I realized Sue was still alive. There was a low howl as my German shepherd got his teeth on the feral-boy's wrist, the wrist holding the blade. Sue didn't have enough remaining strength to clamp hard, to make feral-boy pay for his sins, but his unexpected attack startled the murderous little shit. Feral-boy's eyes widened and he paused long enough for Becky to wind the loop of chain about the boy's neck again and yank outward.

The boy flew backward, arms and legs swinging wildly, but no noise this time, the chain now cutting off his airway. The knife dropped in the commotion as Becky fell backward. I slid Sue off me, gently, and then flew on top of the wild boy. I clasped his hands, kept them from yanking at Becky's hair or getting fingers into her eyes, which left Becky free to pull on the chain, tightening the metal noose about feral-boy's throat, strangling him.

Thirty seconds later, feral-boy went limp.

A full minute after that Becky released her grip on the chain.

I grabbed my penlight off the floor and scrambled to my dog. My glorious alpha male of a German shepherd—the dog that saved our lives twice in two short minutes—lay on his side in a pool of blood, struggling to breathe.

I knelt down in the puddle of crimson and almost wept.

There was so much blood; I prayed most of it was mine.

CHAPTER 9

I heard the blaring of sirens as I carried a rasping Sue up the steps with a trembling Becky Grohl in tow, her hands clenching the back of my belt as we made our way up and out of Nicky Champine's House of Horror. Once in the yard Becky slid gently to the lawn and lay down as though taking a nap. I sank to my knees, turned sideways and vomited. Light washed over us as two squad cars and an ambulance screeched to a halt, officers poured out, guns pointed at yours truly.

An unmarked car skidded onto the dead grass and a door flew open.

"Stand down!" Detective Hanson screamed at the officers as he marched toward me. "Stand down!"

Paramedics poured from the medical van and rushed to Becky Grohl.

I looked up at Hanson. "My dog needs help."

"Jesus, Reid—you need help." Hanson waved over the nearest pair of officers. "What the hell happened?"

"Champine wasn't in this alone," I said, struggling to stand. "Check the basement."

The detective grimaced and helped me to my feet. "After you left, we did more digging. Champine drove a school bus last year in a district where one of the missing girls was from. We found his car—a beat-to-shit Pontiac—and he had laundry cord and plastic sheeting in the trunk."

Hanson ordered the officers to find the nearest pet hospital and get my dog there yesterday.

I squeezed Sue's fur to keep more blood from trickling out from the deepest of his knife wounds. My fist was scarlet, drenched and slippery, and I somehow managed to stumble to the rear of the police car where a cop waited in the back seat. I made damn sure he knew where to apply pressure to Sue's side before the squad car squealed out in search of the nearest veterinary facility.

As they pulled away, I dropped to my ass on Champine's crabgrass. Both Hanson and a paramedic jogged over.

"I broke in," I confessed, looking up at the detective, unsure of what would happen next.

"We got a warrant," he spoke slowly. "I'll make it right in the report." Hanson looked toward the Champine house and then back at me. "You look like hell, son."

"The bastards had her chained down there."

CHAPTER 10

A figure in black stood silently, motionlessly, veiled in the thickets at the far edge of Eunice Champine's property. He'd been there minutes before the initial wave of squad cars and ambulances had arrived.

And he cursed himself for being late.

The figure remained a statue among the trees and brush and watched as cars from Bridgeport PD joined the CPD squads, as neighbors from up the street, having heard the commotion, came out from their homes and milled about in little islands to witness the night's goings-on, as crime scene vans appeared and a team of CSI agents rushed inside the Champine house with their kits and cases and cameras. The figure took in the official activity—the flashing of police lights, the buzz of radios, officers and plainclothes like bees about a hive. He watched as a barricade was swiftly set in place to keep incoming news vans and other media at bay.

An hour later the figure watched as two men in CPD windbreakers carried a body bag on a stretcher into what he believed to be a medical examiner's van.

And he knew exactly what that meant.

The figure in black dropped hard to his knees.

He was in anything but prayer.

Five minutes later the figure faded backward into the darkness.

It was as though Everyman had never been there at all.

CHAPTER 11

Both Becky Grohl and I were rushed to Northwestern Memorial Hospital, where I received four stitches in the skin at the base of my throat. I looked as though I'd really gummed up a morning's shave. I received seventeen more stitches and four staples in my left forearm, which looked torn and ratty and was beginning to itch. Detective Hanson and his partner, a short guy named Marr, took my statement in a conference room at the hospital. Marr promised to drive me back to my truck at the Champine house, but things came up, and the detectives kept getting called away. I sacked out on the sofa in a waiting room of somber faces and awaited further notice from Hanson or Marr. I called Paul Lewis a few times to keep him up to date, then called Dick Weech, my neighbor down the street, apologized like crazy about the hour, told him where I hid a key to my trailer, and begged him to let Delta and Maggie out so they could do their business.

The cops had rushed Sue to a nearby veterinary facility in Bridgeport. I drove the clinic staff batshit with phone calls every half hour—mostly begging for updates and letting them know Sue's home veterinarian was on her way there to help—and got the play-by-play as Sue underwent emergency surgery for a ruptured spleen, three broken ribs, and a foot or two of stitches from feral-boy's knife. Finally, with Doc Rawson's assistance, they got Sue into stable condition. My poor dog had to have a blood transfusion, which likely saved his life. And he'd probably be spending the foreseeable future at Rawson's place.

Sharon Rawson was the veterinarian Paul had recommended a decade back. She's a genius when it comes to animal care and runs the pet hospital I take all the kids to. Nobody's better. Last year, Rawson had guided me every step of the way in the treatment of Amie's renal failure. We both sat in her office and shed tears when it got to the point where nothing more could be done for my sweet, little springer . . . and a decision had to be made. Doc Rawson's a little south of seventy, gray-haired, more librarian than pet doctor, and I live in utter terror of her sitting me down one day soon and telling me she's calling it quits—going to sit in a rocking chair, drink gin and tonics, and gaze at sunsets.

I'm sure I made Sharon's night. And I know I woke her as the phone rang a dozen times before she picked up while the ambulance rushed Becky and me to Northwestern Memorial, but good old Doc Rawson grabbed her bag, jumped in her car, and sped off to Bridgeport.

Eventually, I drifted off to sleep thinking about Vira, thinking back on how her education had kicked into overdrive after I'd caught her miming my commands at the newbie class in Schaumburg. Soon after that eye-opening experience, Vira had become part of the training team and I mixed her in with the others whenever I led orientation classes. And soon after that we began the hard work—playing hide-and-seek with the scented tennis balls.

Vira took everything I could toss at her and, in her own manner, begged for more.

The first time Hanson woke me, I learned that Nicky Champine started fessing up once he was informed of the evening's events at his home in Bridgeport. Champine took the news hard, weeping from his remaining eye as he led the detectives through his statement. The feral-boy was his son, born of his beloved sister who had died—twelve years earlier—while giving birth in the tub in the bathroom of their rambler home. The incestuous lovers had been ashamed, and refused to let anyone know, thinking they could pull the birth off themselves by boiling water and using clean towels like they do on TV shows.

It turned out, after all, that Nicky Champine's sister had never left the family dwelling; in reality, she had only traveled about fifty yards from her Bridgeport home as she was buried in some makeshift coffin of plywood and 2x4s in the woodlands that shrouded half the Champine property.

Nicky Champine claimed he never wanted to kill any of the girls he'd taken, but none of them proved a worthy replacement for his sister-slash-paramour.

"Jesus," I said to Hanson.

"Exactly," he replied.

"Wait a minute." Something troubled me. "I went through that house room by room. Where the hell was the kid hiding?"

"They've got a small attic—mostly joists and insulation—and Champine made a space up there where his kid could hide in case anyone came knocking when he wasn't home. Basically, Champine nailed down some plywood and tossed a doggie bed up there for his son to sit on," Hanson said. "Champine said the kid loved it up there, as though it was some kind of fort."

"Was the access hatch in the hallway ceiling?"

Hanson nodded and I realized the indentations in the walls came from the heels and pads of feral-boy's feet—thumping against the Sheetrock—as he pulled himself up into the attic opening.

A chill swept over me. Feral-boy was a couple of feet above my head, listening as I bumbled about the hallway looking at drywall divots and high school pictures. If he'd removed the hatch cover, he could have reached down and stabbed me in the neck with that knife of his.

The second time the detective woke me it was nearly five in the morning when he and Marr were finally able to return me to my pickup. On the ride back to Bridgeport, Hanson said that Champine's grandmother suffered from Alzheimer's and had, in fact, died in the house six years earlier. Champine didn't notify the authorities out of fear of losing the house, of losing his son, and it also kept Granny's social security checks continuing to be direct deposited into her checking account, to which he had joint access.

"I've got Vira registered in the system as having been put down," Paul whispered though no one else was around. "That way there won't be any bullshit from the cops or the court."

I couldn't sleep when I finally made it home, and Paul had been kind enough to bring Vira back later that morning. I opened the front door and she flew into my arms, knocking me backward, and licking and re-licking at my face. After five minutes of play, I filled Vira's feed dish with Milk-Bones, bacon bits, and a healthy slab of peanut butter.

"I can't thank you enough, Paul." I shook his hand for about the seventh time.

"Don't worry about it, but if anyone asks, you're the dog guy; tell everyone she's just another golden retriever you happen to have. Call her Angie after the Stones' song."

"I love that song."

Paul took a long look at Vira. "Do you think she smelled that poor woman on him? Kari Jo Brockman?"

"Some breeds have three hundred million scent receptors. Humans have only five million. For the most part, that's how dogs like Vira decipher the world."

"So you think she smelled it on him?"

"Maybe." I shrugged, now exhausted. "I really don't know what the hell to think."

CHAPTER 12

I sat next to where I buried Amie's ashes the year before, on a slight incline about twenty yards off my back deck. Plenty of sunshine, and my English springer could be close to everything that was near and dear to her. I missed Sue, who was recuperating at Doc Rawson's place. I couldn't wait to get my German shepherd back home, where he could continue to hold court over all us commoners.

I've got a three-bedroom manufactured house—a glorified trailer home without wheels—located on a nearly two-acre wooded lot in Lansing, a suburb about seven miles south of Chicago's city limits. I'd bought the place the year before Mickie and I were married. One of the happiest days of my life was the day I carried Mickie over the threshold. One of the saddest was the day I helped her move out.

Mickie and I had been high school sweethearts. They say those relationships never last, but that's not what destroyed our marriage. I love Mickie, probably always will, and though she brought a laundry list of my maddening quirks and idiosyncrasies to our marriage counselor, I came armed with only one.

Mickie liked dogs.

Sure, that sounds weird considering what I do, both for a living and with most of my free time, so let me rephrase that. Mickie *only liked* dogs. There's a Grand Canyon–sized chasm between those who *like* dogs and those who *love* dogs. Hell, most everybody likes dogs—that is until you have to deal with the poop and the piddle and the teething—where they gnaw to death your favorite belongings—and the recurrent barking, the vomit messes, the squeeze of the veterinarian bills, late-night toilet trips, you name it.

If I learned anything, anything at all, it's that on the off chance I ever remarried . . . I'd need to find someone who truly *loves* dogs.

Speaking of getting remarried, I'd heard a month back from a mutual friend about Mickie's engagement and upcoming nuptials. Of course I drank a bit too much that evening—I'm a guy, we're wired that way—and, of course, I found myself dialing her number in the wee hours of the morning. Although I knew in my gut there'd been no hanky-panky during the course of our marriage—that wasn't Mickie's style—I was locked and loaded and full of piss, vinegar, and a year's worth of profanity. It may have been the hour, or perhaps she'd seen who it was on her caller ID, as the phone appeared to ring forever. I figured it was about to flip over to her answering machine when Mickie finally picked up.

"Hello, Mace," she said, in a voice more tired than angry.

"I hope you have better luck this go-round," I said after a moment and clicked off.

We've not spoken since.

It's been four days since the incident at the Bridgeport rambler. My statement, with Detective Hanson's lending of a hand, was short and sweet: *I got there first. The house looked empty, but when I cupped an ear against the window, I thought I heard a moaning sound, as though someone were in great pain. I thought it stemmed from Becky Grohl or, perhaps, Eunice Champine—and, knowing backup was on the way, I made the decision to go in. I followed the moaning sound to the hidden room in the basement and was in the process of freeing Becky Grohl when we were attacked.*

I'm not sure if Nicky Champine—killer and kidnapper that

he is—will ever get around to suing me over Vira's attack, as the man now has other pressing legal issues of his own. And though I strive to feel sympathy for Champine's son—the feral-boy who'd never had a chance in life except to get sucked into the vortex of his parents' madness—whenever I think about what he did to Sue with that blade of his, I can't find it in me to feel sorry for the little shit. Becky Grohl is now back home with her parents; and though the press is giving the family the privacy they need, she's become a bit of a media sensation considering the way in which she dispatched one of her two captors. Becky gave me a big hug when I saw her last at the hospital.

I assume I made the final cut for the Grohl family's Christmas card list.

Fortunately, I've only appeared in the news stories as an *unnamed police contractor.* This is fine by me—not only because I'd come across so awkward and bumbling in any TV interview that they'd have to get one of the guys from *Dumb and Dumber* to play me in the movie, but, more significantly, I could potentially venture off script and wind up getting Paul Lewis and Detective Hanson in hot water as well as sending Vira to the head of the canine line for lethal injection.

I cracked open a sixteen-ounce can of Coors Light and got lost in thought as I watched Delta Dawn, Maggie May, and Vira meander aimlessly about the back porch, garden chairs, and picnic table. Of the two collies, Maggie had instantly taken on the role of Vira's surrogate mother, with Dawn co-starring as Vira's know-it-all aunt. Sue, of course, had been one part patriarch and two parts camp commandant. But today my dogs were quiet. I'd brought the girls over to visit Sue at Doc Rawson's place, but he had been heavily sedated and barely able to lift his head before sinking back into sleep. The girls all knew something had occurred, and a sense of sorrow hung over the trio.

Vira glanced in my direction and began to wander my way. She paused over the spot where I'd buried Amie's ashes, where the grass had regrown in a slightly different shade of jade. Vira bobbed her head, almost imperceptibly, and strolled over to sit down next to me.

"Hey, Vira," I said, touching the top of her head.

An instant later Vira was in my arms, wiggling about, licking at my face, doing her best to cheer me up. I had to hold her back from licking at the stitches in my neck.

After a minute, she quieted down, and I held her in my lap.

"Crazy week, Vira," I said, and took another sip of beer. "Crazy week."

As I took the chicken out for grilling the dogs began to bark, and then I heard the car pull into my driveway. Ad hoc visitors rarely appear, especially after Mickie's departure, and I pulled back the window curtain to see who it was. A CPD squad car came to a stop behind my pickup truck. It wasn't Detective Hanson, unless he'd transgendered in the past few days—as well as altered his race—because a Caucasian female officer sat behind the wheel. Something must have occurred and they need human remains detection dogs, I thought, only to immediately dismiss the notion. CPD never wastes time sending me an escort to a crime scene. When CPD calls, I bat-out-of-hell to the location they provide. The officer stepped from the car. Young, dark hair cut medium, athletic build, mid height, and—I caught myself combing fingers through my hair—attractive.

Then it dawned on me. I remembered Paul Lewis mumbling something about a lady cop that had taken a strong interest in Vira, the lady cop that had found Vira alive in that garage—where that drunken nutball had tried his best to kill her. Paul mentioned how this lady cop was interested in taking Vira, if no one else showed up for her. Three seconds later I had my dogs out the sliding glass door, off my doormat-sized deck, and sitting in the backyard.

"Stay," I said sternly, pointing at the yard but staring at Vira.

It was early evening. They could lie in the sun or loaf under the picnic table. A second later I was opening my front door, hoping my Right Guard was working, wishing I'd sprayed some on my face. I stepped outside, explaining how my maid had called in sick, and we began chatting under my awning.

"Nice shiner," she said, after introducing herself as Officer Kippy Gimm and confirmed my notion that she'd been the cop who'd discovered Vira in that pile of blankets and pillows.

"I forgot to duck," I replied, bringing a forefinger up to my eye where feral-boy had kicked at me.

"I hope I'm not disturbing you, but I wanted to ask about your dog."

"CACC put her down after she attacked Champine. They didn't even wait long enough to realize she'd caught Brockman's killer." I felt myself begin to blush as I voiced that packaged lie, an actor missing his mark and blowing the dialogue.

Officer Gimm looked at me like I was a specimen on a microscope slide and said, "I was very sorry to hear that. She was about the sweetest little girl I've ever met in my life."

I nodded without speaking, seeking to limit my deception to a bare minimum.

Officer Gimm glanced at my pickup truck and looked about the yard. "So you train cadaver dogs?"

I nodded again.

"Can I see your dogs?"

"I'd love to show them to you," I said. A drooping Paul Lewis in the unemployment line flashed through my mind. Only Paul wouldn't be receiving any unemployment checks as he'd have been fired for cause. And I'd lose my city contracts and probably wind up driving a school bus and delivering pizzas like Nicky Champine. I made a big production out of checking my watch. "But I've got an obedience training class in Lincolnshire in an hour."

"I don't mean to make you late." Officer Gimm checked her own watch. "Perhaps I could see your dogs another time?"

"Give me a call and we'll set something up," I replied, praying she'd get in her squad car and just go away.

She glanced around my front yard again and then looked me in the eye. "Is everything all right?"

"Of course it is," I said, acting all surprised at her question. I could feel my face turning red, and I couldn't seem to stop shifting my weight from one foot to the other, like a kid in line for a much needed bathroom break. "I'm just running a little bit late."

Seconds passed and she still didn't budge. I felt as though I were beginning to melt.

Mickie had conned me into trying out for *Arsenic and Old Lace* as a senior in high school. Mickie, of course, got a lead role as one of the murderous old aunts, and I got a small role as a police officer who rambles on and on about a play he'd written. Everyone involved in the production was charming—everybody hit their marks, everybody stayed in character, and everybody read their lines with great pizzazz—everyone, that is, except me. I walked onto the stage, looked out into the audience, spotted a bunch of faces staring back at me . . . and froze. Someone offstage whispered my line in order to get me going. I took the verbal cue, stood perfectly still, like an ice sculpture, and zipped through my lines so fast my entire role lasted all of four seconds. Maybe three.

The audience applauded long and loud during the curtain call; however, there was a noticeable lapse in volume—mixed with audible laughter—as I stumbled out before the footlights to take my bow.

If an audience were observing today's performance, they'd be tossing tomatoes and cabbage.

"Okay, then. I'll give you a call to come back and check out your dogs," Officer Gimm said finally and walked around to the driver's side of her squad car, but she stopped as she spotted something by the side of my house. "Who's that?"

I looked sideways. Vira sat quietly at the far corner of my house, staring back at Officer Gimm.

"That's Angie," I said after a tongue-tied moment. This fresh hell had no end in sight. I wanted to bang my forehead against the side of my trailer home.

"But she's a golden retriever, too?"

"Golden retrievers are a breed that make exceptional human remains detection dogs," I said, sounding like some pompous college professor. "They have a very keen nose."

"I see," Officer Gimm replied, her eyes never leaving Vira.

A few seconds or a thousand years passed slowly. I seriously contemplated bolting for the tree line, living in the woods for the rest of my life, eating worms and rabbit for dinner.

"So I drove all the way out here," Gimm finally spoke again, still staring at Vira, "and you're not even going to come say 'Hi,' Honey Bear?"

At *Honey Bear*, Vira flew through the air as though she were Superman and was in the police officer's arms a moment later, licking at her face. Kippy Gimm knelt down and hugged my golden retriever.

"I knew it was you, Honey Bear," Kippy said, her smile as big as Lake Michigan. "I knew it was you all along."

CHAPTER 13

"I'm sorry I lied," I said. Although we were seated at my kitchen table, I felt as if I were in the principal's office awaiting my parents' arrival.

"You weren't very good at it," Kippy said. "I thought about giving you some tips, but it was too much fun watching you dig the hole deeper."

"It's just that some people I know, Vira included, could get into a great deal of trouble."

"No worries." Kippy scratched at Vira's ears. "Although I may blackmail you into shoveling my driveway next blizzard."

"It's a deal."

I poured coffee into the cup I'd set in front of Officer Gimm, and then pointed at a bowl full of creamers and sugar packets I'd lifted from a nearby McDonald's earlier in the week. "Hey—if you knew I was lying, I guess that means I didn't really lie."

"Sure, Buster," Kippy replied. "Whatever you say."

I liked how Kippy called me "Buster," but suddenly I got all nervous and tried to decipher if Kippy was flirting with me or if "Buster" was just a common colloquialism she used with males each and every day. I can't say I'm much of a flirt, certainly not a successful one. The only reason Mickie and I ever got together was because of that time when Mickie sent her best friend to confer with one of my high school wingmen. My wingman duly reported back what Mickie's emissary had to say: *Tell numbnuts Mickie will say "yes" if he ever gets off his ass and asks her to the dance.*

Sometimes guys—and other such numbnuts—need to be led by the nose.

"Earth to Mason Reid," Kippy said. "You still here?"

"Sorry, the pain meds make me a little groggy." In truth, I'd not been on anything stronger than an occasional ibuprofen since I'd left the hospital. Rather, I'd been lost in silly contemplations since Kippy called me "Buster" and missed what she'd just mentioned. "What did you say?"

"I wanted to thank you for going out on a limb for Vira, for saving her life."

"I'm just lucky Paul went along with it. Otherwise I'd have had a hell of a time tying him up."

"We could have used my handcuffs had I known what was going on."

After half a cup of coffee, I told Kippy about what happened when Vira found Kari Jo Brockman's body at the construction site.

"Vira is a special dog, of course, but what are you saying?" Kippy asked. "That she's supernatural?"

It felt good to have someone who cared about Vira voice it in such a mild manner as to not make me sound all batshit crazy . . . well, maybe just a touch batshit crazy.

"I've been around dogs my entire life. I thought I'd seen everything. I don't know if I'm ready to dive into *supernatural* or anything like that. Maybe if we think about Vira like we would about human beings—for every billion lunkheads farting about with a finger up their nose, there's a true prodigy. Like a Mozart or an Einstein." I scratched at my cheek. "Why should dogs be any different?"

"You know she was a hero that night in Forest Glen?"

"She was?"

Kippy had gotten the bulk of the story from Vira's initial master—the woman who'd been staying with the drunken jackass. The woman told Kippy that in the week or so they'd had the puppy, Vira seemed more interested in what Granger was up to, in monitoring him instead of hanging out with the woman and her son. Vira was always peeking Granger's way and once Granger even mentioned he got the feeling the little mutt was judging him—silently peering into his soul—and finding him wanting in some manner or another.

Of this I had no doubt.

And Vira had been a brave puppy that last night, when it all came crashing down. Evidently, Granger took sanctuary in his home office at night, surfing the web, slurping whiskey, and leaving his two houseguests to take care of the dog, to bond, to whatever. On an upper bookshelf sat a large glass goblet into which Granger dropped any gathered pennies at the end of the day. When the mother and son had first moved in with him, Granger had promised the boy that once the goblet was full, they'd run it through the change-counting machine at his bank, and he'd let the kid keep the proceeds. So any pennies the boy came across, or his mother handed him, he'd run into Granger's office and add them to the penny collection.

That night the woman had stood in the hallway watching as her son went rushing into Granger's office with hardly a glance in Granger's direction, his fist clutching a handful of copper and zinc. Her son stretched up to seize the goblet's stem, yanked it off the shelf, but he didn't account for it now being three-fourths full of pennies and the weight spun him off balance. For a half second she thought her son might come through okay as he swayed for balance, like a medieval knight giving a drunken toast, but the chalice twisted sideways, creating a waterfall of pennies, before the kid dropped it altogether.

Shattered glass and a thousand pennies sprayed across the hardwood floor.

Her son stared up at Granger—who now stood beside his desk—saw something in Granger's face, and turned to run. But he wasn't fast enough, not nearly, and the tip of Granger's right shoe connected with her son's bottom side and the boy went sprawling through the open office door, out into the hallway . . . landing at the base of his mother's feet.

And then—out of nowhere—Vira darted in front of them, coming to the rescue, offering Granger a big piece of her mind in a piercing puppy yap.

After that—the harried packing and rushed exit.

"I'll be damned," I said, looking down at my golden retriever. I flicked a pretzel off the tabletop for her to chase. "Of course she did. That's my Vira."

"To be honest, I have no idea how she survived in the garage with that truck running all evening." Kippy sipped more coffee. "Granger died from carbon monoxide poisoning. He was in the kitchen with the door to the garage shut, but the fumes seeped inside and killed him—that's how strong the carbon monoxide was. And when I first spotted Vira," Kippy continued, shuddering at the remembrance, "there was no movement. No movement at all."

"So you're saying Vira sort of died that night and came back, or had some near-death experience . . . and, as a result, she has *certain* abilities?"

Officer Gimm shrugged. "I just know my little girl's gifted, she's a very special dog." She continued scratching Vira's neck. "In fact, she's my Honey Bear," Kippy said, digging a card from a pocket and sliding it across the table. "If Vira ever needs a doggie sitter, call me. Or," she added, glancing from my black eye to the stitches at the base of my neck, "give me a call if you two goofballs find yourselves in trouble again."

Five minutes later Kippy gave Vira an extended embrace, and then stepped outside and headed toward her squad car. Her on-duty shift was soon to begin, but Gimm appeared to have a bigger bounce in her step than when she'd first arrived to question me about Vira.

"Hey," I blurted as Officer Gimm opened her driver's door.

She looked back my way.

"Would, um, maybe, you like to grab a cup of coffee sometime?"

Kippy stared back at me. "We just had coffee." Then she got in her squad car, shut the door, waved goodbye, more at Vira than me, and drove away.

I cringed, both internally and externally.

Perhaps a team of doctors could surgically reverse one of my legs so I could kick myself in the ass. I hadn't asked a girl out since Mickie, in junior year of high school when I was a whopping sixteen years old, and here, just now, I'd made such a complete buffoon of myself. Officer Kippy Gimm shows up because she loves Vira, and she's hoping I'm guilty as sin of pulling a fast one at Chicago Animal Care and Control in circumventing the "kill order," which Paul and I had indeed done, and—after a reunion that would bring tears to the eyes of Ebenezer Scrooge—idiot me asks Kippy Gimm out on a date.

If only I had a dozen bags of industrial-grade lime, I'd get in the bathtub, coat myself in the stuff, and shoot myself in the temple. Then, a few days later, there'd be nothing left of me on planet Earth.

All this time, and it turns out I'm a moron.

Who knew?

CHAPTER 14

Even though it was the middle of the night, and even though he was cutting through a hazy patch of woods, Everyman wore a black ski mask to conceal his features. Mason Reid—Dog Man that he was—would get a glimpse of Everyman's real face if the chance arose, if Everyman got lucky on this first outing . . . and then for only the briefest of seconds.

Everyman held a small flashlight in his left hand, but kept it pointed down at the hard soil to keep from stumbling into some ankle-breaking dip or hollow. In his right hand, a SIG Sauer 1911, also pointed down. His boots, jeans, and sweat-shirt were as black as his ski mask. In all his time in the Windy City, he'd never ventured into the Cook County village of Lansing before and had spent the afternoon driving about the suburb, driving about Dog Man Reid's neighborhood. Dog Man certainly had it good, a little slice of the rustic so close to the big city.

And before venturing into Lansing, Everyman had spent the morning zooming in, using Google Earth to view Dog Man's house and the nearby property from above.

As the forest began to thin, Everyman cut wide left, wanting to study the front of Dog Man's trailer house. He slowed his pace, did his best to keep as silent as possible, and reflected on what had brought him to this point . . . what had set him on this midnight hunt.

Everyman should have killed the two Champines that very first night. It would have been the logical thing to do, the most humane, and possibly the kindest. Two bullets to the head, each, and done the girl as well.

It would have saved the three of them from all the future pain and suffering.

Nicky Champine had fucked the pooch on his initial hunt. It'd been sloppy as hell—clusterfuck would be the proper term—and Champine was lucky he'd not been caught on the spot. The girl's rust bucket of a VW Cabrio had been abandoned at a rest stop off I-57—north of Kankakee—her purse kicked under the car. Nicky Champine should have further thanked his lucky stars that Everyman had gotten there first, lest Champine's burgeoning career would have been nipped in the bud by the local constables.

Everyman knew about the blind spots. Everyman lived in the blind spots.

And Nicky Champine didn't know about shit.

He'd walked about the rest area, verifying that no one from the other cars stopping to take leaks and stretch limbs held any interest in the VW convertible. And when the other cars had vamoosed, Everyman batted cleanup. Thank God the poor woman had dropped her purse in the abbreviated struggle, and Champine had panic-kicked it under her car before diving into his Pontiac and zipping away. Everyman would have hated to drill key-deep and then jam a flat head screwdriver into the Cabrio's ignition while tourists came and went.

Instead, Everyman was able to drive the girl's ragtop to Englewood, ditch it at a run-down strip mall that appeared to have more commerce taking place on the outer walkway than inside the shopping plaza. He left the doors unlocked, the keys in the ignition, and the girl's purse atop the dashboard for all to see.

Everyman figured the Cabrio was gone by the time he'd jumped a downtown bus.

He then spent a small fortune in cab fare getting back to his own vehicle at the I-57 rest stop. He'd bought a two-gallon gas can, filled it at the gas station from where he'd had them call him a cab, and told the driver he was helping his idiot nephew who'd run out of fuel and made it to the rest area running on fumes. The driver could not give a shit and Everyman tipped him forty bucks to keep it that way.

So when Everyman hunted down Nicky Champine's Bridgeport home that evening, he had every intention of killing every last soul in the house for the trouble he'd been put through that afternoon . . . for having to clean up the mess Champine had left on his stomping grounds. Everyman parked his vehicle, now sporting a set of recently lifted plates, a block away, circled Champine's rambler, peeked in windows, and, at three in the morning, he hit the front door like a hot knife slicing through butter. He had his SIG Sauer 1911 in Nicky Champine's mouth a split second before the man's eyes fluttered open. But Everyman heard the pitter-pat of feet in the hallway from where he'd just crept and spun sideways. An undersized silhouette filled the bedroom doorframe, something sharp and shiny in his hand. The shape darted forward and Everyman's finger tightened on the trigger when Nicky Champine screamed something incomprehensible from the bed.

The figure froze mid-room.

Everyman was taken aback, kept one eye on the new arrival and one on Champine as he struggled with the lamp on his bedside table. A moment later the room was illuminated and Everyman got his second surprise of the day. The kid in the center of Nicky Champine's bedroom wore cutoff sweat bottoms, a white T-shirt, and looked to be all of ten years old.

"Don't hurt Junior," Champine pleaded. "Don't hurt my son."

"Then perhaps *Junior* should drop the butter knife and lie down on the floor," Everyman said.

Over blueberry Pop-Tarts and cherry Kool-Aid—they had no coffee to offer him—Everyman decided not to kill father and son Champine. He listened as Nicky Champine told their tale. Everyman had to keep himself from chuckling at certain portions of the man's account—as that would be rude—and eventually he holstered his .45 caliber pistol.

Evidently, the two were all they had in the world as mother-slash-grandmother and sister-slash-mother had both since passed away. You couldn't make this stuff up, thought Everyman, who up till now had thought he'd seen everything. He knew in the back of his mind that shrinks would have a field day with him, but the Champine pair was off the charts.

And since Everyman wore the blond mullet wig, the Buddy Holly frames with clear glass, a John Deere hat, and a thick brown jacket, these two would never be able to pick him out of any lineup the police had to offer.

The Champines were of no threat.

In fact, by the time the sun was coming up, Everyman found himself giving Nicky Champine tips and tricks. Best practices to keep from getting caught, things to sure as hell avoid—meaning everything Nicky Champine had done at the I-57 rest stop. Everyman didn't know if he'd spared the two out of sheer delight at their bizarre nature, out of them being somewhat kindred spirits, or if he remembered how big a fool he'd been when starting out.

Everyman had started ages ago . . . in college.

The first time had been a debacle; he'd half-assed it just like Nicky Champine. Everyman had played at private detective, and followed an elderly couple home from the mall. He found out where they lived and came back to their house in the middle of that same night. Although all the house lights on the block were off, Everyman's first mistake had been parking across the street as though he were visiting their neighbor. His second mistake had been the racket he'd made breaking into the side garage door with the crowbar he'd brought along. Thankfully, the side of the house was shrouded by a redwood fence in order to hide a row of garbage and recycle bins, but after busting open the door Everyman had hidden in some nearby bushes a full ten minutes, watching for house lights to pop on, listening for police sirens, before he felt it was safe to continue.

Then he entered the elderly couple's garage through the busted side door.

And though he'd hurried, he made roughly the same amount of noise prying open the kitchen door as he had breaking into the garage. In fact, the old codger stumbled out of bed and into the hallway, flipping on the hallway light in time to spot Everyman charging him, crowbar held high above his head.

It happened so quickly, Everyman wasn't able to enjoy it. It wasn't what he'd expected or what he needed it to be.

It wasn't *fulfilling*.

He took more time with the spouse.

Then Everyman got paranoid—about fingerprints and hair fibers, blood spatter and his footprints in the bushes. And about any neighbor-witnesses. He was smart enough at the time to know he'd screwed this thing up six ways from Sunday. Everyman went into the garage, found several bottles of lighter fluid, then started in the basement, and as he backed his way through the house, he sprayed the wooden staircase, the carpeting, the sofas and love seats, the tables and walls and curtains . . . anything that would burn. Finally, he lit a chunk of newspaper, tossed it on the steps, paused to verify it took before darting out the garage, across the street, and jumping behind the wheel of his car. His heart beat so fast he thought it'd quit. But Everyman stayed long enough to spot flames through the old couple's front window before gunning it out of the neighborhood.

It had been exhilarating . . . thrilling . . . and what Everyman figured must be an adrenaline rush. He'd caught the news that morning. A fire had burned down a house, sadly killing the elderly twosome—William and Georgia Donovan—who lived there. It was considered a horrible tragedy—that is until the medical examiner performed the postmortems and found, among other nasty tidbits, that there was no smoke in either of Mr. or Mrs. Donovan's lungs.

And the fire department investigators soon found all sorts of indicators that an accelerant had been used here, there, and everywhere.

Everyman lived on pins and needles that semester, expecting the police to yank him out of class or from his campus apartment at any second. It turned out a neighbor had in fact seen his car peel away, but, thank God, had informed the police that he believed it to be the Donovan's estranged son—a drug-addled mess of a man who'd made the old couple's lives a living hell for decades. The neighbors all figured young Donovan had done them in for whatever meager inheritance he'd have coming. And since young Donovan had no alibi outside of another night of passing out, the police got their hooks deep into him.

They eventually dropped charges against young master Donovan for lack of evidence at about the same time Everyman was graduating magna cum laude.

Everyman killed the flashlight as he edged out of the tree line. He held the night-vision goggles to his eyes and spotted Dog Man Reid's pickup truck. It was the only vehicle in the patch of flat grass and gravel that, evidently, constituted Dog Man's garage. Although there were no other cars, that didn't necessarily mean Dog Man was alone, that a spouse or girlfriend or, hell, a boyfriend, wasn't sharing Dog Man's bed. Dog Man's website had been minimalistic, basically blurry pictures of various mutts, a schedule of his upcoming obedience classes, and contact information—a phone number and email link—in case you'd like to set up a training class or have your canine receive private lessons.

Everyman hung the night goggles down around his neck, retreated into the woods, thirty feet, and brought the small flashlight back into play. He cut along sideways, until he was even with Dog Man's backyard. He snapped off the light and again brought the goggles to his eyes—a picnic table, plastic yard chairs strewn about, and a lopsided gas grill that looked to be a dozen brats away from collapse. Dog Man's yard arched upward in a slight mound before flattening out as it worked the fifty-odd yards toward the woodland, toward where Everyman now stood.

Dog Man's place had a small deck, raised maybe two feet, with only a sliding glass door to keep the night away. He let the goggles dangle around his neck and stared at the back of the trailer home. A gap between the drapes covering the sliding glass indicated a light or two had been left on inside.

But everything else indicated the household was lifeless . . . sound asleep.

This was the opportunity Everyman had been hoping for—to score a hole in one. The sliding glass door would be child's play. He could get through that entryway without breaking stride. Once inside the trailer home, and once inside whatever passed for a master bedroom, he'd take out whatever gender of houseguest, if any, with whom Dog Man shared his bed. This would wake Dog Man up of course, unavoidable, but that was okay. Then, he would make Reid pay for what had occurred at Champine's rambler.

He wanted Dog Man Reid to see his face—his true face—before he shot him in the mouth.

Everyman raised his SIG 1911 and stepped into Mason Reid's backyard.

CHAPTER 15

I woke with a start.

I'd slipped down on the sofa, head lopsided on a cushion . . . my heart pounding. My eyes focused on the TV in front of me. Some home fixer-upper show—the kind Mickie had gotten me addicted to—droned on with the volume set at five. I poked at the clicker until the current time displayed on screen.

2:30 a.m.

I'd been having nightmares lately, weird and surreal. Something—a mishmash of ogres, beasts, or some other monster—was always after me, breathing down my neck, and reaching out with gigantic arms or spider legs or tentacles or whatever. None of the dreams made a whit of sense, and I knew they stemmed from my interactions with Nicky Champine and his feral son, nevertheless, I'd taken to nodding off on the sofa—keeping Sue's spot warm for him, I guess—with the TV on low as well as a light from the kitchen.

Vira growled—low and guttural—her warning pitch. And then I realized it wasn't a nightmare that had woken me.

I jumped forward, peeked out the front window, and slapped the porch light on. No one was out front.

"What is it, Vira?" I asked.

My golden did a one-eighty, turned toward the pet door, and began to bark. Delta and Maggie came in from the bedroom, twisted about in concentration, and then joined in with Vira, facing the back door and adding their voices to the cacophony.

"Quiet," I said, killing the kitchen light and TV, making the room dark, making it harder for anyone trying to peer inside.

Something was out there all right. In back, maybe near the woods where I do some of our HRD training. We did get the occasional deer and opossums. Not long ago, Sue had treed a raccoon. Frankly, the kids could give a shit about mere squirrels and chipmunks and most rabbits—unless the little critters pushed the envelope.

And the little critters never felt the need to push the envelope, especially around Sue.

But what worried me most was, some years back, I'd seen coyotes—and more than one. As a result the pet door gets shut down at night. Coyotes can be devious bastards if desperate for food. They can bait dogs, lure them away from their homes, and get them out in the open where the coyote pack can circle their prey.

At that point it's a one-sided fight and over quickly.

I hit the deck light, cut into the back bedroom, and pulled aside an inch of curtain. I scanned back and forth. Nothing on the deck or on the lawn that I could see. Perhaps the barking had scared away some deer. Perhaps a raccoon heard Sue was away and stopped by to thumb his nose and flip us the bird. I worked my gaze farther across the yard, toward the tree line, away from the deck light and toward the darkness.

Maggie and Delta stood in the doorframe watching me while my golden stood sentry at the pet door. And then Vira started in again, a throaty snarl from her perch at the sliding glass. She was informing me that whatever was out there had most certainly not gone away. Vira began barking again and the two sister collies ran back to the living room to join in the choir.

This time I didn't hush them.

The mind wanders down dark passageways in the middle of the night, dark thoroughfares that would be laughed at in the cold light of day. I was frightened. And Mickie was no longer here to help me shrug it off. Quite frankly, I wanted anything or anyone out there in the dark to hear my snarling girls—to hear them loud and clear, and in no uncertain terms—like a blinking neon sign on a dark Vegas night . . . with the sign flashing: *BEWARE OF THE DOGS*.

My eyes returned to the darkness, to scanning the tree line at the outer edge of my property. I no longer thought of coyotes trying to draw my kids outside. I didn't know what to think but kept staring across my parcel of land, hoping for an answer that would make me giggle and allow me to tease the girls for causing such a stir, but no such . . . Jesus Christ . . . I damn near leapt backward but clawed at the windowsill. A shape—I'd taken for some bush or busted tree—receded back into the haze, and farther back, fading away into the shadows.

By the time I was finally able to breathe again, the dogs had settled, growls tapering off to silence.

And though I flipped on all exterior lights, and though I shut and locked all windows, and though I double-checked all doors, and though I had three damned good watchdogs, I didn't sleep a wink the rest of the night.

CHAPTER 16

Everyman backed into the tree line at the first snarl.

He stood motionless, listening as the growls grew louder and a light on the front side of Reid's trailer popped on. He knew that Champine's kid had taken out one of Dog Man's cadaver dogs. He wondered how many Mason Reid had left. Everyman didn't sweat one dog. He'd become pretty handy with the SIG 1911. And he might even be able to hold his own with two of Reid's mutts, but he suspected a third one might eventually connect with an artery.

Especially if Reid had another German shepherd, like the one he'd seen at Champine's house.

As if to answer his query, the dog began to bark and was quickly joined by at least two or three others. The lights then went off in Dog Man's trailer and Everyman took another step backward. The pack of dogs quieted and the deck light came on, illuminating the yard, but by then Everyman had positioned himself far enough back, in the shadows . . . of the shadows.

Can you see me? Everyman knew Dog Man Reid would be staring outside, looking left and right, trying to ferret out what was causing the ruckus—the anarchy—and eventually squinting his way.

Can you see me, Dog Man?

* * *

Everyman had been there that morning, at the demolished sausage shop north of Polish Village. He'd seen firsthand what Dog Man's golden retriever had done to Nicky Champine. He'd also seen the aftermath of what Dog Man and his German shepherd had done at the Bridgeport house near Bubbly Creek.

That had been a most unpleasant day.

Everyman had been on his way to the office, wearing his everyday mask—his true face—when he heard the call on the police scanner he kept in his car. A summer dress—blue chiffon and lace—had been tied to the front gate at the construction site. The police feared it was the work of the Velvet Choker Killer.

It was out of the way, but Everyman had a certain amount of leeway at work, so he got in the turn lane at the light and took a morning detour. He sat in his car, down the block, and watched the gathering crowd. He watched as a young guy in a pickup truck parked out front of the construction site, and as the young guy and his golden retriever were hustled inside by a pair of cops in blue.

And then he couldn't believe his eyes.

That goddamned Nicky Champine was intermixed in the crowd of onlookers gawking at the police activity. It was one of the first things he'd warned that numbskull against ever doing.

Jesus Christ—he should have killed Champine that first night in Bridgeport.

Everyman sat and steamed. He was so pissed off he thought of doing something stupid himself. He thought of walking over and yanking Nicky Champine away from the ad hoc get-together, but Champine wouldn't recognize Everyman's true face.

Champine only knew him as John Deere hat, blond wig, and black glasses.

After an instant, he knew he'd be damned before he'd ever show fuck-up Nicky Champine his true face.

So Everyman watched as the scene unfolded. He watched as the Dog Man came out with his golden retriever and figured they'd just found the girl. Everyman watched as the cadaver dog became agitated, began barking uncontrollably. He watched as the golden retriever charged across the street.

And he watched as the dog ripped into Nicky Champine.

So I guess that's that, he thought after the ambulance carted Champine's ass off to the nearest hospital. Everyman went on to work and spent the rest of the morning drinking tasteless coffee and staring at his monitor. He had no doubt that sometime soon the authorities would get around to popping open Nicky Champine's rambler, and then they'd be in for one hell of a discovery. But it wouldn't blow back on him as the Champines only knew Everyman by the absurd disguise he wore whenever he stopped by. He'd never shared private information or any information whatsoever about himself with them; he'd always worn his driving gloves when he'd visited, even while eating. And all the gifts he'd picked up for them had been paid for in cash and handled with the utmost care.

Too bad about the kid, though. When he thought about it, Everyman knew the boy was five times as smart as his old man. Hell, it was only the kid that kept him from killing his fuck-up clown of a father that very first evening.

Everyman shook his head. It was really too bad about the kid.

But by lunchtime Everyman said *screw it.*

And he went to get the boy.

Everyman stopped by his home long enough to don his hat and glasses, blowing off the mullet wig this time. As he drove slowly down the secluded lane toward Nicky Champine's rambler, he tapped lightly on the brake. A squad car was at the house, a single officer knocking on the front door. Everyman turned into a neighbor's driveway, backed out, and headed back up the street, away, and holed up in a coffee shop a few miles away from the Champine house.

Everyman knew the kid would never answer the door. And he knew if the cops had anything on the Champines, they wouldn't send a single officer in a squad car. But it wasn't only the police that made Everyman step back. One neighbor up the street had been out raking leaves, another neighbor was out front kicking a ball around with her two toddlers.

Too goddamn many eyes.

Not good at all for a man who lives in the blind spots.

Everyman went home. Lay on the couch, lost in thought. He'd get the kid out of the house under the cover of darkness. Make him know his father had been injured, was in the hospital, and, in a few days, when everything broke, the kid could watch the story play out on TV.

Hell, Everyman thought, maybe I can even get the kid to a dentist while I'm at it.

He made it back to Bridgeport at half past midnight and—what the fuck?—there was an empty F-150 parked across the street from the Champine house. Something nagged in the back of his mind and, as he wheeled his vehicle around, it occurred to him. The damned pickup looked suspiciously like what that dog handler had been driving at the crime scene this morning in Avondale.

Which meant cops.

It had to . . . but where the fuck were they?

Everyman parked where he had that first night—when he'd come to kill—on another block, and, with flashlight aimed at the ground, he cut through the woods, coming out on the edge of Nicky Champine's back property. He tried the night goggles. Worthless. Then he heard a noise, some kind of fracas coming from inside the rambler. What the fuck, he thought for the tenth time, then reached down for his SIG 1911.

Guess I'll be killing the Dog Man while grabbing the kid.

But then he heard sirens, getting louder, and he took a fast step back into the trees. He heard a commotion out front so he jogged through the undergrowth to get a better look. Two figures spilled out onto the front lawn. The one in front holding something . . . holding a limp dog. And then the street exploded with squad cars, one after another, and he took several more steps backward into the woods. There were so many lights now he didn't need the night-vision goggles. He stood behind an oak and watched the scene play out.

He stood motionless, observing everything, right on up until they hauled the kid out in a body bag.

Can you feel me, Dog Man? Everyman didn't get scared, not in the traditional manner, but he felt the hair on the back of his neck begin to rise. It was . . . thrilling . . . invigorating. He smiled as he took another step backward, and then another. *I think you know I'm out here, Reid.*

Everyman wished he'd anticipated this late-night uproar so he could have brought a special treat for Reid's pack of cadaver dogs—a little something he could toss into the yard for them to find in the morning. Just a little snack for them to enjoy, perhaps those green blocks of rat poison, perhaps crushed glass mixed in with hamburger. Or maybe ground chuck with strychnine.

Everyman turned from the trailer house and headed back into the woods. After a dozen cautious steps, he brought out the small flashlight. By the time he got back to his car, he had another plan in store for Mason Reid.

A plan filled with irony.

Everyman loved irony.

CHAPTER 17

Three days later Sue came home.

His absence had left a giant void in the household. There was no one around to keep all us peasants in line. I drove Sue from Sharon Rawson's pet hospital and lifted him down from the passenger seat of the pickup. He shot me his Benito Mussolini expression, chin arched far upward and disapproving, as if to demand why there was no ticker-tape parade for him. Sue's left side had been shaved into a buzz cut with a foot-long line of stitches marking where the knife had struck at his ribs and slid along his side. I had to admit Sue's scar looked badass. So did Sue. He strutted, head held high, about the womenfolk as the assemblage mingled in my driveway, making sure they each got a good, long look at his injuries.

I'm glad they don't have VFW posts for heroic dogs or I'd be driving Sue there every other night for bingo, dancing, and poker.

I continued Sue's regimen of antibiotics—mixed with his dog food—plus an application of salve along his stitch marks each bedtime. Almost immediately I realized how exhausted my German shepherd was most of the time. Sue moved slowly, and lacked the get-up-and-go he'd always had before the incident. He didn't care to take any walks, preferring to spend the days perched on the living room sofa staring at the TV. Sue didn't—or actually couldn't—struggle through the pet door so he trained me to slide open the screen door whenever he ambled over in order to head outside to take care of his business. Doc Rawson had warned me about this, about how Sue might take months to recover his energy . . . and how Sue might never be the same. This wasn't surprising, not only due to the extent of his injuries, but Sue was the oldest of my flock; he'd turn ten in November.

No doubt he'd expect some kind of masquerade ball and fireworks to mark the occasion.

Sue drove me crazy going after his stitches, licking and scratching at the stainless-steel sutures. I finally gave up trying to stop him and placed his paws in booties and strapped the cone of shame around his neck. I hoped it would be a humiliating experience, and one that would at last teach him to keep from scratching at the sutures. Despite this, Sue still managed to look all regal, sitting with his back arched on the sofa as though he were Henry VIII wondering which wife to behead.

I like to think my German shepherd lived because of Doc Rawson's veterinary magic or because he has moves that would make an NFL running back green with envy or because he's too cantankerous to die, but I knew the truth. If it had been a full-grown man wielding that butcher knife in the Bridgeport rambler, the three of us would have been hauled out of Nicky Champine's basement in body bags.

Last night I sat next to Sue on the sofa and scratched at his shoulder blades. "What do you think about retiring?"

He looked at me, and then turned his attention back to the ball game on TV. I continued to scratch at his shoulders as we watched the Cubbies strand three runners in the bottom of the eighth.

"Just give it some thought, Sue—that's all I'm saying."

They'd already removed my stitches; unfortunately, I looked anything but badass. I currently sported a thin white scar along the base of my throat a lover might question were she interested in bestowing a hickey; as usual, there were no such offers on the table. There also remained some discoloration on the skin around my right eye. Paul offered to bring over a tube of his wife's concealer. I politely declined.

Although I've spent most of my late afternoons and early evenings teaching obedience classes, Vira and I made it to a handful of uneventful hunts. One was for a lost toddler in which we searched the acres of forest behind the child's house. The trademark scent of human death is, of course, unique to human beings, which means that cadaver dogs can differentiate between human and animal remains. That said, Vira did drag me past an interesting array of dead critters during our lost-toddler search, but, fortunately, no human remains.

Thankfully, as it turned out, the child had been grabbed by her estranged father and, days later, was returned unharmed.

Paul stopped by after work for a quick beer before shuffling home where Sharla waited to fatten him up with a homemade meatloaf she'd tossed in the oven. Paul shared with the kids a handful of dog biscuits he'd no doubt lifted from CACC before joining me at the kitchen table where I had a cold Coors Light waiting. We watched as Delta and Maggie slipped out the pet door to play in the backyard and as Vira jumped up on the couch to watch TV with Sue.

"Sue's on disability, gonna roll his 401(k) into gold or Alpo or something," I said. "You got any prospects for me?"

"A new recruit for the cadaver games, huh?" Paul said. "No HRDs at the moment, unless you'd like a chubby Shih Tzu who farts like a dragon."

"I'll pass."

Paul sipped his beer and kept looking over at Vira. "You bring her to see Doc Rawson?"

"Yeah, she did the checklist. Vaccinations—up to date, duh; no discharge from Vira's ears or eyes; temperament—Vira's a happy camper; there's been no vomiting or diarrhea; and her appetite's great."

"You tell Rawson how Vira picked Champine out of a crowd?"

"She agreed it was *extraordinary*, but not that bizarre as Kari Jo Brockman had been held captive by Nicky Champine for over three months. He'd . . . done things to her—Champine's stench was all over the poor woman—and the doc figures Vira caught hold of the scent."

"So no extrasensory perception? Or spooky shit?"

I chuckled at how Paul and I thought alike. "Okay, just for fun I surfed the internet last night, and the closest thing I could find was an article on *mediumistic sensitivity*. It wasn't about dogs, but, evidently, certain folks are highly sensitive and somehow able to serve as conduits for . . . psychic communication."

"But communication with whom?" Paul asked, still staring across the room at Vira. "The dead?"

"I have no idea."

"Do you think any of this has to do with what happened the night they found Vira?"

"I just train dogs, Paul." I tossed a hand in the air. "But that's what she brought up."

"Who? The lady cop?"

"That's Officer Kippy Gimm to you," I said.

"You talk to her again?"

"Not since the castration." I'd shared with Paul what had occurred at my trailer home. How I'd asked Kippy out and was quickly shot down. Sad to say I'd been thinking about Kippy Gimm a lot lately, and it still stung like a son of a bitch. "Too bad there's not a call for carny geeks anymore. I could be the guy who eats his own shit."

"First off, you've got to stop clobbering yourself," Paul said. "Second off, welcome back to the land of the living. Sharla and I have been worried about you this past year, since the—well—you know."

"The divorce?"

"Yes, the divorce," Paul said. "Last year, Mace, you got reclusive, all turtled up and withdrawn into yourself. And I know what you were going through had to be about as much fun as rubbing your kidneys against a cheese grater, but the Mace from a year ago would never have asked a girl out much less said 'Boo' to her. But now look at you—asking some hottie out."

"She blew me off, basically said *no way in hell*."

"I can't remember how many times Sharla said no before she realized how suave and debonair I was and finally caved." Paul finished his beer and stood. "You should really call that lady cop. Pretend it's about Vira."

> Dear Officer Gimm,
>
> I want to update you about Vira's progress as she continues her training as a human remains detection dog, but first I must apologize for asking you out in such a boorish manner. It was inappropriate, and I deeply regret that there is now a tinge of awkwardness between us.

I stared at the email and then hit delete. Paul was right, I've got to stop beating myself up. I had felt a connection between Kippy Gimm and myself, and I went for it. Sure, maybe I came across more like Peter Lorre than Cary Grant . . . so sue me. Sorry I tipped my cards. It's not like I had walked over and snapped her bra strap for Chrissakes.

It was nearly midnight and I was following Paul's advice and contacting Kippy. However, the card Officer Gimm handed me contained a phone number as well as an email address, and I was taking the chickenshit route. I decided I'd send an email regarding Vira's recent training activity and not bring up anything weird that may or may not have occurred between us when my cell phone rang.

I recognized the number—of course I did—as it had been sitting on the table in front of me. A lump the size of a bowling ball caught in my throat, but I answered anyway. "Hello."

"Remember our talk about Vira?" Officer Gimm said without salutation.

"Yeah."

"How she's special in a *certain* manner?"

"Yeah," I repeated.

"I've got a test for her."

CHAPTER 18

I'd never driven through Koreatown at one in the morning before. Vira and I cruised along Lawrence Avenue, nicknamed Seoul Drive by my fellow Chicagoans due to the Korean-owned shops crowded together along both sides of the street. I took a right on Pulaski and then let the navigation app on my phone guide us through the remainder of the route in order to arrive at the North Mayfair address of the bungalow Kippy had texted me. Somehow, I massaged my pickup into the only spot available—across the street and two doors down. Perhaps a newborn could slip through the space between the F-150's bumper and the Subaru BRZ parked in front of me.

Two squad cars were parked in front of the bungalow in question. Between the police cars sat a nondescript white van with no signage, which I assumed was owned by the body removal company contracted by the city. Eventually, after the detectives and forensic specialists finished their chores at the scene, the van would be used to run the victim to the ME's office for the mandated autopsy. I also assumed a couple of the cars congesting the street in North Mayfair at this hour of the night were unmarked police cars utilized by detectives working out of CPD's 17th District. In fact, as I let Vira jump out of the passenger seat, I noticed a couple of shadows talking in the front seat of the BRZ I'd parked behind and figured them for plainclothes.

Showing up at an active crime scene, where there's not a smidgeon of ambiguity as to the location of any human remains, and not having received an *official* request for my attendance, is not in my wheelhouse. I looked at Vira, wondered if we should jump back into the F-150 and get the hell out of town before a nearby detective started posing questions I couldn't answer, but then I spotted Officer Gimm on the bungalow steps staring at us, so we headed in her direction. Regretfully, I fitted the choke collar around Vira's neck and clipped it to the leash. I wanted to keep any of her potential *overenthusiasms* to a minimum—didn't want to risk a repeat of the Nicky Champine attack—and, as we cut between the body removal van and one of the CPD squad cars, I got a bit of a jolt when I spotted a figure sitting quietly in the rear seat, arms folded behind his back.

Vira and I crossed the sidewalk as Kippy came down the steps to meet us. She placed a hand on Vira's head in greetings, and took two minutes to whisper a truncated version of the evening's events. The guy in the back of the squad car, Tomás "Tom" Nunez, had blown a point-two-five, but he'd not been driving and that wasn't the reason he was cuffed in the back of the patrol car. The reason Tom Nunez was cuffed in the back of the patrol car lay on the floor of the kitchen inside the nearby bungalow in a pool of her own blood.

The two-story bungalow belonged to Mrs. Nicomaine Ocampo, a Filipina who'd migrated with her husband, Dr. John Ocampo, to the United States—first to Oahu and then to Chicago—in the mid-1990s. Her husband had been a surgeon at the Northwestern Orthopaedic Institute but died young after a short bout with pancreatic cancer, leaving Nicomaine—without family in town—to raise their infant son, John Ocampo Jr., all by herself. She'd purchased the bungalow outright with the proceeds from her husband's life insurance policy and worked long hours assisting a local tax accountant, but her primary focus over recent decades had been single-parenting her son.

John Jr., now in his early twenties, had been living on his

own since he left for college, so Nicomaine meets Tom Nunez at a social gathering—neighborhood get-together or something—and they hit it off. Nicomaine has been lonely for such a long time that it became a whirlwind romance. Within months they're married. At first John Jr. is happy for his mother but soon comes to realize that she is Nunez's main source of support. Nunez is an occasional manual laborer, more often than not on unemployment. Nunez supplements his unemployment checks by selling marijuana and hits of speed. John Jr. informs the police that he's embarrassed to admit having purchased marijuana from Nunez in the past, and that, based on conversations he's had with his stepfather, he believes Nunez sells a lot more than he lets on. Nunez had been arrested twice previously for selling drugs, albeit small amounts. He's not Scarface or anything that dignified but does manage to keep a number of people happy with a variety of recreational drugs.

Soon the Nunez-Ocampo marriage becomes stormy. Turns out Nunez is also an alcoholic. He drinks himself to unconsciousness most nights. Nicomaine becomes unhappy with her matrimonial choice, a giant step down from husband number one. The couple begins to argue all the time. And, when Nunez is drunk, basting in that hot Latin temper of his, he gets slappy and shovey . . . and sometimes chokey. A restraining order was issued; but, after time passes, they rekindle. *De jure*, he's not supposed to be within a hundred feet of her; but, *de facto*, that's how these things sometimes play out. The woman gets lonely, feels guilty, or, quite frankly, she phones the guy for sex.

Evidently, that was the fatal mistake that occurred this evening.

Nunez comes over. They have sex. They have a meal. He starts drinking. They argue. Nunez, wasted and angry, figures he's tired of taking her endless shit, and lets Nicomaine have it with a steak knife. He realizes what he's done, drinks more, and ultimately passes out on the couch. He comes to an hour or three later, sees her lifeless body . . . and calls 911.

Nunez doesn't deny killing Nicomaine, claims he remembers nothing, but he'd been holding the knife, and the crimson trail leads to him and the sofa. And, considering his blood alcohol level, Nunez was still intoxicated when the police arrived at the scene.

"They're about ready to haul Nunez to the station for booking," said an impatient-looking cop who came up from the street to join us.

"Can you buy me five minutes, Wabs?" Kippy said.

I got an obligatory four-second introduction to Gimm's partner, Officer Wabiszewski—"Wabs" to those in his inner circle. He looked about my height, hovering at that six-foot-nothing mark, but appeared as though he spent all of his free time at the gym. Not being a member of the inner circle, I got the stink eye.

"How do I stall them? Pull my gun?"

"Talk balls or pucks for Christ's sake—this is Chicago," Kippy said. "Better yet, tits and ass 'cause you're all shitheads."

"Three Grey Goose," Wabiszewski said, as though bidding on a used car.

"Screw that. I'd flash my chest for three Greys," Kippy bartered back. "Three shots of the house brand."

Wabiszewski gave a slight nod to seal the deal, spun on a dime, and headed back to the police car containing Nunez, shouting something enthusiastic about the Blackhawks.

"I could spring for some Grey Goose, if you'd like," I mentioned.

"What?" Kippy's verbal cues indicated time was of the essence.

"Nothing."

"You ready to go in?"

Internally, I turned and ran, abandoning Vira and sprinting as fast as I could back to Koreatown, where I hid behind an alley dumpster. Externally, I looked into Kippy's brown eyes, wondered what it'd be like to run my fingertips along the curve of her neck, and announced, "I'm ready."

CHAPTER 19

"I can't have that mutt compromise my crime scene," Detective Alan Triggs said immediately after introductions. "Stay the hell out of our way and, if there are no narcotics, get the hell outside and we'll talk later."

"Understood," I replied.

Kippy had led Vira and me in a serpentine manner about the entryway, keeping us hugging close to the wall as we crossed the living room, until we stood a few paces outside of the kitchen and peeked at the drama currently unfolding in there. Detective Triggs was a short man, balding, with gray nasal hair in dire need of snipping. Behind Triggs, I spotted a pair of pink slippers lying haphazardly on the tiled floor, the feet that once fit them lying near the stainless-steel dishwasher. I saw the lower portion of a pink robe, its down-side soaked in crimson. There was blood spatter the size of silver dollars about the floor, and several CPD forensic experts huddled about what I took to be the late Nicomaine Ocampo Nunez. A forensic photographer was hard at work documenting the scene.

"What the hell's your dog doing?"

Detective Triggs's question tore my attention away from the kitchen scene. I looked down at Vira. Even though we were thirty feet away from the body, Vira fought through another one of her episodes, jiggling, mouth wide open, face scanning side to side like a windshield wiper.

And then it was over.

I looked back at the detective. "She's getting her bearings."

"Bearings?" Triggs said. "I thought she stuck her tail in an outlet."

"Should we check upstairs, sir?" Kippy cut in. "See if Nunez has a stash in one of the bedrooms?"

"That and the basement, too, but stay the hell out of the living room and kitchen. Don't fuck up my blood trail."

"You saw it, didn't you?" I asked as Kippy and I stood alone in the second-floor master bedroom.

"Yeah."

"Vira can catch the scent or vision or whatever the hell she does at ten yards away."

"It started as soon as she caught sight of Nicomaine Ocampo lying on the floor," Kippy said. "What the heck do you think happens to her?"

"That's the million-dollar question," I said. "Remember, this is all new to her. Vira's still a novice as a cadaver dog, and now she's dealing with this other thing. It's like she takes it all in, inhales it or something—disappears for a moment, inside herself or somewhere—and then comes back with some kind of . . . *insight*."

"Insight?"

"I guess that's as good a word as any." I shrugged. "What do we do now?"

"Now we walk Vira by the squad car; let her get a good look or sniff or whatever at the suspect. You need to hold tight to her leash, Reid, because that restraining-order bastard Nunez stabbed his wife to death. Vira will go ape at the sight of him and prove our theory."

Officer Wabiszewski was leaning against the driver's-side window, smiling, and chatting away as though he and the cop behind the wheel were a couple of old veterans who'd not seen each other since they'd stormed the beach at Normandy. As we walked toward the rear of the squad car—where a cuffed Nunez sat—I caught Wabiszewski staring dagger eyes at Kippy. I also noticed the cop behind the wheel glance at his watch, likely for the tenth time in ten minutes. Kippy walked around to the driver's side to buy me a few seconds, and I wasted no time.

"Him, Vira?" I whispered, crouching next to my dog and the rear passenger door. I pointed a forefinger at Nunez, who slowly turned his heavy-lidded gaze our way. His eyes were bloodshot and cloudy; the man looked like he was still more than several sheets to the wind. Blunter yet, Tom Nunez looked shitfaced. "Is it him, Vira?"

Vira jumped up against the back passenger door of the squad car. She and Nunez stared at each other through the window for several seconds. Neither one said a word . . . nothing spoken or snarled.

"Hey, hey, hey," the officer behind the wheel began yelling at me, his head turned my way. "Get that damned dog off my car. I've got to go."

We pulled back and an instant later the squad car was heading toward Pulaski Road.

A moment after that, Officer Wabiszewski said, "Either of you want to tell me what the hell that was all about?"

"I call bullshit," Wabiszewski said, his sole focus on his fellow officer.

Kippy shrugged. "It was a test."

"I don't get it," Wabiszewski replied. "I know you're punking me somehow, but I don't get the joke."

"It wasn't Nunez," I said. I'd taken a knee next to Vira and started to remove the choke collar from around her neck.

Wabiszewski stared down at me as though seeing me for the first time and said, "Who the hell are you again?" Then he turned back to his partner. "You might want to tell this guy the stats behind court-issued restraining orders."

"It wasn't him." I had confidence in my golden retriever; she'd dismissed Nunez with hardly a second glance . . . or sniff.

"If something happens to some poor girl, always grab the shithead with the order out on him. Slam dunk, case closed."

"It wasn't him." I held firm. "Nunez didn't kill his wife."

Wabiszewski sighed. Kippy stared at Vira, a meditative look in her eyes.

Across the street, a couple of car doors shut. Vira went wild. She sprang into the street, snapping and snarling. My fingertips were still working the choker, and I flew forward, rib cage landing on the curb. I lost my grip on her collar but landed on the leash and was able to latch on to it as it strafed forward under my jeans and T-shirt. I grabbed the strap with both hands, an anchor in a tug-of-war contest, which snapped Vira to a halt. She continued to strain against the leash, growling and barking.

"No, Vira," I spoke into her ear, using my command voice, my arm now firmly wrapped around a pair of golden shoulders, keeping her from any further sprints. "Sit."

Vira froze and then sat, suddenly quiet, but her focus stayed on the car parked across the street. I glanced up and spotted the dark figures that I'd first assumed were plainclothes police officers in the Subaru BRZ I'd parked behind. The two had stepped from the vehicle, stood in the avenue, but now stared our way. In the streetlight, I could somewhat make them out. One was a woman, salt-and-pepper hair—maybe late fifties—who clutched a satchel to her chest as though to protect her from the attacking beast. The man standing next to her was much younger, dressed in khakis and a dark polo shirt. He also appeared stunned at the turmoil in front of him.

"Who's that?" I asked Kippy, who had stepped beside me.

"The son," she said. "John Ocampo Jr."

CHAPTER 20

"I was at home, streaming Netflix," John Ocampo Jr. told Kippy. "Why are you asking me these questions? You've already arrested the drunken bastard who killed my mother."

I made Vira sit and stay still by the front tire of my F-150, several yards from where Kippy dove in headfirst, confronting the Ocampo kid. I kept Vira's leash in both hands just in case. At first, she'd shot me a questioning glance, but had since kept her eyes focused on John Jr., watching him closely for any false move.

"Why *are* you asking John these questions?" said Evelyn Shertzer as she stepped between Kippy and Ocampo. Shertzer was the grief-counselor-slash-social-worker who'd been assigned to help Ocampo Jr. deal with a host of bereavement issues—sadness, regret, anger—as well as help him manage the thousand and one arrangements to be made. "You're not even a detective."

"What the hell is going on out here?" Detective Triggs crossed the road with Officer Wabiszewski—who'd run inside to fetch him—in tow. "First we hear what sounds like a goddamned werewolf movie, then Officer . . ." the detective pointed at Wabiszewski as he stumbled trying to remember his name and quickly gave up, "then this guy comes to grab me about some ruckus in the street."

"I've been discussing with John the various stages of

mourning over a significant loss, especially one that occurred in such a distressing manner," Shertzer spoke first, "and suddenly that dog nearly attacks us. Then Missy here runs over and starts giving John the third degree. That's what happened."

"I'm not so sure Nunez did it," Kippy said to the detective. "And I think you need to start looking at *other* suspects."

Triggs stared at Kippy for several seconds, as though she were a fresh pile of something Vira may have pinched off in the road. He then looked at Officer Wabiszewski. "Get your partner out of here immediately." He turned back to Kippy. "Expect a conversation with your lieutenant."

Vira's leash strained tight in my hands. Somewhere in the unfolding excitement, Vira moved to the back of Ocampo's Subaru BRZ, placed her front paws on the back bumper, stared straight at the trunk, and started to bark. A second later she began batting at the back of the BRZ with a right paw.

I looked up to find five sets of eyes staring back at us. Triggs's, Wabiszewski's, and Shertzer's were filled with confusion . . . bewilderment. Kippy's eyes were full of righteous indignation. But John Ocampo Jr.'s eyes were filled with fear.

"She smells something in the trunk," I said.

"You need a warrant," Ocampo said.

"You're making me suspicious, kid," Triggs said.

"It's just the principle of the matter . . . civil liberties. I've been at protests over this kind of stuff."

"Exactly what I need in the middle of the night," the detective replied. "A revolutionary."

Somewhere in the mix Officer Wabiszewski pulled a vanishing act. He had been standing right there, staring at Vira, his mouth agape as though he were being fit for braces and then—poof—he was gone. It seemed an odd moment for a bathroom break, but the muscle-bound cop returned and said, "The car is registered to Nicomaine Ocampo Nunez."

John Jr.'s head twitched. "The car is mine. Once I get done paying Mom back the loan, the title goes into my name."

Triggs had been grinning since Wabiszewski's reappearance, since he'd heard who truly owned the vehicle—the corpse in the bungalow's kitchen. "Time to open the trunk, son."

I'd just backed up the F-150 as far as possible, till my rear bumper kissed the Altima parked behind me. I dropped a fistful of Jerky Treats on the passenger seat for Vira. She gave me a look that said *Seriously?*

"You earned them, kiddo," I told her, and then jumped out to join in the excitement.

Ocampo Jr. twisted the key, popped up the trunk lid, stepped aside, and extended both arms in a *what'd I tell you* gesture.

The trunk was empty.

Triggs turned to me and said, "Hell of a dog you've got there." Without another word, the detective headed across the street, back to his crime scene.

Kippy began working her way through the Subaru's vacant cargo space, methodically, with her flashlight, inch by inch. I climbed back into the cab of my pickup and hit the headlights to make her task easier. I then watched from the curb as Kippy scanned the carpeting in the floor of the trunk. A few seconds later, she stopped and straightened her back.

"Detective," Kippy called, her eyes never leaving the cargo hold. "I see blood-spotting, drops the size of dimes."

Triggs had made it halfway up the bungalow's steps, but he came jogging back. Somehow—in the sprint—a pair of glasses appeared on his face. He looked where Kippy pointed, took her flashlight, and bent deep into the cargo hold.

"Looks fresh," he shouted, though we all stood nearby. "I need Pauline," he ordered, "have her bring the kit."

Kippy scampered back to the bungalow to flag down the CPD forensic specialist known as Pauline.

Triggs pulled himself upright from the tight space and stood. "Your dog caught that through a locked trunk?"

"Although I'm training her in drug detection," I continued the lie and then peppered in some truth, "she's originally a cadaver dog."

"I'll be damned."

Vira began to bark from inside the cab of my F-150, and all heads snapped her way. Shertzer hadn't moved an inch. In fact, she clutched her satchel so close to her chest, she looked in need of bereavement counseling her own self. John Ocampo Jr., on the other hand, had taken the opportunity to softly step backward and was now two car lengths away, hovering at the edge of the beam kicked off by my headlights.

Officer Wabiszewski gave Ocampo Jr. his undivided attention. "Don't make me chase you, sweetheart."

CHAPTER 21

"So your mother is still quite active?" Silver Years Retirement Home director Shelley Fedorchak said.

"God yeah," the caller replied. "Not as much since Dad passed, but my wife, Maureen, and I are always on her to keep busy, you know, keep doing things with her circle of friends."

"That's very caring of you," Director Fedorchak said. "At Silver Years we make it a point to get all of our residents—our guests as we call them—involved in some activity or another, no matter how big or how small. Did you see the list of pastimes on our website?"

The caller said, "Yes, most impressive."

"We don't want to push these activities on our guests too hard. In a perfect world, we'd like for them to show up of their own accord. But we worry about any shut-ins and work with their families—their sons and daughters and even grandchildren—to try to assist in getting them to participate, to try to get them to come out of their shells."

"You won't have to worry about Mom being a shut-in," the caller replied. "The main thing Maureen and I worry about is Mom staying fit."

"We do have an exercise room, with classes on fitness led by certified physical trainers."

"That sounds great," the caller said. "But, you know, even with Dad gone, Mom loves her nature walks, being out and about in the fresh air. Does Silver Years have anything like that to offer?"

"Funny you should ask," Director Fedorchak said. "Gomsrud Park is just down the street—within walking distance—and it's full of both hiking trails and bike paths."

"Hiking trails?"

"I'm positive there's at least a mile or two of footpaths," the director said. "They twist and circle about, and are enclosed by trees and flowers and foliage. And, if I remember correctly, sculptures by art students at Thornton Fractional—Thornton's the local high school—are positioned at every turn."

"Wow."

"If your mom likes to hike, I know she'll love it here. We have one guest—a lovely spirit by the name of Weston Davies—who spends half his day on the Gomsrud trails. Mr. Davies heads out after breakfast and we're lucky if we see him back by lunch. I know Weston would be willing to share the ins and outs and best pathways with your mother."

"That would be awfully nice of Mr. Davies."

"Can I schedule a time for you and your mother to stop by and take the nickel tour?" Director Fedorchak asked. "I believe Silver Years is the best assisted living facility that our little village of Lansing or, quite frankly, all of Chicago has to offer."

"Maureen and I are in Orlando next week, but I'll be in touch as soon as we return," the caller said. "Personally, I think your retirement home is going to be an excellent fit."

"I look forward to meeting your mother."

"Thank you," Everyman told the Silver Years director. "You had me at hiking trails."

CHAPTER 22

The dogs began to bark—a Greek chorus announcing an imminent arrival. I peeked from behind a blind. A white Chevy Malibu parked in my driveway. A second later Kippy Gimm stepped out in jeans and a denim shirt, not on duty this time round.

"Hey," I said, stepping outside.

"Hey," she replied. "Sorry I'm so early, but I thought I'd see if Vira and the others would be up for a walk."

"Think you could handle all the girls?"

"Of course."

As soon as Kippy and the thrilled trio rounded the corner of my driveway, I bolted back inside, hit the bathroom, squeezed an earthworm-sized line of Crest onto my toothbrush and polished the ivories for a minute. I ran a hand through my hair, twice, then three times, and then tore through a bottom drawer in which I had an indistinct memory of tossing a bottle of cologne that Mickie had once picked up for me. Of course it was lying sideways and leaking in the far back. I sprayed both wrists as well as the front and back of my neck before I spotted Sue sitting in the hallway staring up at me.

"What?" I said.

Sue turned and headed back to his couch, but I'll take a polygraph my German shepherd shook his head in incredulity before departing.

I ran to my laundry closet, yanked a clean shirt from the dryer and swapped it out with the one I'd been wearing.

Twenty minutes later Kippy and the three amigas returned.

"He hid under the bed?" I asked in amazement.

Kippy laughed. It was her day off and she'd called ahead of time, asked if she could stop by—toss a Frisbee around the yard with Vira—and bring me up to date on the rest of the Ocampo murder case, the bits and pieces that would never make the evening news.

Who was I to say no?

I even set out coffee.

"Ocampo Junior knew his mom and Nunez were rekindling, restraining order or not. He also knew—spoiled little shit that he was—his mother's bungalow was worth a small fortune. You see, North Mayfair is listed on the National Register of Historic Places. Junior also knew his mother had some savings in the bank, a sizable 401(k), and a small life insurance policy through work. So if Nunez goes away for her murder, Junior winds up with the entire pot of gold."

"But he hid under the bed?"

Kippy dumped a couple of my shoplifted McDonald's creamers into her cup of java. "Ocampo left work early, parked the BRZ a couple blocks over, and got to the old house before Nicomaine came home from her job. And, yes, he hid under the queen-sized bed in the master bedroom. Mom comes home, cooks up some Thai salmon with ginger for her and Nunez. They have a little wine with the candlelit dinner, get amorous, and shake it down on the bed Junior's hiding under."

"Icky."

"Did you just say *icky*?"

"I think I did."

"Very icky," Kippy agreed.

"So where was Nunez when his wife was killed?"

"Nunez is truly an alcoholic. He finished the rest of the wine from dinner, had a couple of tallboys, and then started sucking down some brandy before crashing on the couch in front of the TV while his wife cleaned up the kitchen. Junior had crushed up some sedatives—Restoril, which is a benzodiazepine—and spiked the brandy to ensure that Nunez would stay passed out if any subsequent struggle got out of hand."

"Charming."

"After it was done, Junior lays the knife gently on Nunez's lap on his way out the door. A couple hours later Nunez comes to, he's groggy as hell, grabs the knife out of confusion, walks to the kitchen, sees his wife, and calls the police. He's heavily intoxicated and sedated and has no memory of seeing or hearing anything."

"How did the blood get in the trunk of the kid's car?"

"That's the thing of it, Reid."

"Call me Mace."

"That's the thing of it, Mace. If Junior had brought along a plastic garbage bag or grabbed one at the house, he'd be home free. Instead, he took off his pullover hoodie—his killing shirt, if you will, as he's got a T-shirt on underneath—and folds that in half and uses it as some kind of makeshift bag. He shoves the goalie mask he wore and gloves inside, hightails it back to the Subaru, and tosses his hoodie bag into the trunk where some of his mom's blood began to seep through."

"So Nicomaine sacrifices everything to raise the kid, all by herself . . . and she ends up with a psychopath for a son who kills her because he wants her stuff." I shook my head. "That's just depressing."

"You want to know the weird thing?"

"It gets weirder?"

"Junior told Detective Triggs he wished he could take it back—all of it. He told Triggs he wore the goalie mask and tied down the hoodie so his mother wouldn't recognize him—would think it was a burglar or home invader in her last seconds of life—but she kept whispering his name, over and over again, as he stabbed her to death."

"She knew."

"Probably recognized his eyes through the hockey mask."

Vira lay on Kippy's feet, resting herself for a round of Frisbee. Delta Dawn and Maggie May sat on opposite ends of my old leather couch and stared straight ahead. Sue sat in the middle looking only mildly perturbed. I think the three were doing a more-than-fair impression of me watching a Bears' game on a Sunday afternoon, sans my frustrated theatrics. Kippy had brought along enough treats and toys to pass around so, in Delta Dawn and Maggie's view, she cut the mustard. And the near-empty jar of peanut butter Kippy handed off to Sue made Kip an ally for life.

I reached for a cream at the same instant Kippy grabbed for a sugar packet. I pulled my hand back.

She smiled. "I owe you an explanation."

"About what?"

"Remember when you asked me out for coffee?"

"I did?" I said. "Completely slipped my mind."

Kippy smiled again.

"I want you to know my *no* wasn't a personal rejection," she said. "It's just that I'm off guys."

"You're off guys?" I said, and then it dawned on me. "Oh, okay. I see."

"No, I'm not a lesbian," Kippy corrected me. "Although I'd probably have better luck if I went that route. You see, I just came off a relationship that ended poorly."

"I'm sorry to hear that," I said, although I wasn't too saddened to learn she wasn't currently in any relationship.

"And by 'poorly,' I mean really shitty," she continued. "It was heartbreaking. He really hurt me. So I'm taking a timeout."

"Emotionally speaking, right? He didn't physically hurt you?"

She smiled, but this time I could tell she didn't mean it. "I wish it had been physical. Then I could have kicked his ass into Lake Michigan."

After the events of the past year—in this, my post-Mickie

era, that is—I was on a first-name basis with heartache. Heartache had moved all of his shit into my spare bedroom. Heartache and I were about to restore a 1968 Ford Mustang from scratch. Heartache and I were getting serious about forming a garage band. And, just for the record, Heartache never flushes.

After a while I asked, "How long is your self-imposed exile?"

"I don't know. I guess I'll just kind of know when it's safe to get back in the water."

"It was that bad, huh?"

"You're dying to know what he did, aren't you?"

"I don't mean to pry."

"I thought he might be the one. I really did. We'd even begun talking as though the two of us were in it for the long haul. So one Sunday I slid out of bed and ran a bath. He was sound asleep so I left the door open in case he wanted to join me. I'm taking this marathon soak when he woke up. He thought I'd left and gone back to my apartment, so he called up a pig friend of his and I laid there in the tub listening as the son of a bitch bragged about everything he'd ever done to me—sexually—including half a dozen things we'd never done. The SOB even talked about how I was *almost as good* as some one-nighter he'd picked up after a softball game a couple of Fridays earlier. I slipped out of the bathtub, quietly dried off as he prattled on to his pig friend about my . . . anatomy. He even used this X-rated language that I'd never heard him use before to describe our sex life."

"He made it sound like a *Penthouse* letter?"

"You read *Penthouse*?"

"No." In truth, I'd not seen a *Penthouse* since Mickie caught me paging through one a buddy had snuck into class in high school over a decade earlier. "God no."

Kippy shrugged. "I guess he made it sound like a *Penthouse* letter."

"What did you do?" I steered the conversation away from *Penthouse*.

"Put on my clothes, gathered all of my stuff in a grocery bag, and left."

"What did he have to say for himself?"

"Well, he was certainly stunned when I walked out of the bathroom—that's for sure. He hung up on his pig friend and tried to *Hey, Honey* it as though I were an idiot. Then he started in on how all guys talked like that, even though the most benign thing he'd said in the previous ten minutes had been to describe the circumference of my areolas."

I tried to kill a grin in its infancy, but failed miserably.

"See," she said. "You're laughing about this. You Y-chromosomes are all alike."

"That's where you're wrong, Kippy. We're not all alike," I said. "I would have made sure your car was gone before I started calling my friends."

"Cute."

"Look, Kip," I said, instantly realizing I showed familiarity by shortening her name. "Maybe your premise is right and all guys are pigs. So you need to find one who can suppress it, keep it hidden, and camouflage it up. My grandma didn't realize Grandpa was piglike until her late sixties, and by then it was too late to do anything about it, and she had accumulated some affection for the old codger."

Kippy took a long sip of coffee, put it down, and said, "Why haven't you been snarfed up? You've got that campy, outdoorsy thing going."

"I don't go camping that much, but you think I'm a rugged, outdoorsy guy?"

"Did I say rugged?"

"Rugged goes hand in hand with outdoorsy. It's a given."

"But you needed a girl to save you from that twelve-year-old."

I put my coffee down. "Feral-boy was strong as hell. And that knife was like a machete."

"Relax, Mace, I'm just joshing," she said. "But you didn't answer my question. Why haven't you been snarfed up?"

I shrugged. "I guess I'm in the spitting-out phase of having been snarfed up."

"You're divorced?"

I nodded.

"And you didn't want it?"

I shifted about in my chair and shook my head.

We sat in silence for a few seconds.

"Did you do a shitty?"

"*A shitty*," I said. "No, I didn't do anything shitty. We just grew apart. Or maybe it was Mickie that grew apart. I'm not sure what happened to be honest. We were high school sweethearts . . . and they always say those never last."

"I'm sorry."

I leaned back in my chair. "I've been in the spitting-out phase for quite a while now, actually. Mickie's getting remarried."

We sipped coffee in further silence. I regretted how my remembrance had cast a pall over the entire conversation. I was scraping the bottom of the barrel for a stupid joke when Vira stood, walked over to the Frisbee laying by the sliding glass door, got ahold of it in her teeth, and then delivered it to Officer Gimm's lap.

"You just got served with a summons."

Kippy laughed. I laughed. The world righted itself.

CHAPTER 23

Goddamned fixed income.

Weston Davies's social security check got direct deposited into his bank account on the third Wednesday of every month, no matter what date that Wednesday happened to fall upon. Of course the bulk of his SSA check went to living in this dump. And no matter how Davies budgeted, crunch time always came the week before his money was deposited.

Which meant the dry spell came mid-month and Davies found it next to impossible to get a drink around here. Especially since the bean counters at Visa had frozen his credit card and kept sending him those threatening letters and making downright unsociable phone calls. Weston Davies snickered—it was almost as though he owed Visa more than twelve grand or something.

The idea came to him as he watched TV in the community lounge yesterday afternoon. Someone at Silver Years, or possibly the family of one of the old farts warehoused here, had brought in a baker's box stuffed full of them saucer-sized ginger snap cookies. When no one was looking, Davies grabbed a dozen of the ginger snaps—six in each hand—and jogged them back to his room. Then he went down to the kitchen and asked a staff member for a Ziploc bag. Then Davies went to the craft's room where a flock of the usual biddies sat farting around with yarn and paste and shit all day every day as though they were in preschool. He asked the least-constipated-looking one if he could have a ribbon. Plus some construction paper, some tape, and a couple of colored markers.

Then Davies sat at a corner table, jazzed up the Ziploc bag, and made a colorful label reading *Bake Sale Charity*.

All that had been the easy part. This morning, however, was going to be the hard part.

Weston Davies had been called into Director Shelley Fedorchak's office on more than one occasion in order to provide his version of some grievance that had been filed against him by one of the other residents at Silver Years. Plus, there'd been that unpleasantness at the start of last year where he'd been informed that Silver Years didn't permit liquor store deliveries. Or was it just *his* liquor store deliveries? He'd forgotten which had caused the ruckus and, to this day, Davies wondered which of the retirement home's octogenarians had brought the matter to Fedorchak's attention and made such a federal case out of it. It could well have been the craft biddies, or perhaps those checkers-playing chuckle-fucks from the commons, or perhaps some other asshole.

Davies put on his single dress shirt and black pants. He combed his strands of white hair to the side, stared in the mirror a moment, and then used the comb on his unclipped eyebrows. On more than one occasion some damned fool or another had mentioned that with his white hair and eyebrows, his rosy red checks, he'd just need a fake beard to pass himself off as Santa Claus, albeit a thinner version of Kris Kringle. In fact, in his first Christmas at Silver Years, Director Fedorchak asked him if he'd dress up as jolly old St. Nick for their holiday party.

Of course he had declined.

So, as spruced up as he'd been in over a decade, Weston Davies held the decorative Ziploc bag and glanced in all directions before heading into the wing of the facility that housed those residents who could no longer live *completely* on their own—those who required extra care and attention when taking their medications, those who required help in their journeys to and from the restroom or shower, those currently wheelchair bound—an entire assortment of requirements for those senior citizens rounding third and heading home on the baseball diamond of life. Davies had absolutely no business being in this wing and figured a Silver Years' staff member might go all Gestapo were he to bump into one.

Davies knocked on three doors before he heard a grunt and took it as an invite to enter. The name outside the room read *Barry Anklan* and that's whom Davies assumed the man in the stained terry-cloth robe and wheelchair to be.

"Barry," Davies said with a welcoming smile. "The cookies are here."

"What?" the man in the wheelchair asked.

"The cookies from the charity bake sale have finally arrived." Davies walked in and handed the Ziploc bag to Anklan. "Ginger snaps, right?"

"Cookies? I didn't order any cookies."

Davies looked confused. "I volunteered to help them deliver, and they told me Barry gets a dozen."

Anklan held up the proffered bag. "Ginger snaps?"

"Remember—they stopped by last month to take orders."

"Are these free?"

"I wish," Davies said. "I went with four dozen and it cost me forty dollars, but it's all for a good cause."

Anklan looked up at him. "What's the cause?"

Davies stared back, wishing it wouldn't have gone on this far. "What?"

"What's the bake sale for?"

"Charity."

Anklan frowned. "What charity?"

Davies was getting pissed, but kept a stiff upper lip. "They need a dialysis machine over at the hospital."

Anklan looked baffled. "A hospital's throwing a bake sale to purchase a dialysis machine?"

Davies glanced about the room and said, "I think it's so poor people can get treatment. Something like that."

"All right," Anklan said. "What do I owe you?"

"Ten dollars."

"Christ." Anklan spun the wheelchair sideways and rolled himself to a dresser, opened a middle drawer that appeared to be stuffed with underwear and socks, and then glared back at Davies.

"Oh, sure, okay," Davies said and turned away. Great spot to hide your wallet, you old gimp, Davies thought. The Somalis on the night shift will never think of looking there.

Anklan wheeled back to face Davies, handed him a crisp ten-dollar bill, and said, "Tell Shelley never again. In fact, have her take me off the list for any of this crap."

Davies bristled at Anklan's mention of Director Fedorchak. "You and me both, brother. I'm just volunteering to help out in my free time and, like I said, they knicked me for forty bucks. You know," Davies caught Anklan's eye and continued, "this fucking place."

"I'll talk to Shelley."

"Let me handle it, Barry. You've got all this other stuff going on," Davies said and pointed at the man's wheelchair. "I'll make sure she understands. This shit's got to stop."

Davies almost made it out of the *extra-assistance* wing home free when he found himself face-to-face with the director of Silver Years. Shelley Fedorchak entered the hallway and appeared, mercifully, to be in a hurry—maybe another one of her *guests* had croaked in the night. His heart skipped a beat at the director's double take, but Davies smiled and kept on moving, praying Reichsführer Fedorchak hadn't seen him slip out of Barry Anklan's room . . . and hoping she wouldn't go sleuthing.

Davies had a few sips left in his flask, but with the ten spot he'd liberated from Barry Anklan and the five in his money clip he could maybe get him 750 milliliters of the cheap stuff at Dean's Liquor. They'd be open by the time he made it across the park. Hopefully, the fat cashier wouldn't be working today. She always got pissed whenever he grabbed at the pennies in the change tray by the register, as though it were her own private copper mine.

Weston Davies smiled and headed out the front entrance of Silver Years Retirement Home.

CHAPTER 24

The Silver Years director had been correct on both counts. Gomsrud Park did contain well over a mile of hiking trails. The director had also been right about a certain white-haired gentleman who trekked about the park's pathways—beginning slightly after nine o'clock each and every morning—as Everyman had shadowed Weston Davies the past two mornings. From his perch on a park bench facing the retirement center, Everyman had spotted the senior citizen exiting Silver Years' front entryway. He stood up and headed toward the nearest of the park's footpaths, past an abstract metal sculpture that looked like something the cat screwed, and worked his way ahead so he could lay in wait, off the trail and among the shrubs, for old Mr. Davies to pass by.

Everyman had never told the Champines when he'd be stopping by, but he turned up at the Bridgeport rambler on four additional occasions. The first time was not long after his initial visit, bringing boxes of children's vitamins, apples, oranges, and bananas for the two to eat, bags of frozen vegetables as well, plus a half-dozen tubes of toothpaste and a couple of new toothbrushes for the dentally challenged youngster—Everyman had gotten a long glance at the kid's teeth on his first visit. He'd also brought bars of antibacterial soap, bottles of shampoo, laundry detergent, a few picture books, and some first-aid creams. Corny, but when Everyman returned again at Christmas, he brought with him a roast turkey with all the fixin's. He showed up again in the spring—with additional supplies, coloring books, and puzzles—to see how the two had survived the winter.

Everyman had last visited the Champines in July, when he handed the kid more coloring books, crayons . . . and a jungle knife.

He and Nicky Champine would talk about life while the kid colored. He'd ask how the boy was doing, if he was learning new things, if he was keeping hygienic. But Everyman never discussed with Champine any visitors the two of them may have tucked away in their basement room.

Though he'd followed the Velvet Choker Killer's exploits via the news, it was none of Everyman's business.

The kid could speak, but stuck mostly to "Yes" or "No" for food or in response to a direct question. The boy combined his words with nods or shakes of the head, along with finger points at anything of interest. The kid wasn't going to recite the Gettysburg Address anytime soon, but Everyman could tell the lights were on upstairs.

When Everyman got up to head home at the end of his last visit, the kid ran over and gave him a long hug, likely for the gift of the jungle knife.

Taken aback, he patted the boy on the head.

Everyman hated the usual dime-store psychiatry. No, he didn't strangle the neighborhood dogs or cats. No, he didn't pull the legs off spiders when he was growing up. Well, maybe he yanked a few legs off of daddy longlegs, but no more so than the average rugrat did. His parents had been normal . . . enough. He'd even made it to Webelos in Cub Scouts until the anal-retentive den mother made his troop clean up one park too many. And he wouldn't ascribe a sexual-like necessity to his *extracurricular* activities, although, in years past, there'd been a certain amount of that.

No, Everyman thought, it was something that had always been inside him, something he'd been born with, flowing quietly beneath the surface; a river running silent and deep, endlessly cutting through his psyche. Everyman would further define it as an internal gnawing that never left—an irrepressible itch from which he could not escape—until he was drawn, like metal shavings to a magnet . . . until he could no longer deny his true nature.

On the flip side, Everyman wondered if he was capable of human affection.

If he was capable of love.

But he knew; his entire life had been in answer to that query.

It was during his time in Houston that Everyman received the only moniker he felt suited him. And that had been the result of a massive screwup as well—likely a second reason he took pity on Nicky Champine. Back in the day when cameras weren't ubiquitous, his disguise was maybe a baseball cap, an old pair of glasses, and a heavy jacket. It was supposed to be a simple shove-and-snatch in one of the parking ramps that serviced the Galleria. She was a small thing he'd been following for a week or two, young, dark-haired, maybe all of five feet tall and a hundred pounds. But the girl had a tiny can of Mace hooked to her key chain and she wielded it like a gunfighter. It took a couple hours of waiting for an opening to get the old van into the spot next to her vehicle. And a half hour after that she came trekking out, shopping bags in hand, heading to her driver's door.

He took a quick glance about the lot.

No possible witnesses in sight.

Perfect.

He jumped out from the sliding door, had a hand around her throat, pulling her backward. He almost had her inside the van when she went Wyatt Earp with the pepper spray. He was lucky she dropped all bags and ran back to the Galleria as he was vulnerable, had sunk to his knees, was wiping at his eyes, when he realized he needed to get the hell out of there.

To this day he had no idea how he raced the van out of that

parking ramp without side-swiping a dozen cars. A block from the Galleria, he double-parked, thanked God he had a Perrier sitting in a cup holder, which he used to rinse his eyes as best he could before being physically able to get the hell out of Dodge.

As for the girl, the description she gave the Houston police that got fed to the newspapers was basically, "I don't know, it all happened so fast. Not fat, not thin. Not tall, not short. Glasses, I think. Maybe brown hair. He could be everyman."

And the name stuck.

Local murders and disappearances, most of which he'd not been responsible for, were blamed on *Everyman*. Be careful was the theme that humid summer, lest *Everyman* get you. Some pencil-necked scribe at the *Chronicle*—obviously a lit major—even juxtaposed his current activity with some medieval Middle English morality play, *The Somonyng of Everyman*, where some poor sap representing mankind must account for his deeds before God in the great hereafter.

If twenty-first-century Everyman had to justify his deeds before God, he'd be in one hell of a bind.

Fortunately, Everyman didn't believe in God.

A month later he left Houston.

Everyman hoped to return there someday, to look up the girl from the Galleria parking lot, to see how she'd been doing. He knew her name—after all, it had been in the papers at the time. Sure, she might have gotten married—if memory served, she was a looker—but in the age of Google and Facebook, he could find the breadcrumbs and track her down.

She'd seen his true face and he hadn't changed all that much. Not really. A few more lines, a few more pounds. Perhaps he'd hold a can of Mace in front of her so she'd make the connection.

Then they'd get reacquainted . . . and make up for lost time.

Everyman spotted Weston Davies walking along the Gomsrud trail. The resident of Silver Years strode past at a solid pace for a man north of eighty. Everyman didn't make any attempts at camouflage. If Davies peered right, he might have seen him standing motionless in the foliage, but the old man's concentration clearly lay only on the trail in front of him.

It made no difference to Everyman if he'd have been seen or not.

This was only going to end one way.

After Davies passed, Everyman stepped onto the trail, picked up speed, gaining quickly on the elderly hiker.

"Mr. Davies," he shouted, now thirty feet behind the senior citizen, too far to trigger a panic response. "Mr. Davies, please."

Weston Davies stopped and turned around, his face a wrinkled question mark. "Do I know you?"

Everyman approached, breathing as though he'd just run a marathon. "I do the accounting for Silver Years and was in a meeting with the director."

"Fedorchak?"

Everyman remembered the name—Ukrainian or something—and nodded. "She got a call about your son."

"I don't have a son," Davies said.

Everyman swung again. "Son-in-law?"

"Jerry?" Davies said, his face scrunched tighter. "Jerry and Paige haven't spoken to me in over a decade."

I wonder why, Everyman thought. Up close, Weston Davies had a drinker's face—blushed red cheeks and nose due to enlarged blood vessels. He bet if he frisked the old guy, he'd find booze.

"I imagine it's pretty serious then," Everyman said. "Director Fedorchak told me you walk the trails and I ran here to get you."

"Well, what the hell do they want from me?"

What had Silver Years director Shelley Fedorchak told him earlier over the phone? That Weston Davies was a *lovely spirit*? Christ, the staff at Silver Years was probably ecstatic—jumping with joy—that this geriatric prick disappeared for half of each day to sneak drinks in the woods. And the other inhabitants at the retirement home probably hoped Davies wouldn't return until after eight p.m., when they were all in bed and asleep.

Hell, he'd be doing the residents at Silver Years a favor.

"To let you know what happened to Jerry," Everyman said softly. "Perhaps discuss funeral arrangements."

"Why would I have to make arrangements?" Davies said. "Jerry grabbed me by the shirt once."

Everyman contemplated doing Weston Davies right here and now but didn't want to lug the old man's carcass a couple hundred yards through the undergrowth, toward the ravine, toward the desired spot in the clearing. Instead, Everyman made do thinking about how he was going to do so much more to this geriatric prick than son-in-law Jerry ever thought possible . . . much more than grabbing at the old fucker's shirt.

"That is regrettable," Everyman said. "But what I meant was they'd inform you about Jerry's funeral—you know, day and time, what church."

"Christ on a crutch," Davies said and looked at his watch as if the news of Jerry's passing had gummed up his already brimful agenda. "I needed to pick something up."

"If it's close by, I can drive you there after you've talked with your daughter."

Davies stared at Everyman with renewed interest. "If Jerry's gone, I'm going to need a stiff drink. Any way you can pick me up a fifth of vodka?"

Unbelievable. Everyman thought again about doing Weston Davies right here and now, but instead said, "I don't think Shelley would approve."

"How 'bout a pint?"

Everyman shrugged. "I'll pick up the vodka while you're calling your daughter."

"Jerry would thank you," Davies said without emotion, not even attempting to feign sincerity.

"Let me show you a shortcut to the north trail, Mr. Davies," Everyman said. "It'll shave off ten minutes."

CHAPTER 25

Silver Years director Shelley Fedorchak was with the book club in the library. Today was guest author day, but Everyman told the aide or receptionist or whoever answered his call that it was of paramount importance that he speak with Fedorchak immediately—that time was of the essence—and off the aide ran to retrieve the director. He doodled on a piece of scratch paper as he waited, thinking about winter, how it was only a couple of months away, and coming fast. They say absence makes the heart grow fonder, but Everyman knew that to be a lie. It was the absence of snow and bitter cold that made the heart grow fonder.

And Everyman recalled his days on the West Coast fondly.

Someday he might return.

It was in San Francisco where he honed his craft, where he actually got good. No more wild bullshit after the pepper spray incident in Houston. When Everyman went out, he used makeup and wigs from a theatrical supply store off Haight Street. Whenever he went on the hunt, his looks would be altered—sometimes realistically, sometimes absurdly—so he'd look nothing like himself.

Never anything like Everyman . . . at least until the final moments, where he revealed his true face. He felt it only right that they should know.

He owed them that.

When he lived in San Francisco, Everyman had been an executive salesman—before the dot-com bubble burst, ruining everyone's good time—and his true homes had been the nation's Hyatts, Sheratons, Embassy Suites, or The Fairmonts and Hiltons of Chicago, Seattle, Dallas, Los Angeles, New York, and Toronto. But it wasn't the tech bubble crash that led to Everyman yanking up roots; it was his boss and chief executive officer at Screen-Com Software, a highly likable man by the name of Eugene Knox.

Everyman thought the world of Knox, liked reporting to him, and enjoyed the good-natured give-and-take—the warm rapport—they'd developed. He also knew Knox to be meticulous, sharp as a tack. Eugene Knox missed nothing. So it was regrettable that upon returning from a London conference, when Everyman went straight to his downtown office from San Francisco International Airport to submit his expense report and list of new contacts, he found Knox waiting for him, a bit shocking considering the time of night.

He asked Everyman to come into his corner office and poured him a glass of bourbon.

Knox was jovial at first, told Everyman he had the silliest of notions to share with him, but Everyman knew all about masks, and saw behind the one Knox was wearing that night. He sipped the Maker's Mark and let his boss say his piece. Everyman had always passed his expense reports on to Knox, who was a cost accountant at heart—by choice and by profession—and something in the news had tripped Knox's trigger, a call to a clerk at the Sheraton in Seattle to get a copy of an illegible invoice had led to a brief conversation about something that had occurred during Everyman's stay there. Evidently, some poor woman had spent a great deal of the evening drinking cocktails in the hotel bar, as business travelers are wont to do, often in excess. The woman returned to her room, ran a brimming tub of hot water for a bath, and, evidently, had been so intoxicated that she passed out, slipped down, and drowned.

Everyman was astounded at how the synapses in Eugene Knox's brain worked. How connections were made and, like a bloodhound, Knox kept on the trail. The man was truly incredible. He had all the tools right there in front of him. The expense reports were at Knox's fingertips. He had all of the exact dates and cities. Knox tapped into the internet, performed a website search of the different newspapers from the various cities Everyman had frequented. Going back an arbitrary year and a half, he plotted out each one in great detail. The records nerd in him, Everyman guessed.

A maid at the Hyatt Regency in Washington, D.C., had been found dead in a room she had been cleaning. She'd been strangled with the curtain cord that, left tied about her throat and anchored to the base of the ceiling fan, had kept her swaying in some warped, slow dance macabre, facing the window, her bulging eyes staring blindly out over the nation's capital. The *Dallas Morning News* article told of how a woman had left an Italian restaurant, alone, walked to the ramp in which she'd parked her car. She was found the next morning, sitting in front of the steering wheel, with the shoulder strap of her seat belt wound tightly around her throat. Her larynx was crushed. Everyman's expense report, yanked from the electronic files, showed that he had eaten dinner at that same restaurant that very same evening. It was odd in that Everyman's dinner receipt indicated that he'd paid for this particular outing in cash.

How . . . unlike him.

The *Los Angeles Times* told a similar story. A business woman enjoying the nightlife had been grabbed from behind, dragged into a dark ally, and choked to death with the leather strap of her own purse. Her body then stuffed into a dumpster. Everyman had made several profitable leads at that Los Angeles Tech Show while he stayed four days at the JW Marriott that very same week.

At the Hotel Sofitel in Minneapolis, which coincided with Everyman's conference with the Honeywell Group, a female chef, who worked the coffee shop's lonely overnight shift, was found in the meat freezer, strangled with her own apron.

At the Toronto Hilton, during a Screen-Com–sponsored lobbyist convention, the one that Everyman had spearheaded, there had been another drowning, much like the one in Seattle. It had been ruled an accident. No foul play. No robbery. Her door had been locked. But then again, how much does it take to wipe up a one-sided struggle in a hotel bathroom, then let the door latch lock shut behind you as you slip silently out into a midnight hallway?

At New York City's Emerald Plaza Hotel, coinciding with Everyman's signing of the Hexcon Industries account, a cocktail waitress in the hotel bar left for a quick break to call her boyfriend and never returned. Janitors found her early the next morning in a desolate, downstairs hallway. Her body was stuffed inside one of those old-fashioned, wooden phone booths. She'd been strangled with the phone cord.

And the list went on. All in all there was a trail of twelve incidents in eighteen months. Twelve incidents of Everyman being in the same city, in the immediate vicinity, of the reported homicides. It was as though Chief Executive Officer Knox was walking through each and every one of Everyman's per diems.

"You can't be serious, Eugene," Everyman said, setting his empty bourbon glass on a coaster on his side of Knox's desk. "If it bleeds, it leads . . . and murders lead the news in every single city on every single day."

"I know," Knox nodded faintly in agreement. "I know."

"All the selling I do for you, all across the globe," Everyman said, chuckling, "I'm in bed by nine, Eugene. Way too pooped out to go on a—what?—killing spree?"

"I told you it was a silly notion," Knox said, taking a last swallow of his bourbon.

A minute later Knox's ergonomic high back desk chair shattered through Knox's office window and plummeted thirty flights to the street below. Three seconds later, Screen-Com chief executive officer Eugene Oliver Knox followed suit. And though Knox had been divorced for over a year—a divorce that he had requested—the note typed on his PC said simply: *Without her I am nothing.*

The month after Knox's funeral, Everyman left for Denver.

"This is Shelley," the director of Silver Years said over the phone line, having finally returned from the book club. "How may I help you?"

"Hi Shelley," Everyman said. "You might remember me. I called a few days ago about finding a place for my mother."

"Of course I remember," Shelley said. "I thought you were in Florida."

"That fell through."

"I'm sorry to hear that," Shelley replied. "Shall we schedule a tour for your mother?"

"I've got a confession to make, Shelley. And, to be honest, I'm a bit embarrassed by it."

"Don't be."

"You don't record these phone calls or anything, do you?" Everyman said, followed with a nervous laugh.

"Of course not." The assisted living director added a short chortle herself. She was in on the joke. "We value our guests' privacy."

"Good, Shelley. That's good. You see, I wasn't as forthcoming with you as I should have been," he said. "Not forthcoming at all."

"How so?" The director now spoke with a more professional timbre.

"But on my behalf, Shelley, I don't think you were all that forthcoming with me, either."

"I have no idea what you're talking about." The director was no longer in on the joke.

"I think you do, Shelley. I believe you said that Weston Davies was a, quote, lovely spirit, unquote. I found Weston Davies to have anything but a *lovely spirit*. Anything but, Shelley. And we both know his daughter would agree with me."

"How do you know Mr. Davies?" The director's tone was now direct, accusatory.

"I bumped into him on those trails, Shelley. The trails you told me about. Don't you remember? The ones at Gomsrud Park."

A pregnant pause, then, "What was your name again?"

"Does Silver Years do a head count at lunch, Shelley? I doubt you do, but if you did, you'd have noticed Weston didn't make it back in time for SpaghettiOs," Everyman said. "Quite frankly, Shelley, Mr. Davies won't be attending any more of your scheduled meals or pastimes."

"This isn't funny," the director said—some grit, some uncertainty, but mostly fright. "I'm calling the police right now."

"Ah, Shelley, I think you're going to have to. There are so many acres between the trails, I can't begin to remember where I misplaced our dear friend," Everyman said. "Sorry to say but I think they'll need one of them—what are they called?—cadaver dogs."

PART THREE

THE VISITOR

A dog is the only thing on earth that loves you more than he loves himself.

—Josh Billings

CHAPTER 26

"My money has the old coot on a bar stool laughing his ass off and buying drinks for whatever barfly he got to make the prank call," a Lansing police officer named Ennis informed me when we connected at the playground parking lot at Gomsrud Park. Ennis was big, bald, and looked as though he could bench-press Mars. He continued to fill me in. "Davies had his license taken away in the nineties—too many drinking-and-driving episodes—which is probably why he's used to all this walking around bullshit. Plus, he got ticketed a couple years back for sitting on one of those kid swings and sucking down schnapps at ten in the a.m. I think that's why he walks the trails or, more likely, finds a secluded bench to sit on and then tosses back a few."

I took the call fifteen minutes ago. Lansing PD had contacted Chicago PD, gotten my name and number, and dialed my cell. I was stunned to hear the job was practically in my own backyard. I'd never had a closer gig or an area I was so familiar with. I loaded all three girls into the F-150 and was at Gomsrud Park eight minutes later. Officer Ennis had parked his squad car on the grass in back of the playground, at the mouth of the north trail.

"Hell, I shouldn't bitch about the old guy. I'll probably be doing the same thing when I reach his age. Better than sitting in one of them homes twenty-four/seven, alternating shuffleboard with jigsaw puzzles while waiting on the Reaper." Ennis continued bringing me up to speed on the search for the missing senior citizen. "We got another officer checking the local bars, looking for the old codger, but I drew the short straw so I'm out here with you. No offense. You know the call the old folks home got was total bullshit. If you whack someone and drag them into the woods, you don't turn around and ring up their landlord about it for Christ's sake. So this is all a bullshit waste of time, but we've got to go through the motions." Ennis scratched at his cheek. "I figure I'll walk the trails, looking left and right as far into the woods as I can see because who'd want to lug a body any farther than they'd have to?"

"Sounds like a plan," I said. I tend not to quibble with guys who have biceps bigger than my head. "I'll follow the dogs into the tree line and we'll cut through to the ravine and up to where it butts against Knob Hill."

"It's good you know the area."

"I used to go inner tubing at Knob—that bunny hill they have." Mickie and I had done that together, often, in winters past. Good times. Better days. "If we don't find anything, we'll cut across to the other side of the trails and work our way back."

Ennis and I talked logistics. He called my cell phone so we'd have each other's numbers in case one of us found something or had a good joke to share. I showed him the stainless-steel sports whistle I wore around my neck like a referee, told him it was loud as hell and how I used it in order to alert others on broader hunts, but he shook his head.

"I'd run around for an hour trying to figure out where that fucking noise was coming from," Ennis said and held up his phone. "Just call me with some directions, you know, like base of hill or middle of the ravine."

"Can do," I told Ennis. "If there's a body in there, my dogs'll find it."

CHAPTER 27

Everyman lay prone beneath one of the numerous pine trees that curved about the clearing. The pines signified where the woodlands at Gomsrud Park came to an end. The curve of pine trees was out of the shadows, and able to get their much-needed sun.

Everyman had picked the perfect spot for an ambush.

He was dressed in all black, exactly as he'd been the other night in the woods outside the Dog Man's trailer—black jeans, boots, sweatshirt, and ski mask. His thin backpack beside him contained the John Deere cap, mullet wig, and black glasses he'd worn on his trek from where he'd dropped the rental car at the outer edge of an apartment complex's parking lot less than a quarter-mile hike from the top of Knob Hill, from where he'd called Director Fedorchak on the burner phone. The burner had since been shut off, smashed with a boot heel, and deposited in a storm drain.

The rental car called for a driver's license and credit card. In the course of his travels, Everyman had come across the name of a devilishly clever artist located in Manila—a man he'd never met and never would—whose identity documents would convince your own parents that you were someone they'd not raised since birth. And though the man in the Philippines provided him with a handful of IDs and credit cards in which to set up hotel or car rental reservations—on days or nights involving Everyman's *pastime*—he always settled up in cash.

It was best that way.

Weston Davies's remains lay in repose no more than forty yards in front of Everyman. Davies's resting spot was a flat slice of undergrowth in the center of the clearing, before the ground dipped toward the ravine. His now-still hands cupped the small flask of vodka that, sure enough, Everyman had found inside the old drunk's right front pocket. Davies looked almost serene in death—that is if your eyes didn't linger too long on the jungle knife protruding from the center of his chest or the black velvet choker necklace he sported tightly about his throat.

Or looked into the old man's eyes—dry green marbles staring vacantly into the sun.

Everyman had made his final moments with Weston Davies last.

Compared to what he'd done to Davies, Dog Man Reid would be getting off easy.

Everyman had his SIG 1911 near his right hand. Near his left hand—a 9.2-ounce canister of bear spray. If it could neutralize an eight-hundred-pound charging grizzly at thirty-five feet, the bear deterrent should make short order of any *undesirable behavior* on behalf of Mason Reid's dogs.

Assuming that Reid's dogs lived up to their name, they'd lead the Dog Man straight to Weston Davies's remains. And as Reid mentally processed the meaning of the jungle knife jutting out from the dead man's chest, the significance of the choker necklace wrapped around the dead man's neck, and as red flags went off in Reid's mind, red flags about the Champines' modus operandi, Everyman would make his move.

He'd slip out from under the pine tree, creep as close as possible before the dogs' attention would switch from the moist blood covering Davies's torso to the newcomer approaching them from behind. He'd spray the scene, including Reid—the bear deterrent had piqued Everyman's consumer curiosity—

and as Dog Man and his team of canines crouched and sputtered and coughed, he'd take out any dog that so much as looked at him with any degree of alertness.

Then he'd shoot Reid in the stomach.

And—as Everyman stood over a writhing, gut-shot Mason Reid—he'd pull off his ski mask and show the Dog Man his true face.

Everyman owed him that much.

CHAPTER 28

Vira led in the middle, with Maggie fifty yards to the left and Delta at an equal distance on the right. I hung back, keeping a leisurely pace, watching my golden retriever and two collies work as a team. They'd been to Gomsrud before, to the acres of woodland behind the park, all those times when I'd been too lazy to cart them someplace more complex for training exercises.

I love my sister collies even though they do their damnedest to gaslight me. The two are inseparable; in fact, they're so symbiotic they may as well be Siamese twins. Now and again I'll catch them staring at something, then they'll send sideway glances at each other before turning back to the original item of interest. It makes me paranoid, gets me thinking the canine duo knows a hell of a lot more than they're letting on. Just last week I picked up a couple of Quarter Pounders on the drive home for dinner. I made a quick pit stop in the restroom before returning to the kitchen table, but they pulled their shtick on me as I lifted the first burger up to my mouth. The bag of food had only been out of my sight a minute or two, but I got all apprehensive and stopped everything to lift the bun and examine all condiments before I took a bite.

We continued our walk together in the shadows of elm trees and oak, ash and maple.

They say that humans have lost much of their sense of smell

as we've continued to evolve, placing a greater emphasis on our sense of sight. I'm not so sure this is true. If I miss two meals in a row, I swear I can smell the hot dogs over at Wrigley Field.

I watched my dogs sniff at the ground as we moved deeper into Gomsrud's jungle of trees and underbrush. Then a site to behold as three snouts lifted into the air, a trio of bobbers coming to the surface. My dogs had caught a waft of something in the nearly nonexistent breeze. A second later they came together as one and took off in a mad dash toward the ravine. The scent of decomposition had tripped their radar . . . they'd zeroed in on the death trail. This was where I'd get my cardio workout as I jogged behind in their wake.

I tapped at my iPhone. I should have made a wager with Officer Ennis. Turns out the old coot wouldn't be found on a barstool laughing his ass off.

"Sup?" the cop from Lansing answered his cell phone.

"The dogs got a hit."

"No shit," he replied. "Already?"

"It's what they do."

"You got eyes on the body?"

"Give me a minute," I said. "You'd have to be an Olympic sprinter to keep up with my girls."

"So where are you headed?"

"You know that grassy area or clearing before it drops down into the ravine? About fifty yards in front of Knob Hill?"

"Ah hell, I started on the southern trails—the farthest side," Officer Ennis said. "If I jog over and they're chasing a squirrel, I'm going to be fucking pissed."

"You won't be fucking pissed," I said. "It's what they do."

I pushed forward, got my second wind and scampered faster, finally slipping into the weed grass and sunlight from behind a row of pines. Maggie May and Delta Dawn sat motionless, ten feet apart, staring into the grass in front of them. Vira sat as well, nearer Maggie, but gently patting at the soil. I couldn't see the body yet, but I knew.

My dogs had discovered the scent's origin.

"Good girls," I said—my happy voice—as I walked over to join them. "What good girls I have."

I stared down at the body.

What the hell?

A knife identical to what feral-boy had done his damnedest to use on me was stuck in the center of the old man's chest. And a black choker necklace—like the kind clasped about Kari Jo Brockman's throat—had been fastened tightly around the old man's neck.

My heart began to race.

And Vira began to growl.

CHAPTER 29

I stumbled backward, staring numbly into the line of pines from where I'd emerged only seconds earlier, where Vira had laser-focused her snarls and howls of warning. The sister collies turned about, scanning, and then joined in with Vira; I suspect more on principle and team solidarity than from a perceived threat.

"Girls," I said in a hushed voice, even though my fight-or-flight response clamored for us to flee the scene, to get the hell out of there.

And then a figure dressed head to toe in black stepped slowly into a narrow gap between two pine trees.

I froze to the ground, an ice sculpture—too terrified to breathe—but my golden retriever launched herself like a rocket, thundering down toward the dark figure. Instead of retreating, the man took a single step forward. His left hand lifted—he held something, some kind of tube—and that broke my trance.

"No!" I screamed.

A blast of mist—a thick funnel of fog—hit Vira at twenty feet out. She went down on her shoulder, yelped, rolled sideways, spun about a circle—becoming a whirling dervish of coughs and yaps and cries.

I stepped forward. "Run, Vira! Run!"

And my golden retriever ran. And it wasn't pretty. I'm not

sure how Vira did it—blind and choking on tear gas—but she scurried diagonally under a pine tree. We heard a thump and piercing yelp as she slammed into the trunk, then another second of scuttling noise . . . then she was gone.

"Drop the canister, Motherfucker!" Officer Ennis shouted, stepping into the clearing, sidearm drawn, his gun sights on the man dressed in black. "Drop it now, Motherfucker!"

The figure in black released the cylinder with his left hand, letting it drop to the ground.

I'd forgotten about the cop from Lansing, tears of relief came to my eyes . . . and then something bad—and I mean something very bad—happened.

Ennis approached from the side, from where the trail curved around the clearing. He'd spotted the dark figure a step in front of the row of pines—saw the man sported a ski mask as though to knock over a savings and loan—and witnessed what he'd done to Vira with the can of pepper spray. Ennis had walked into something all right, something much more than a dead man lying in the weeds.

Officer Ennis came in slowly, cautiously, gun leveled in a two-handed grip, held directly in front of his eyes. The only flaw was that the dark figure faced forward, still looking at me, and Ennis could only see him in profile.

"Hands in the air where I can see them, Motherfucker." Officer Ennis's voice was authority incarnate, the man was all business.

Bit by bit the figure's left hand—his canister hand—began to rise. His right hand swayed inward, by his thigh now, no longer blocked by pine branches.

And I could see what he held.

My jaw dropped. "He's got a—"

It's like when frames have been removed from a movie in order to make the movements speed past. It happened so fast I can't say I saw the dark figure drop and twist toward the Lansing police officer, his right hand outstretched. Three shots were fired in the blink of an eye, another blink later and Ennis crumpled to the ground.

"Run," I screamed at my sister collies. "Run!"

There was no time to ponder or debate.

I either make it to the ravine . . . or I die.

CHAPTER 30

Everyman didn't know how Dog Man's golden retriever had gotten a bead on him so quickly. He'd not even begun sliding out from under the tree when the cadaver dog tipped off Reid. He'd researched human remains detection dogs and knew they keyed in on decomposition scents—on blood and bone and decaying flesh.

And he'd purposely made a mess of Weston Davies's chest to keep the damned mutts in hog heaven.

Reid's golden retriever had gummed up the schedule all right—he'd wanted to work his way much closer before being detected; Everyman wanted point-blank range—but it was worth the price of admission to douse the critter in bear spray. The golden furball had such high hopes and dreams and lofty ambitions—plans on how it would destroy Everyman's afternoon—only to have those hopes and dreams go up in smoke or, more accurately, come crashing down in a cloud of capsaicin, which is basically the active component of chili peppers. When the furry fucker dropped to earth like a bag of cement, spun like a kid's top, scuttled blindly under the pine tree, and smashed against the trunk, Everyman almost held up a palm to ask Reid for a truce, so they could go out for a beer and relive the sight from every angle.

Unfortunately, Everyman's mirth and good cheer nearly did him in. It kept him from noticing the hulking ape of a cop as he snuck in from the sidelines. Of course Everyman dropped the can of bear spray and began to raise his left arm. Everyman watched in his periphery as the police officer approached. To get off a good shot he needed the cop to come closer, and closer still, but Reid began to shout a warning and Everyman went O.K. Corral.

Afterward, Reid began to scurry, his collies ahead of him—already leaping into the ravine. Everyman tore after the Dog Man, wasting a shot, realizing at this distance that a running man trying to peg another running man wasn't going to happen. But it was a clearing, basically a meadow, so Everyman went into an Isosceles stance—feet shoulder-width apart, support foot a little in front, elbows locked, two-handed grip—keyed in on center mass, and pulled the trigger as Dog Man Reid lunged over the side of the ravine.

And damned if he didn't tag him.

CHAPTER 31

Something punched at my armpit, twisting me sideways as I plummeted into the ravine. I bounced off the mud eight feet below, somehow scrambled to my feet, and took off after my collies. The creek ran at a trickle this time of year. I stayed to the side, near mangled branches and exposed roots, hoping they'd provide cover, and damned near cheered when I cut right around the first bend without incoming fire.

It finally registered I'd been shot. Each step stung like a beehive. I squeezed my arm to my chest with my right hand, stumbled forward, and then poured it on, running as fast as possible on the muck and uneven dirt. I breathed hard, sucking in air and performing mental gymnastics, figuring another hundred yards before I hit Cohansey—one of the side roads that sections off Gomsrud Park—maybe double that if the creek serpentined its way toward the street.

My collies came back for me, but I nudged them along with my chin. "Run, girls. Run."

Then I heard sirens—screeching and piercing—from the front side of Gomsrud, maybe they were pouring into the lot where I'd parked my pickup. I thought maybe Ennis had called in the dead body or maybe Lansing PD overheard the skirmish through Ennis's radio or maybe there were multiple reports of gunshots.

The knife in Davies's chest and the choker necklace clasped about his throat flashed through my mind. I peeked down at my shoulder, saw my shirt turning crimson, and staggered ahead as best I could.

When I hit Cohansey I felt giddy and thought I might be slipping into shock, my arm now numb as though it were asleep. I lurched across Cohansey during a gap in traffic, flagging the two girls along with me, turning to look for Vira, feeling sick when I remembered she was still in the park, recovering from the pepper spray, hoping she stayed in hiding, hoping that pepper spray would soon wear off my poor little girl.

I cut inside the nearest shop—an A&W—and stumbled to the front of the line. The guy ordering seemed upset at first, but after a glance at me—covered in muck and blood—he backed away, maybe even left.

"Call 911," I shouted at the staff, all now milling about on the other side of the counter, knowing that Lansing's entire police department was likely at Gomsrud Park as all of us in the A&W could still hear the sirens. "And those are my dogs," I said, pointing outside their front door as I slid down to the floor. "Don't let anything happen to my dogs."

Fearing I'd pass out at any second, I kept repeating the *don't let anything happen to my dogs* refrain to anyone who passed my orb as two squad cars and an ambulance arrived. I parroted it to the paramedics as they cut off my sleeve, examined my underarm, applied bandages and pressure.

The paramedics must have determined my wound was not life-threatening as I kept repeating my mantra to the wide-eyed officers who took my truncated statement: "Officer Ennis and I were attacked in the field by the north trail, between the pine trees and the ravine, before the landscape breaks upward into Knob Hill, near the bunny hill; we were attacked where we'd found the body of the missing senior citizen."

The officers wanted to know about their friend and colleague.

"I think he's dead," I could barely choke out and felt tears rush to my eyes. "I'm afraid he's dead."

Before they shut me in and closed the back of the ambulance, I caught a glimpse of Vira standing next to Maggie and Delta—blinking her eyes and staring my way.

Thank you, God, I thought. Thank you.

CHAPTER 32

Everyman tore off his ski mask in his mad dash to the lip of the ravine, hoping there was time for the Dog Man to see his true face before taking his last breath. He hit the edge at full tilt, nearly tumbled into the hollow himself and . . . goddamnit, there was no Mason Reid.

Everyman scanned right, his SIG 1911 sweeping along with his line of vision, and he caught sight of the Dog Man stumbling around a creek bend. He'd winged the son of a bitch—saw blood in the filth and mud where Dog Man had crash-landed—but it wasn't a kill shot. It took every ounce of self-control to keep from leaping into the creek bed and tearing off after the lucky son of a bitch. Everyman knew he'd catch Reid in a minute or less, he knew he could make Reid look into his eyes—make him look into his true face—and then he'd aerate the pesky fucker once and for all.

But the police sirens clinched the deal.

Everyman stormed back; grabbed his backpack, canister, and mask; did two seconds crossing the ravine; and then bolted for the bunny hill. By the time he'd made it to the park's "shut-for-the-season" tow rope, he'd donned the John Deere hat and Buddy Holly glasses. Ten feet later he sported the Chicago Bears windbreaker. Everything else went into the backpack, now covered by his windbreaker. Any eyewitnesses turned up during police canvassing might mention they saw some nimrod cutting up the Knob Hill tow rope from Gomsrud, and just assumed the silly-looking dork lived nearby.

Everyman didn't want to kill the police officer, had been hoping Lansing PD wouldn't take his call to Silver Years too seriously—at least until a body showed up—and would only send Reid and his dogs to scour the damned park. Killing a cop would mean a handful of detectives might actually put down the donuts and start asking questions.

Killing a cop would bring beaucoup heat.

Everyman figured the squad cars were at the park's entrance by now, filling the main guest lot. Soon, if not already, they'd figure out their cars could fit on the hiking and biking trails. He had to assume the dead cop had radioed in where Weston Davies had been found—field before the ravine—which meant he only had about a minute. Everyman picked up his pace. He didn't take off in an uphill sprint, as that might signal his being the cause of the police sirens to any potential witnesses, but at a quicker, more-sturdy hiker's aerobic stride. Near the hilltop, he turned to look back. Knob Hill did have a hell of a view, he had to admit, and squad cars had yet to roll into the clearing. From his elevation he could see his handiwork—both bodies—the dead cop and Weston Davies and . . . Jesus Christ.

At the bottom of Knob Hill sat a golden retriever, motionless, staring back up at him. Even at this distance Everyman knew it was the goddamned dog he'd blasted with bear spray. Everyman gazed back at the golden—like a staring contest when you were a kid—then realized what he was doing and got his ass back into high gear.

At the top of Knob Hill, he glanced back down. A squad car was pulling into the field, slowly, not wanting to get stuck or mess up the crime scene, but that goddamn golden retriever was nowhere to be found.

Three minutes later Everyman was in his rental car.

Five minutes later, he was leaving Lansing.

CHAPTER 33

"This makes zero sense, Reid," Detective Hanson marched into my hospital room at nine p.m. sharp and spoke without preamble while his partner, Detective Marr, stood in the doorframe. "Hell, I'd arrest you if I could figure out how you managed to shoot yourself in the armpit from behind."

They were keeping me overnight at Community Hospital in Munster, a five-minute skip east into Indiana. With feral-boy having already slashed my left forearm and me now getting shot in the left armpit, the only decent takeaway is *thank God I'm right-handed.* They had a cop sitting outside my room, like you see in the movies, and the hospital had its own security guards making their rounds. It didn't really matter; I was too medicated to feel frightened. The doctors had me on morphine to control the post-surgical pain and, though groggy, I did my best to answer any questions the Lansing investigators—boomeranging in and out of my room—had for me.

At some point along the way someone must have paged the two CPD detectives.

"Tell me you've contacted the Grohls," I'd voiced my concern about Becky Grohl's safety to every officer, detective or not, who'd wandered into my orbit. If this was tied into Nicky Champine and his feral son, Becky Grohl might also be in danger.

"They're heading to a friend's cabin in Oregon," Hanson

replied. "We were at their house right after this broke. Marr even carried her dad's rifle to the minivan."

Marr lifted a hand my way from the doorway. "Least I could do."

"From the look on Mr. Grohl's face, they're probably halfway there by now."

"Did you see the old man's body?"

Both detectives nodded in unison and Hanson said, "The knife is the same make and model as the one the Champine kid had. The black velvet choker necklace is *newish*—at least as those go—so likely not from Nicky Champine's sister's collection."

"But no missing girl," I said. "And why the old guy?"

"No fuss, no muss," Hanson said. "Weston Davies lived in an old fogey home down the street and walked those trails every morning. He more than served his purpose."

"What was his purpose?"

"I think you know," the detective said to me. "To lure you into the woods, Reid. To lure you in and kill you."

I then shared with the two investigators how someone had been poking about the woods near my trailer home in the wee hours of the morning last week, and how Vira and the collies had gone crazy—waking me, warning me. And how I no longer believed it to be a trick of the light . . . how I truly saw someone fade back into the shadows of the trees and the brush.

"That was your dogs saving your life," Hanson replied. "Sort of like they did today."

CHAPTER 34

Everyman took I-94 out of Lansing. He stayed in the right lane and followed the speed limit as though it were gospel. He pulled into a McDonald's drive-thru at Roseland and ordered three Big Macs, a large fry, and coffee.

Killing made him hungry.

Everyman parked in a spot farthest away from the restaurant's entrance and, between sips of black coffee, made short order of one burger as well as the entire batch of fries. Then he smeared the remaining two burgers and special sauce over the ski mask, crumpled the remaining mound of mush together as though he were kneading bread dough and dropped it into the bag his order had come in. Everyman walked inside, stuffed the bag into the nearest trash bin, hit the restroom and washed his hands.

Although he'd paid cash, he tore up the receipt and flushed it.

Everyman then sat in the car again and took apart the SIG Sauer 1911—ejected the magazine, cleared the chamber, field stripped the frame, and removed the barrel from the slide. He went through the drive-thru a second time, refilling his coffee and buying a couple items off the dollar menu. He dumped the small burgers onto the passenger seat and put the pieces of the SIG 1911 into the McDonald's bag. He thought about popping the trunk and putting the bag with the rental's spare tire but said *fuck it* and headed out.

Everyman headed straight into the city, took Lake Shore Drive, and found a parking spot near the Chicago Yacht Club. Everyman put on a hat—not John Deere this time, a Cubs baseball cap—and sunglasses. He stuffed the McDonald's bag filled with SIG Sauer parts into a side pocket of his oversized windbreaker and headed out for a pleasant stroll along the lake.

A mile later the throng of walkers thinned in the late-afternoon sun. Everyman rounded a bend and found the spot he'd been looking for. He walked to the shoreline—the color of the water was beautiful—smiled in the sun, and began tossing pebbles and small stones into Lake Michigan. As Everyman continued his walk along the shore, he mixed in SIG Sauer parts—frame, barrel, springs, magazine—with the pebbles and stones until his McDonald's bag was empty.

On the way back to his car, he dumped the bag in a trash bin along the walkway.

Everyman wouldn't want to litter.

He returned the rental car—speed checkout, again settling in cash—tossed the burgers in his backpack and used their restroom. He washed the canister of bear spray with towels and half the soap from the dispenser, and used more towels to wipe it down and placed it back in his pack. As he hiked a few blocks to the nearest bus stop, he dropped the canister inside a fence at an empty playground. Kids would find it after dinner, dick around with it, and that would be that.

Everyman thought about how the movies make their villains omnipotent, and ghostlike. They never screw up until the final minute and perhaps not even then if there's a sequel in the works. In those films there are never a hundred potential eyewitnesses capturing the killer on their cell phone cameras, the heavy never leaves prints or DNA at the crime scenes, and, when cornered, the baddie is able to fight like a cross between Bruce Lee and Godzilla. Quite frankly, Everyman grew philosophical on the city bus returning him to his regular vehicle, when you get right down to it, killing was easy—thirteen-year-old gangbangers did it all the time—getting away with homicide was the tricky part.

Everyman was left-brain dominant, high in analytical skills, sound in logic, and talented in math and science. Left-brain dominant or not, he was also aware of his *faulty wiring*. He'd read studies on people like himself—years ago, back when he felt a need to know the things the experts knew, what the profilers knew—back when he thought the knowledge might matter, that it might be useful. He'd read so much *abnormal* psych it became tedious. Everyman knew he didn't process emotions normally. Fear and love meant nothing, they were mere abstracts—constructs—otherwise Everyman could never have accomplished the things he'd achieved.

Sure, he cared not to get captured and would do everything in his power to avoid that . . . what with prison cuisine being what it was.

There were only two large-scale sensations that in some manner or another got through to him. First, the absolute adrenaline rush of doing what he did. Perhaps that's what it was all about, the ultimate in a thrill-seeking addiction. And that addiction went hand in hand with the complete anarchy Everyman had discovered in murder.

The second large-scale sensation was the anger.

The anger didn't come often—in fact, *anger* was too weak a word for it—and he was shocked the few times it washed over him, flooding his senses. It was debilitating, nearly uncontrollable. He couldn't think straight.

Instead he saw red.

Blood red.

Just like the night in Bridgeport when he spotted the forensic pathologists carrying the Champine boy out in a body bag. It was all he could do to keep from rushing forward into Nicky Champine's front yard and emptying his SIG 1911 into every cop and every detective and every ambulance driver in his path, and then drawing his knife to finish off the rest.

Of course that would have been a suicide run.

Instead, he'd forced himself to his knees that night in Bridgeport, a migraine of fury drilling into his cerebellum. Everyman was stunned to find he had this level of feeling—perhaps some kind of affection—for the little fucker . . . as there he was, on his goddamned knees, crippled in rage over the boy's death. He knelt there on the ground for five straight minutes until the answer came to him and, with the answer, the blood red passed.

The Dog Man put that boy in the body bag, ergo, Everyman was going to kill the Dog Man.

Although Mason Reid had been wounded today, he'd been saved by his dogs twice so far . . . three times if you count his night in the basement of the Bridgeport rambler.

But Everyman had all the time in the world.

And he was left-brain dominant.

There would not be a fourth.

CHAPTER 35

"Can you hear me, Mace?"

I opened my eyes and may have mumbled something to effect of, "Perfyzzertquees."

"Mace." Kippy's face hovered over me. "Are you awake?"

"Of course I'm awake," I said, slurring, my brain detached as though I were speaking in the third person. "I got shot, Kippy."

"I know, Mace," Kippy replied. "The doctor said you're going to be okay."

I looked at her several seconds or maybe a decade and finally said, "You have the prettiest eyes."

"Yes, two of them," she said. "I came here to let you know that we have your dogs. Okay?" Kippy nodded her head as though to prod me along, to help me grasp her talking points. "Wabs and I sprung them from Lansing PD earlier tonight."

The clock on the wall read quarter of twelve—whatever *quarter of twelve* meant—and I did my best to focus on what Kippy was saying to me but she seemed to be floating in and out of a dark tunnel, or maybe I was the one floating in and out of a dark tunnel. Not long after Detectives Hanson and Marr had left, the hospital had upped my pain meds and/or given me something to help me sleep.

Eventually I said, "Are the girls okay?"

"They were spoiled rotten, Mace. They even got to eat people food."

Eventually I said, "Fucker tear-gassed Vira."

"She's fine. I called a vet and they told me what to do. Wabs held her while I rinsed her eyes with saline." Kippy stared into my face to see if anything she was telling me was getting through my medicated skull. "And I used up that entire bottle of doggie shampoo you had under your laundry tub scrubbing it out of her fur."

Eventually I said, "How did you get in my house?"

"We're cops, Mace."

The red flag cut through my grogginess. "But he knows where I live," I said to her. "And the bastard wants me dead."

For some reason this notion struck me as funny as hell and I cackled like a chicken—louder and longer—until I caught sight of Kippy gazing down at me without the slightest hint of a smile. After my cackling stuttered and came to a stop, I spent another decade telling her about the watcher in the woods from last week, and how I knew for a fact it was the same man hiding in the pines at Gomsrud Park.

"Don't worry," Kippy said after piecing together my semi-coherent ramblings. "If anyone tries to break in, Wabs will shoot them in the face. I'm heading back to your trailer now and the squad car will be sitting in your driveway all night."

"Kippy?"

"What, Mace?"

I forgot what I wanted to tell her, but eventually I said, "Can I drive the squad car sometime?"

"Sure, Mace, but it's time for you to go back to sleep. Okay?" she said. "I just stopped by to let you know the dogs are safe."

I don't remember if I did but I'd like to think I thanked her, and then I said, "Kippy?"

"What, Mace?"

"The prettiest eyes."

CHAPTER 36

Three days had passed since the shooting.

After spending the bulk of a second day at Community Hospital being poked and prodded and fed pills, Detectives Hanson and Marr got me into a three-bedroom, split-level safe house in Park Forest. Hanson had stopped by every evening to fill me in on the day's investigation. His briefings didn't take long, unfortunately, but at least he brought pizza.

Now if I could only talk him out of pineapple toppings.

Then, the next morning, Kippy brought Sue and the ladies over. I blinked back tears when the kids showed up. I hugged them with my good arm, shook paws, scratched ears and chins, and then ushered them into their new playground; the safe house had a spacious backyard surrounded by chain link. All the jostling with the dogs hurt like hell so I verbally thanked each officer a baker's dozen times or more.

Even Wabiszewski gave me a soft pat on my good shoulder in salutation.

The wound wasn't deep; the projectile only absconded with a teaspoon of flesh. I'd been lucky, according to one of the surgeons who told me I could have been stabbed in the armpit with a knife and then bled to death or choked on my own blood. The doctors had cleaned the wound, sterilized it, stitched me up—thirty stitches not counting the liquid skin adhesive—and pumped me full of antibiotics. For being so lucky, my entire left side throbbed with every bump or jolt or beat of my heart. And unlike the heroes on TV, I doubted I'd be good to go after a short commercial break. The bandage had been replaced this morning. The doctor wanted it kept dry another few days before I could begin washing it with that strange-smelling liquid soap they'd provided.

But the other wound, the real one I worried might never heal, was my sense of guilt over the death of Officer Roderick "Rod" Ennis. The man had single-handedly saved my life. If Officer Ennis had taken a leisurely stroll on his way to the clearing, I'd be a dead man. If Officer Ennis had decided to scroll Facebook as he waited for LPD's finest to arrive at Gomsrud, I'd be a dead man.

Rod Ennis had interrupted my murder.

I'd read the officer's obituary. Repeatedly. The man had a two-year-old son with another on the way. A couple of kids would never know their father and a wife would never see her husband again. It's irrational—I understand that on some gut level—and maybe it's a form of survivor's guilt as Kippy had pointed out when she'd brought the dogs over.

"You were a victim, Mace," Kippy had told me. "Officer Ennis would know it's not your fault. It's the son of a bitch in the ski mask, Mace . . . and we're going to catch him."

When I had shared the news of Vira's having had another *episode* after her discovery of Weston Davies in the clearing at Gomsrud Park, and her ensuing warning of a monster hidden among the pines, Kippy took it in stride. A case could be made that she was a bigger disciple of Vira's mysterious abilities than I; after all, Kippy had seen her in action first. However, Officer Wabiszewski was a tougher sell. He'd been struggling with Vira's unique *skill set* and hadn't quite advanced beyond the doubting Thomas phase. Fortunately, however, Wabiszewski was a skeptic on most matters. He didn't appear to have a lot of trust in anyone not named Kippy Gimm or Dave Wabiszewski.

In fact, Wabiszewski looked about the room after my tale of Vira's Gomsrud warning and said, "We can't go running to Detective Hanson or his partner, Detective Marr, and, when they ask how you knew Weston Davies's killer was lying in wait to polish you off, tell them we've got this clairvoyant dog. 'No shit, Detective Hanson, really, little Fido's right out of *The X-Files*—she has second sight or ESP or maybe she even knows God—and that's how we knew about Nicky Champine and North Mayfair and the prick in the woods.' "

We absorbed Officer Wabiszewski's analysis in silence.

Wabiszewski went on, "Listen, I wouldn't be here if I hadn't seen in person what went down in North Mayfair. We can buy it maybe, maybe not, but how do we convince an assembly of high-ranking cynics without getting our asses tossed in Lakeshore?"

Chicago Lakeshore was the city's major psychiatric hospital.

"Look," I said, picking pages off the printer Hanson and Marr had helped me lug to the safe house and bringing them to the kitchen table, "here's some stuff I got off the internet, and we all know how everything on the internet is true." I'd read an article once that recommended beginning a presentation with a joke or some kind of lightheartedness. Unfortunately, Kippy wasn't guffawing and Wabiszewski didn't appear to be rolling in the aisle, so I continued. "It all makes for an intriguing read but it's kind of awkward to talk about, you know, out loud and in front of people—I feel as though I should check myself into Chicago Lakeshore . . . but just bear with me." My homework assignment had been short and sweet—to try and figure out Vira's *special* ability. "We've already touched on mediumistic sensitivity, where some folks are highly sensitive and can serve as conduits for psychic communication. But there's also a phenomenon known as clairolfaction, which is a form of clairvoyance. It's where a person is able to access their mediumistic ability through their sense of smell."

Wabiszewski smirked.

"Okay, okay," I said, a palm in the air. "I know it sounds as though I'm talking out of my ass, but remember, we're talking about a dog . . . and dogs in the *normal* world already have this absurdly powerful sense of smell."

"I smell dead people," Wabiszewski did a passable imitation of the clairvoyant kid from *The Sixth Sense*.

"Shut up, Wabs," Kippy said. "Vira's a cadaver dog. It's what she does."

"Wikipedia also coughed up some interesting information." I shuffled my stack of sheets to another page with my good hand and began, "Retrocognition is when a person has knowledge of a past event, but could not have learned about that past event via ordinary means." I paused a second, shrugged, and then dropped my stack of sheets onto the kitchen floor. "Look, I feel as though I should be humming the theme from *The Twilight Zone*, so let's return to the land of the living. Training dogs is what I do—day in and day out. That said, Vira is the smartest, most-intuitive dog I've ever trained. The girl communicates with her eyes and, hell, her entire body better than any mime I've ever seen," I said. "She recognizes voices and seems to comprehend more words than I do. This is miles beyond discerning gestures or being able to follow some simple pointing. And we're fluent in each other's cues. Vira can read my face, she can tell if I'm sick, she knows my moods—and I can be a moody son of a bitch."

"Most dog owners would say similar things about their precious little Fido or Rover," Wabiszewski said.

"But Vira is off the charts; she's a freaking genius."

"So forget supernatural; rather, she's a canine Madame Curie?"

"I don't know. Intelligence ultimately boils down to brain size relative to one's body size—that's why having a brain one-fiftieth the mass of our bodies puts us at the top of the food chain," I said, amazed I recalled the fraction. "But dogs are no slouches either, their brains are at a ratio of 1:125 the mass of their bodies, and that holds true across all breeds. Most other animals would be in special-ed classes compared to dogs."

I could tell I was losing them in the math. "I have a final thought, though, and you two were there that first evening in Granger's garage—maybe there's some kind of uptick in neural activity or canine IQ or whatever caused by suffering heavy trauma at such an early age."

Wabiszewski smirked again.

"You know her best, Mace." Kippy stared my way. "No more BS. What is Vira's special gift?"

I had trouble making eye contact. Perhaps an extended stay at Chicago Lakeshore would be for the best. "Scent DNA."

"Scent DNA?" Wabiszewski said, his face scrunched like wrinkled laundry.

"I tossed and turned last night, couldn't sleep a wink, and it came to me around three a.m. Murder's an intimate act, right? And killers leave all sorts of DNA that the CSI teams sort through. Now stick with me a second here. Why wouldn't there be scent DNA—some kind of scent aura—left at crime scenes as well? Of course there would be. In terms of the Velvet Choker Killer, Nicky Champine had Kari Jo Brockman in his basement for three months. Ultimately, he'd strangled the poor girl and stuffed her in his trunk. And Nicomaine Ocampo's son, John Jr., stabbed his mother to death in their kitchen." I took a second to catch my breath. "Now Vira—and maybe all HRD dogs—receive this avalanche of stimulus, this smorgasbord of scent data, but she's kicking it up to the next level. Seriously. Vira visits a crime scene and then attempts to process this smorgasbord, to perform some kind of forensic analysis on the various smells and odors—the scent DNA—and decode them."

We chewed quietly on this morsel before I continued.

"I need a Stephen Hawking or someone light-years smarter to explain what I'm getting at, but the scent receptors in a dog's nose are beyond amazing. You want supernatural—these scent receptors are supernatural and they enable dogs to identify thousands and thousands of different smells and, in Vira's case, I think she interprets these odors. She makes links, she makes relationships . . . connections—she connects the dots," I said. "So do I think Vira is some kind of ghost dog? Hell no. Vira's just Vira—she's the LeBron James of cadaver dogs."

CHAPTER 37

"Why does it always have to be Hawaiian?" I asked as politely as my taste buds would permit. The two CPD detectives and I sat at the safe house's kitchen table eating pizza with paper plates and plastic forks. The dogs were all in other rooms. I think even they'd gotten tired of the same scent night after night.

"He's screwing you with Canadian bacon and pineapple every evening?" Detective Marr said.

"Hey," Hanson said, plopping a third slab onto his plate, "the man who buys the pizza gets to pick the toppings."

"But the Department's picking up the tab," Marr replied.

I looked at Detective Hanson.

"Okay, the man who physically picks up the pizza and brings it to the safe house gets to pick the toppings."

CPD's policy of my not ordering food to be delivered to the safe house had been explained to me. They didn't want me handing out this address to anybody, not even my parents. I considered myself lucky they allowed Kippy and her partner to swing by now and again. In fact, those two would be arriving any minute, hopefully with more beer. "You tell the kid what that lady at Silver Years said?"

Hanson finished chewing. "The kid's got enough to worry about."

"You know I'm right here, don't ya?"

Hanson looked at me and said, "When the shooter called Silver Years the first time—with that bullshit ruse about finding his mother a place to live—the director jotted his name down on her calendar."

"And?"

"He told her his name was *Reid Mason*."

"Good to know my murderer's got a sense of humor," I said, pushing my half-eaten first slice aside. I was no longer hungry. "I train dogs, and I try to help you guys out whenever stuff pops up, and now I'm walking around with this giant bull's-eye on my back."

"See what you did?" Hanson said to Marr. "You got him all riled up." He turned back to me. "As long as Marr and I aren't the killer, you're safe here. You even got your girlfriend stopping by."

"She's not my girlfriend."

"Well," the detective replied, "that's a damn shame."

"I've canceled all my training classes. If anyone calls me with work, I have to say no," I said. "As of now, I'm down to six hundred bucks in the bank."

"We should set up a GoFundMe page," Marr said. "A picture of you and the dogs with a note: *Please don't let us get murdered.*"

"That'd probably go viral?" Hanson said.

"If I do the page, kid, can I have ten percent?"

"Sure," I said, unsure if the two detectives were joshing or not. "Anything new today?"

"This should cheer you up," Hanson said. "When I was talking to that lady at Silver Years, she told me the guy on the other end of the phone had a white voice. I'm sure her hearing my black voice clued her in. I don't know if I should be insulted or not."

"You're too old to be insulted," Marr said and turned to me. "It's too bad you don't have midget feet."

"Why?"

"You're a size nine and nine's the same size shoeprint they got from the dirt in that strip of woods by your house. They also got a size nine from the soil around the pine trees at Gomsrud."

"Is there anything you can do with that?"

"We've got some photographs and casts from the impression," Marr replied, "but I don't think our perp's dumb enough to hang on to any designer boots he wore to a double murder."

"Look, kid, I know this sucks out loud for you—it's a kick in the nuts—but believe me, you're the first one I'll call if anything breaks," Hanson said. "We've interviewed and reinterviewed Nicky Champine's neighbors. No one remembers there ever being any other cars parked in Champine's driveway or on the street in front of his house besides that Pontiac of his, which he always kept in the garage. We're fingerprinting every square inch of his rambler. But having ruled out Champine's prints and his kid's, your prints, the prints of the female victims," the detective shook his head, "that's looking to be a dead end."

"Something'll pop soon," Marr said. "A cop was killed, and though we do our best to solve all murders, this cuts close to home. If it makes you feel better, when we get him—and we'll get him—it's fifty-fifty he comes out feet first."

"It's not just us," Hanson added. The two were tag-teaming to lift my spirits. "This is front burner if you've been watching the headlines. We're working with Lansing PD, with their detectives. Even the FBI, their Chicago field office, has offered to help."

"Of course all those guys are a bunch of pussies," Marr said, "but they let us use their database."

"Can't they do that profiling thing?" I asked.

Marr thought a moment and said, "You want a profile, kid? White male between thirty—'cause of experience, 'cause of what we've seen him do—and sixty. I go with sixty because I'm fifty-five and I'd be a hell of a serial killer if I put my mind to it. Our guy appears to be average height, average weight, hell; he's even got an average shoe size."

"Fifty-fifty on him having served in the military based on the skill with which he used both the gun and knife."

"And he's a cunning son of a bitch," Marr continued. "Look how he put all of these pieces together in order to lure you out to Gomsrud. I'd even toss in that he's a college grad, just for shits and giggles."

I made no comment.

Detective Hanson finally said, "And killing's easy for him."

"Yes," Marr replied. "Killing is easy for him."

"You know it's a popular misconception that African Americans aren't serial killers," Hanson said, switching topics. "That's simply not true—we hold our own."

Turned out I'd been right about Detective Hanson. He'd been divorced for three years and, after I shared a bit about my marital situation, he looked at me and said, "If you didn't want the split, it never heals."

I already had enough things to worry about and I hoped Hanson had been speaking more to himself than to me.

What I'd kept from Detective Hanson—we'd been chummy, but I didn't know him that well—was my observation that he was already in another marriage of a sort. The bond he had with his partner was palpable. If anyone messed with Detective Marr, they'd best be prepared to deal with Hanson, and if anyone messed with Hanson . . . well, vice versa.

To me, that's as good a definition of marriage as any.

I knew the detectives were trying to lighten my mood with the nightly visits and updates, and I enjoyed watching as Hanson and Marr jostled and ribbed and gave each other shit. And, unless I find myself on the wrong side of the grass in the impending weeks, I assume the partners do good work.

"I'll be pissed at you two if I wind up a statistic in a documentary on NBC or some cable channel," I said. "You know—*back after commercial, we'll tell you where they found the charred remains of Mason Reid.*"

Marr grinned and said, "Don't worry; we'll say nice things about you in the interview."

"Too bad the killer followed us from the station to Reid's safe house," Hanson said as though he were in front of a row of microphones. "In hindsight, we'd have done things differently."

Marr grinned again and said, "When are your cop friends going to get here and what the hell do they want from us?"

Since all of my left arm's toil had been reallocated, I glanced at the watch on my right wrist. "Any minute now. Kippy's done some research and would like to bounce it off you two."

Of course there was more to it than that—much more—but I'd wait till the gang got here so we could all team up and make our case.

The safe house was killing me.

If I get a flat tire, I change it. If my roof leaks, I patch it. If my dog catches a serial killer and winds up on death row, I'll do whatever it takes to save her. But this waiting around shit was driving me crazy. I'm not wired to lounge about all day, sitting on the couch, eating bonbons, and getting hooked on afternoon soap operas. It's not in my DNA. I'd read somewhere that sharks must remain in constant motion or they'll die. And I'm beginning to understand how they feel.

I'd passed from denial to acceptance in about fifteen minutes. I'd accepted the fact that an unknown stranger—a cold-blooded killer—wanted me dead. Okay, not necessarily where I'd pictured myself at this juncture in my life, but I'd hurdled acceptance and was now onto the final stage in my development . . . the *pissed-off-what-can-I-do* stage?

Sure, shrinks might insist I'd never left the anger phase; but, not wanting to quibble with the American Psychiatric Association, both *anger* and *what-can-I-do* led us to the real purpose of tonight's meeting.

"You keep grimacing, kid," Hanson said. "How's the arm?"

Five days had passed since the incident at Gomsrud Park and my pain management was down to acetaminophen and beer.

"Healing, I suppose. Sure wish it were a month from now."

"Just say the word and I'll see if I can scrounge up some fentanyl from the evidence locker."

"Good to know."

"Seriously, kid. You look like all your dogs ran away from home," Hanson said. "Anything we can we do to cheer you up?"

I glanced at the detective and said, "A pepperoni with black olives."

CHAPTER 38

"Generally speaking, we think of serial killers as lone psychopaths, outcasts driven by an unquenchable thirst to make their twisted fantasies come true," Kippy said and held up a folder stuffed with papers. She'd come prepared. "However, studies have indicated that upward of twenty percent of serial killers, and maybe even higher, hunt in pairs. That's more than a fifth."

"Think about it," Detective Hanson chimed in. "For every four Dahmers, you get a couple of assholes like the Speed Freak Killers."

Both detectives were playing nice; egos had been kept in check. Either that or the two were busy with the twelve-pack of Heineken Wabiszewski had handed off to them upon entering the safe house.

"History provides countless examples of murderers working together as teams—Leopold and Loeb, Bonnie and Clyde," Kippy continued. "Leonard Lake and Charles Ng—the Operation Miranda Killers—collected women as sex slaves before killing them. Angelo Buono and Kenneth Bianchi—cousins for crying out loud—stalked LA as the Hillside Strangler. Bianchi even wanted to become a police officer, but, thankfully, got tossed on his ear by the local sheriff's office."

Kippy had handed out photocopies of her research. While the others followed along on their hard copies I enjoyed watching her present. I got the sense that fellow students would have loved to crib Kippy's notes in high school.

Something I never had to worry about.

"There are even a number of duo-sex teams. You've all no doubt heard of Charles Starkweather and the killing spree he went on with his fourteen-year-old girlfriend Caril Ann Fugate. Another couple, Paul Bernardo and Karla Homolka, were quite the match—abducting teenage girls, taking sexual turns with them, killing them." Kippy glanced down at her handout, frowned, but continued, "This next one's a hometown story—a guy by the name of Robin Gecht who, along with his several accomplices, were known as the Chicago Rippers as they raped, tortured, and murdered prostitutes, other single women, housewives. I only bring them up to point out how *killing partners* can go beyond pairs."

"Gecht and his asshole friends were part of a satanic cult," Detective Marr piped in this time. "I imagine like Manson, Gecht was able to bend others to his will."

Kippy nodded. "Now in the case of the Velvet Choker Killer, we know all about Nicky Champine and his son by incest, but what if there was a third *killing partner* in the mix?" Kippy cut to the heart of the matter. "What if this third partner is the one who laid the trap for Reid at Gomsrud Park?"

"But Champine and his kid seem so low-rent," Wabiszewski said. "Gruesome to read about, like Jeffrey Dahmer, but Nicky Champine hardly seems to be *able to bend others to his will*."

"Think the other way around," Hanson rose and stood next to Kippy—Heineken in hand, a most-contented professor—and faced the room. "In terms of these teams of killing partners, let's also talk about what we call the *dominant predator*. These dominant predators have an uncanny eye for recruitment, and for grooming potential accomplices. They're able to recognize certain traits—say young, needy, extremely insecure, mentally unstable, low intelligence—and work these individuals, manipulate them, wrap them around their little finger, and train them as co-conspirators."

"So what if there's a dominant predator hiding in the weeds?" Kippy got the last word. "And what if he's got it in for Mace?"

I carried out a one-handed battle with the bottle of Tylenol—damn those childproof caps—and eventually shook two extra-strength tablets onto my plate and looked at Hanson and Marr. "Can I ask you guys a big favor?"

"You can ask."

"I know you've already grilled him," I said to the detectives. "But can you set up another meeting with Nicky Champine?"

CHAPTER 39

The main ground rule was that there would be no questions of any kind regarding any of the charges the State had already brought against Nicky Champine. The Velvet Choker Killer had been charged with four counts of first-degree murder, four counts of kidnapping resulting in death, and sexual assault. Compliments of the Illinois Department of Corrections, Champine was being held in remand—in detention—at Stateville Correctional Center.

It had been a no-brainer for the presiding judge; Nicky Champine had been denied bail.

And no matter what Champine said or did today—even if he coughed up the name, address, and golf handicap of the man who murdered Weston Davies, Lansing police officer Rod Ennis, and then attempted to kill me—Champine could have no plea bargain with the prosecutor. In fact, the only reason Detective Hanson figured that Champine agreed to talk to us at all was to score a short outing from his cell at the correctional center in Crest Hill.

The detective had provided me with my own personal set of ground rules. I was *to sit in a chair on the side of the room and shut the hell up*. It had been a massive step forward from Hanson's initial reaction to my request to hold palaver with the Velvet Choker Killer. The detective's initial reaction had been a loud, "You have got to be fucking kidding me."

We'd gone round and round until Kippy dropped the bomb, "Nicky Champine might react differently with a woman in the room."

"That's fucking insulting." Hanson opened his mouth to add more but stopped, took a step back, took another sip from his bottle of Heineken, and looked at Kippy as though she were a long-lost relative. Wheels began to spin, gears began to shift. "Can you wear your hair down, Officer Gimm?"

"Of course," Kippy said. "I can also tinker with lipstick and makeup, maybe get a skirt at Hollister."

"You don't need to go Pippi Longstocking, but . . . yes," Hanson said. "Central casting—girl-next-door meets college freshman."

Although the pictures of Nicky Champine's late sister showed her to be one part plain Jane, one part homely, and one part overweight, Champine had set his sights higher when he began the abductions.

The detective looked at his partner. Marr gave an almost-imperceptible nod.

That was the moment I knew it was a go. The detectives had initially returned from Crest Hill empty-handed. Hanson told me Nicky Champine muttered nothing of help when he felt the need to mutter anything at all. The Velvet Choker Killer had an interest in what occurred at Gomsrud Park, a passing curiosity he claimed, wanting to hear anything that went beyond the nightly headlines on the local channels. But Champine had played coy, uncommunicative, as the detectives peppered him with queries about any friends—old or new; colleagues—pizza delivery or bus drivers; neighbors or general acquaintances.

Ultimately, Nicky Champine turned to his lawyer and asked if he could return to his cell for an afternoon nap.

Kippy knew I was restless. All of our conversations spun around our conviction that Nicky Champine damn well knew who was behind the Gomsrud Park ambush. My name hadn't made the papers, so I was a nobody. But suddenly, out of a clear blue sky, someone wanted to take vengeance—wanted to kill me.

It made zero sense, as Detective Hanson had first told me that night at the hospital.

None of us, as Wabiszewski had opined, believed Champine to be some kind of charismatic leader able to bend others to do his will. No way in hell. Nevertheless, Nicky Champine—the Velvet Choker Killer—had to be the link.

Kippy had stopped by after her shift last night. We'd been nibbling cold pizza, chatting again about the case as I scrolled down articles on Nicky Champine for the millionth time. An account in the online version of the *Chicago Tribune* contained pictures of Champine's four victims, all young—high school, early college—and certainly attractive.

"Five years younger and you'd have fit Champine's bill," I mumbled aloud, regretting it instantly.

"Really," Kippy said instead of tossing a piece of crust my way. She took the kitchen chair next to me, hijacked my laptop, browsed through the article, taking lengthy looks at each and every photograph.

That's when we hatched our scheme.

Kippy and I discussed being subtle with the detectives, let Hanson and Marr, over the course of the conversation, think they'd come up with the bright idea, but, as they say, no battle plan survives first contact with the enemy. Realizing subtlety was getting us nowhere, Kippy switched gears—went heavy-handed—and hit Hanson over the head with it.

But I credit the CPD detective with how quickly he came around . . . and adapted. Perhaps having a young woman in the room, perhaps dangling a *pretty* of the opposite sex in front of Nicky Champine, a woman who roughly fit his pattern, with the assistance of hairstyle and makeup and youthful attire, might get him to open up—essentially, per Marr, *make the sad sack of shit more talkative.*

I, on the other hand, wasn't expected to undergo a makeover or even tease my hair. My entire job, as Detective Hanson made abundantly clear, repeatedly, on the ride to Crest Hill was to *sit in a chair on the side of the room and shut the hell up.* I had the back seat of Hanson's unmarked Chevy Impala all to myself as Detective Marr was sitting out round two with the Velvet Choker Killer. Marr didn't want too many people flooding the interrogation room; he didn't want to intimidate or swamp Nicky Champine into silence. So I listened from the back of the Impala while the adults spoke cop lingo and plotted strategy as we took I-55 south on our field trip to the Stateville Correctional Center.

Perhaps somewhere along the way they'd stop and pick me up a Happy Meal or kiddie cone.

I'd read online that Stateville sits on over twenty-two hundred acres, has an operational capacity of almost thirty-eight hundred with about twelve hundred dubious souls in maximum security. SCC's maximum-security facility houses general population, segregation, protective custody, and temporary writ inmates—whatever the hell that term signified. But all of these facts and figures meant nothing until we began our approach and I spotted the thirty-three-foot wall studded with guard towers.

Suddenly it got real.

"If I ever got sent up here," I said, reminding the two police officers that someone was in the back seat, "I'd own the place in a month."

I tend to make bad jokes when I'm nervous, still I felt a bit insulted at how hard the two cops chuckled.

"Maybe if you had Vira," Kippy said after she'd finished guffawing.

Though maximum-security visits ended at two-thirty p.m., we were at SCC on *official* police business. Nevertheless, it took us fifteen minutes, four sets of harsh eyes, one metal detector to pass through, and, in my case, two forms of ID to get in. Once inside we were taken down an unoccupied hallway in the opposite direction of the family visitation wing. Eventually, our guide—an aloof corrections officer with a name tag that identified the wearer as Kent Hall—opened a door and deposited us into the windowless interrogation room we'd be using for today's meeting.

Kippy and Detective Hanson got set up at the table and, sure enough, there was a wooden chair, no cushion, along the far wall—the parking stall for yours truly. Hanson even pointed me toward it as though I'd forgotten my lot in life on the trek inside.

A few minutes later the door opened and Corrections Officer Hall ushered in another attendee—Nicky Champine's attorney. Upon arrest, Champine had obtained a court-appointed public defender, which he had for about fifteen minutes before J. Sidney Rice—already well known on the Chicago legal circuit—had swooped in and taken over the Velvet Choker Killer's defense. Rice sat opposite Detective Hanson, who, in turn, introduced Officer Kippy Gimm. As an afterthought, Hanson looked my way, said I was a contractor on the case, and, no kidding, muttered my name as *Masonry*—like the stonework—instead of Mason Reid.

I suspect the detective did it on purpose.

From my remote island along the side of the room, I watched their interactions. I don't imagine there's a great deal of love lost between Detective Hanson and Defense Attorney Rice. J. Sidney Rice had been a constant fixture on local TV, but never there to say terribly pleasant things about the actions and motivations of the Chicago Police Department. He even screamed to the media about how the search of Nicky Champine's Pontiac was illegal and how it spit in the face of Champine's Fourth Amendment rights. But maybe it was all a game. Hanson had told me that Nicky Champine was *going down no matter what tricks J. Sidney pulled from thin air or out of his headline-hungry ass.* Any judge that let the Velvet Choker Killer free on some bullshit technicality would soon find himself friendless, unemployed, and possibly tarred and feathered.

I wanted to ask J. Sidney what the "J" stood for, but knew it would fly in the face of my assigned ground rule of shutting the hell up. Since he went by the initial, I imagined it was something mundane like John or Jim. Detective Hanson had told me Rice wore these thousand-dollar suits, but I wasn't urbane enough to tell the difference between the dark suit Rice currently wore and what you'd walk out with at the Men's Wearhouse during their two-for-one sale. And if he made that kind of dough practicing criminal defense, how come he had a toupee that looked like something Howard Cosell had discarded back in the seventies? Rice seemed to be in his early sixties, but the thing on his head was as black as Poe's raven and made it look as though his hairline began a half-inch up from his eyebrows.

"Twice in a week, Detective," Rice said after the introductions were complete. "You're adding a great deal of wear and tear to my Mercedes."

"Don't you have a few dozen other clients you can visit as long as you're up here?" Hanson replied.

"If they're at Stateville on a *permanent* basis, I can't imagine they'd be happy to see me."

The two men laughed and I tried to make sense of our legal system. J. Sidney Rice was representing Nicky Champine on a pro bono basis, but it wasn't as altruistic as that may sound. Rice was no Atticus Finch, and that had been Gregory Peck's real hair. Sure, J. Sidney would pound on the table and scream about illegal searches and seizures, and Champine would still get about a dozen life sentences. But Rice was media savvy; he gained a boatload of free publicity from a high-profile case such as this one. It cemented his celebrity status and, as Detective Hanson mentioned on the ride to Stateville, Rice would probably walk away from this one with some kind of book deal.

And this offshoot of the Velvet Choker Killer's case—involving the murders at Gomsrud Park—would add an extra twist and turn to Rice's supposed nonfiction.

Five minutes later and a different corrections officer, this one the size of a Neanderthal tribal leader, guided Nicky

Champine—decked out in a powder-blue jumpsuit and slipper-shoes—to a chair next to his attorney. Champine was handcuffed and the guard took a moment to connect the cuffs to a metal ring set in the table, not all that dissimilar to how Champine'd had the girls chained up in his hidden basement room. Champine would have to be Houdini to escape his manacles and do any real damage.

Perhaps it was Stateville protocol for these types of visits, or perhaps Detective Hanson was taking no chances on Champine making a lunge for Officer Gimm.

If it were the latter, my money would be on Kippy.

There was no getting around the flesh-tone bandage tightly and completely covering the hollow where Nicky Champine's right eye had once been. Any other observation about the Velvet Choker Killer came in a distant second, though I noticed how his hair could use a shampoo and/or lice check. Champine seemed to have a naturally greasy complexion—that or he'd yet to acclimate to the community showers at his new habitat.

Although it was mid-afternoon, I saw no trace of a five o'clock shadow and wondered if Champine shaved at all. He was taller than I'd remembered, maybe six-two. Of course I'd mostly seen him in a prone position, squirreling about the sidewalk in a puddle of his own blood as I pulled Vira off him. The man was more pudgy and doughy than overtly plump. In terms of the four girls he'd kidnapped and eventually put to death, he certainly had a weight advantage.

Once settled in his chair Nicky Champine began to twitch, his head and neck in perpetual motion, turning and twisting about the interrogation room. Champine's remaining eye moved from the tabletop to Kippy, to the back of his hands, to Kippy, to the floor and back to Kippy, the wall, to Kippy's chest, to the guard leaving and closing the door behind him, to Kippy again, a quick glance at me, at Detective Hanson, to Kippy, at his lawyer's profile, and then back to Kippy.

Like a compass needle pointing north, all roads led back to Kippy.

His disconcerting peeks put me on edge. They might have been charmingly endearing in a high school nebbish manner—unless you'd been aware of the deeds Nicky Champine had been up to in his free time.

"Gentlemen and Officer Gimm," Rice began the meeting, "I just want to reiterate our ground rules that these discussions have nothing to do with the State's case against my client. Obviously, Mr. Champine was a guest at this very facility when those most unfortunate events occurred at Gomsrud Park." Rice looked from his client to Detective Hanson on the opposite side of the table. "Quite frankly, I'm not sure if Nicky has more to say than he did when you previously visited, but shall we get started?"

CHAPTER 40

"I'm going to keep the Band-Aid eye," Nicky Champine said after an abbreviated glance in Detective Hanson's direction before flashing his gaze at Kippy and then to the wall.

The Velvet Choker Killer talked in a soft hum that was little more than a murmur. He'd be all but impossible to hear at any kind of ball game and the continual darting about of his cranium made me wonder if he'd be able to follow any activity on the field or court. I leaned forward in my chair to pay close attention, my remote island straining toward the mainland.

"I thought you were thinking about a glass eye," Hanson replied, happy the kid was talking, wanting to keep it that way. "What did you tell me those things were called?"

"An ocular prosthesis, but they're fussy to wear and not as hygienic," Champine said—head peeks from his hands to the clock on the wall and back to Kippy. "I can draw pictures on each new Band-Aid if I want, before they get put on of course."

"No eye patch in the running?" the detective said.

"I don't want to be a pirate." Champine's shoulders began to quiver and I realized he was giggling to himself. His head continued its orbit from the floor to his lawyer's briefcase before pausing on Kippy for the briefest of seconds. "You're very pretty."

Albeit creepy coming from Nicky Champine in that understated drone of his, I couldn't argue with his proclamation.

Though I don't think Kippy needs an ounce of makeup, she'd had her hair cut in a shoulder-length pageboy, wore clear gloss over naturally pink lips, and sported a white button-down shirt with a gray pinstripe skirt she'd gotten on sale at Water Tower Place.

All in all, it sliced off a few years. Kippy looked early twenties.

And the image she projected fit squarely into Champine's profile.

"Thank you," Kippy said, acting all prim and proper. She adjusted her yellow legal pad in front of her, checked a few notes, and peered up. "As Detective Hanson discussed previously with you, several factors at Gomsrud Park indicate the existence of a copycat killer."

Champine's lone eye peered from his lawyer's chin to my feet to the pen in Detective Hanson's hand, again to Kippy's chest, and then to the closed door.

"These factors, as Detective Hanson discussed with you in Tuesday's visit—strangulation via laundry cord, positioning of a choker necklace about the asphyxiation marks on the throat, stabbing via jungle knife, as well as a specific human resource *element*—are tied directly back to the Velvet Choker Killer." Kippy spoke to Nicky Champine as if he was not the Velvet Choker Killer, as if that aspect of his life was metaphorical—more figurative than flesh and bone—there was no judgment in her tone. It had been determined that Kippy was not here either to confront or to antagonize.

Kippy Gimm was here to enchant.

She placed a sheet in front of Champine. "The first list contains the names of the managers and staff you worked with at Domino's pizza. The second list contains your supervisor and associate drivers at the bus company. The third column lists immediate neighbors as well as nearby ones, including those who have moved in the past ten years."

Champine gazed at Kippy's list of his known acquaintances for maybe all of five seconds before the head twitching kicked back in—at the corner of the table, the floor, at me, and back to Kippy. Champine was doing that shoulder-quiver thing as well—chuckling noiselessly to himself—in on some joke only he was aware of.

Kippy cleared her throat and pushed on. She handed Champine a second sheet of paper. "The investigators found a high school yearbook at your Bridgeport home. Your senior high school yearbook. This list contains the names of all of the classmates that signed your senior yearbook."

I'd gone over the materials and this was the shortest of all the lists.

Kippy looked up from the document and said to him, "Would this be a list of your old friends, Nicholas?"

The room fell quiet.

At Kippy's use of Nicky's given name, Champine's head bobbed in her direction and froze. Like the Cyclops of Greek mythology, his lone eye stared at the woman across the table. "I've never had any friends," Champine finally replied, still no more rotations about the room. "And my sister and my son are dead."

Kippy crossed her hands as though in prayer and looked back at the Velvet Choker Killer. "I'm sorry to hear that."

Champine added, "You look like Kari Jo."

Indeed Kippy did.

"Nicky," Rice placed a warning hand on Champine's forearm. "These people are not here to talk about any of that."

"Kari Jo was my favorite," Champine continued. "We had talks about how it could be for us, but later—when I came back downstairs—I could hear Kari Jo crying."

"They're not here to talk about any of that, Nicky." Rice now began to squeeze Champine's forearm.

"She didn't know I'd come back down. Kari Jo didn't know I'd heard her crying." His head scanned from me to Hanson and then stopped again at Kippy. "You can't have love if you cry." Champine shook his head and said, "You can't."

The room fell silent again. I worried that our gambit had

worked too well. Champine needed to explain to Kari Jo's doppelgänger why their *affair* had come to an abrupt end . . . why Kari Jo had to die.

I feared we'd driven him over the brink, but then his head twitched my way.

"I know you, don't I?" Two of Champine's fingers touched the flesh-colored bandage near his temple. "You were there that morning."

I said nothing.

"You were with the dog, the one that did this to me," Champine said, a forefinger slipping across the bandage, in the hollow where his right eye should be.

J. Sidney Rice sat upright, clicked his pen, and looked my way. "Who the hell are you again?"

"Calm down, Sidney," Detective Hanson said. "Reid contracts the search dogs with CPD."

"Was it his dog that attacked my client?"

Hanson nodded.

"We're done here," Rice said. He began tossing papers into his briefcase but stopped to point a finger at Hanson. "This is beyond outrageous, Detective, and you know I'm going to raise a fucking stink."

Champine, whose remaining eye hadn't wavered from my face during the attorney-detective squabble, asked, "Were you the *human resource element* at Gomsrud Park?"

"What?" I said, confused, and disobeying my only ground rule.

Champine's head bobbed to Kippy and back to me. "She said several factors at Gomsrud Park were linked to the Velvet Choker Killer . . . and one was a *human resource element*."

I looked at Detective Hanson, who leaned back in his chair and tossed up a hand.

"I was at Gomsrud," I admitted.

Champine asked, "Is that where that happened to your arm?"

I nodded in reply. The shoulder sling wasn't required and

I planned to toss it out in a day or two, but it helped keep my arm immobilized—less movement, less pain.

Champine said to me, "He was taken with my son."

The room fell silent a third time.

"If my visitor is coming for you," Champine continued in that gentle drone of his, "you don't have long to live."

CHAPTER 41

"He came to your house five times and you never got his name?"

"I knew better than to ask and he never would have told me anyway," Nicky Champine replied to Detective Hanson. "Remember, that first night he came to kill me."

"But your boy interrupted."

"I'd be dead now if my son hadn't walked in."

Since the *breakthrough*, Champine's head centered on his lap with only sporadic peeks upward at Kippy. With the floodgates open, Hanson had resumed control of the interrogation. Kippy took copious notes as the detective walked Nicky Champine through each of the five visits with his mystery man. J. Sidney Rice also took copious notes but I suspect his annotations were geared more for his next TV appearance. Visions of an international bestseller likely danced in the defense attorney's head.

As for me, I sat back and listened as the Velvet Choker Killer told his tale.

Hanson glanced over at Kippy's notes. "Green John Deere hat, black glasses, thick brown jacket and boots. He wore this same getup every single visit?"

"He had blond hair in back, long, but I don't think it was really his," Champine said. "He sometimes had a sandy-colored mustache but I'm sure that was fake, too."

"You said he came the night of your first abduction—when Ashleigh Mueller was taken—but how did he know about you? How did he find your house?"

Champine's head popped up in what appeared to be an *I've-been-a-naughty-boy* gaze at Kippy and then dropped back toward his lap. "I think he was out *looking* and bumped into me or maybe he was tracking Ashleigh and then saw what happened . . . and then followed me home."

I'd read somewhere that it takes three kills for one to qualify as a serial killer. Nicky Champine had four to his name. Becky Grohl would have been his fifth had he and his son not been stopped. Ashleigh Mueller had been the Velvet Choker Killer's first kill.

"You said you took Ashleigh from the rest area," Hanson glanced again at Kippy's notes, "at mile post 333, north of Kankakee, yet her VW Cabrio was found on the south side of Chicago. Did you move her car?"

Ashleigh Mueller was the only Champine victim that wasn't a native of Chicago. She'd been skirting Chicago on her way back home to Decatur when she'd pulled into the I-57 facilities at mile post 333.

"No," Champine said. "I left it there."

"Did he take it?"

"I don't know."

"After your son interrupted—when your visitor decided to let you live—you said you sat at the kitchen table and he gave you *tips* on how best to proceed?"

Champine nodded.

"What kind of tips did he give you?"

"He said to be aware of video cameras, and to assume they were everywhere. He said to wear a disguise, no matter how stupid, for the cameras or any onlookers that happen by." Champine continued to stare downward as he spoke. I suspected he was too ashamed to glance up out of fear that Kippy—his Kari Jo replica—would stare back at him with an unforgiving severity. "He said for me not to *shit where you eat—*

but I had nowhere else to bring *my new friends*. And he told me to swap out cars with something untraceable whenever I went out *looking*, but I don't know how to do any of that," Champine said. "And he told me I should never hang around the scene to watch the police do their work." Champine peeked quickly in my direction. "I should have listened."

A thought occurred to me, something I'm sure had already crossed Kippy's and Detective Hanson's minds. Nicky Champine would likely have been caught at the get-go, at the rest stop at mile post 333, if his visitor hadn't entered into it . . . become a part of it. Instead of running to the police, Champine's visitor cleaned up after him—possibly driving Ashleigh Mueller's VW Cabrio to a different location and ditching it there. Without the aid of Champine's visitor, the state police would have discovered Mueller's abandoned vehicle in a day, maybe two at the tops, and a serious search for Ashleigh Mueller would have begun much earlier.

Champine kept the girls alive—captive in his basement for months—until he eventually moved on to the next one. So if not for Champine's visitor, Champine likely would have been picked up within that first week—he was clearly disturbed but not a rocket scientist—and Ashleigh Mueller would have been set free.

And the next three victims of the Velvet Choker Killer would never have taken place.

And Nicky Champine would never have entered the serial killer pantheon.

"You said your visitor was taken with your son?" I asked and spotted Hanson frowning my way. "Why would he give a shit?"

"I think he was surprised at first. It was a novelty. And, later, he brought us food and presents and cleansers and books and that jungle knife—but it was all basically for my boy, it was all basically for him." Champine's head bobbed my way again. "I suspect underneath everything he's lonely. I suspect he doesn't have a family . . . or really anyone."

"So his heart grew three sizes that day like in *The Grinch*?" I asked Champine and noted that Hanson's frown had grown into a scowl. If they hadn't taken the detective's sidearm upon entering Stateville, he might have used it on me.

"Not like that," Champine replied. "But on his last visit, my son ran over and gave him a giant hug. I was a few feet away, and I can't be sure, but I think his eyes got moist." The Velvet Choker Killer focused his single eye in my direction. "Were you there in Bridgeport that night, when my boy died?"

"Yes," I told the truth.

"They've never given me a clear story of what happened. Just that he attacked with that knife he loved so much," Champine said. "Was it painless for him?"

"Yes," I lied.

PART FOUR

THE PREY GROUNDS

Pray tell me, sir, whose dog are you?

—Alexander Pope

CHAPTER 42

"I'm Bernt Landvik," Illinois Department of Transportation's security guru greeted Kippy, Wabiszewski, and me as we filed into a small conference room on the second floor of CPD's Headquarters Building on South Michigan. "Yup, it's Norwegian, but call me Bernie." He shook hands and pointed at a young guy with slicked-back hair who was busy working two laptops on the other side of the conference table. "That's Jake Saunders. Jake's an equipment engineer. He does the real work while I drink Dr Pepper and ride his coattails."

In response, Saunders shot both thumbs in the air, and then went back to working away on his two PCs.

"Jake and I work out of the IDOT office on West Washington, but once a month we make the pilgrimage to see our overlords in Springfield. Worry not," Landvik said, "they put us up at a Motel 6 where all our coffee and cable whims are met."

I'd finally gotten a first name out of Detective Hanson—Eric—but still lacked the requisite courage to use it. Hanson and Marr—still on an adrenaline high after the Nicky Champine interview—had allowed the three of us to tag along to the presentation. The investigators ushered us into chairs surrounding Saunders while Landvik—middle-aged, suit and tie, wire rims—took a sip of, evidently, his favorite soft drink and began his presentation. Although the man from the Illinois Department of Transportation kept his spiel on surveillance cameras informative, short, and lively, I got the impression he gave the same presentation weekly, perhaps even daily, and struggled with ways to keep it fresh.

It turns out Illinois was the first state in the union to equip its fifty-something rest areas with security cameras—closed-circuit television surveillance equipment—and call boxes—emergency signaling communications systems—as well as lighted walkways in an effort to keep their interstates safe for both tourists and business travelers, as well as fellow Illinoisans.

IDOT saw this surveillance installation as a key deterrent to crime, which had already resulted in the arrest of car thieves, muggers and pickpockets, smash and grabbers, graffiti artists and vandals, as well as those apprehended for a wide variety of other offenses such as domestic assault—what is it about family vacations that brings out the best in humanity?—also road rage incidents and, unfortunately, rape. In one case, rest area surveillance recordings proved a useful tool in tracking a suspect after a murder had occurred. Busted-open vending machines, broken displays, and vandalized restrooms were becoming a thing of the past.

"Jake's booted up the IDOT network to show you real-time video footage from the CCD cameras at a couple of our rest areas." Landvik addressed his young apprentice, "Right, Jake?"

"Yup," Saunders replied, and made short eye contact with Kippy, Wabiszewski, myself, and the two detectives before pointing at his right monitor. "I've brought up six separate video feeds from the six security cameras at the Rend Lake rest area, mile post 79, on I-57. Note how our various cameras are centrally located in the car parking lots, the truck areas, as well as inside the building. In fact, we have cameras focused on both doors in order to capture video of the entire lobby."

Sure enough, Saunders's screen on his right laptop was split into six squares, with each square displaying video from Rend Lake's rest stop by way of a different angle. In one box we watched cars entering the parking lot, from another we could watch them exit. Still another camera covered the lobby, currently a person was taking a camel-length drink of water from the fountain, others were mingling about a wall map, and one more was off to the side doing leg stretches. Another square covered the walkway and parked cars, while another covered the eighteen-wheelers lined up on the rest stop's opposite side.

After a few seconds, Saunders continued. "My left monitor has the seven security cameras at the wayside rest on I-90, at mile post 2. These, of course, cover the rest stop from similar angles as Rend Lake illustrated."

Kippy, her partner, and the CPD detectives studied each monitor as though they were portals into another universe. I tried to feign their level of intensity as I watched an endless procession of automobiles pulling in and a parade of other vehicles exiting, as I watched drivers and passengers rushing in to use the restroom facilities—to take care of their business—and those ambling, more peaceful in nature, back to their cars.

I think Landvik caught on to me as he dived back into his presentation.

"These cameras record to DVRs—digital video recorders," Landvik continued. "We're able to remote access in at the request of the ISP—the Illinois State Police—as well as other law enforcement agencies," Landvik pointed at Detectives Hanson and Marr, "such as the Chicago Police Department. If instructed, we can monitor the rest area in question on a routine basis, like what Jake has set up for us, or we can access specific cameras for, say, when a call box is activated."

"So if my car is ripped off while I'm in the restroom," Kippy said, "I can use your call box or 911 it on my cell phone and you can remote in and get a digital recording of who stole it?"

"Exactly," Landvik said. "And since we're able to capture license plates on vehicles moving upwards of forty miles per hour, we should also be able to get the plate numbers of the vehicle that dropped off your pesky car thief."

"How long do you archive these video recordings?" Hanson asked, pointing at Saunders's laptops.

"Our retention policy is sixty days before the system begins overwriting the old footage. In a perfect world, we'd love to keep a year of video, but that's cost prohibitive. Quite frankly, Detective, we're lucky it's not thirty days considering the number of cameras IDOT utilizes as well as the corresponding quality settings. The higher the video quality—resolution, compression type, etcetera—the more storage space it consumes. The belief is that two months should be more than sufficient time for criminal activity to have been detected and reported."

Landvik took another hit off his sugar water. "Bear in mind that specific incidents—unpleasant incidents—are exported and therefore stored separately. For example, if an alarm or alert is triggered, we can get the video to the requesting authorities ASAP and that becomes," he motioned at the two detectives again, "a permanent part of your investigation. To continue Officer Gimm's example regarding the stolen car, if your Porsche Boxster gets taken while you're in the restroom, and we're alerted within a normal timeframe—that is, immediately—life is good and we likely captured the theft on digital. But if you show up three months downstream to inform us of your stolen Boxster, well . . . quite frankly, you're shit out of luck."

"If it takes you three months to report a missing Porsche," Marr said, "you need to get your head examined."

"Exactly, Detective. And Jake'll probably tell them that same thing."

Kippy raised a hand as though in class. "Any way a person can get around these cameras?"

"You could come in on foot, I suppose. Let's say you walk in from the woods or someplace behind the building, sit back on the grass, and wait for the Porsche Boxster to arrive. Then put a bag over your head or wear a Halloween costume as you hotwire it." Landvik thought for a second. "But five minutes later the state police will have the plate number on the stolen Boxster and be out looking for it."

Kippy followed up, "You ever get calls about anyone looking suspicious, loitering or casing the joint?"

"The state police answers those types of calls, of course, and they'll send a car. But if anything seems amiss—or if a crime has in fact been committed—they'll contact us and, like referees in a football game, we'll go to the tape."

"What about in cases of abduction?" Kippy pursued a new line of inquiry. Hopefully, Hanson and Marr could recognize a detective in the making. "A girl drives in, the place appears deserted, but she gets taken—either driven away in her own car or the abductor has a partner who leaves with the girl's vehicle."

"Unfortunately, that situation could very well occur, but remember, these places maintain a constant stream of traffic, a constant stream of eyewitnesses—ninety-nine percent with cell phones at the ready. And many of these rest stops have a variety of trucks parked there day or night for hours at a time."

"But if there are no witnesses, and sixty days go by," Kippy had dug in, "the video recording gets overwritten and no one will ever know."

"If a person disappears—goes missing—and an officer like Detective Hanson or Detective Marr finds reason to believe the person may have been abducted at or had passed through a particular rest area, we will by all means go to the tape."

Landvik sipped at his Dr Pepper and glanced about the room for additional questions.

"What's the weirdest thing you've ever recorded?" I finally asked, assuming it was on the tip of everyone's mind, but the looks I received from Kippy and the others informed me otherwise.

Saunders said, "Tell him about the sex videos."

"Great. Thanks a lot, Jake," Landvik said. "Okay, as bizarre as it sounds, and on more than one occasion, we've come across a couple getting *passionate* in the lobby of one of the rest areas."

"You're kidding," Marr said. "And here I thought I was a cheap date."

"I guess the heart wants what the heart wants," Landvik replied.

"They weren't very explicit," Saunders said. "No major close-ups or anything. Not even NC-17, maybe an R rating."

"Jake and I thought of selling the videos to Cinemax or Showtime for their after-midnight fare, but realized no one would want to watch." Landvik put down his can of pop. "Alas, the people who have sex at rest stops look exactly like the people you'd imagine having sex at rest stops."

CHAPTER 43

"Going back an arbitrary three years, I've got a list of fourteen travelers that have been reported as missing. And none of these were teenage girls running off to LA or New York. All fourteen travelers were on road trips and never made it either to or back home from their destinations. What do these fourteen travelers have in common?" Kippy had been working this angle in all her free time for the past day and it was now time to share. Her partner and I were handed a two-page printout. "Each and every one of the fourteen was making their way through Illinois."

It was after midnight. The two CPD officers had come over to casa-de-safe-house after their shift with a twelve-pack of beer. We were in the kitchen—five times the size of the one in my trailer home—drinking Heineken, eating pretzels, and listening to Kippy lay out her case.

"That's a pretty big net you've tossed out," Wabiszewski said.

"Based on the police reports, interviews with family and friends, and locations of last phone calls made, all fourteen were traveling, or were soon to be traveling, through some part of Illinois."

"The Land of Lincoln is what? Sixty thousand square miles? So we each take twenty thou and meet back here in a hundred years."

"Don't be such a wiseass, Wabs," Kippy said. "You know where I'm heading."

Kippy was a gunner and, unlike the vibe I got off her partner, wouldn't be content with the natural advancement through the CPD ranks to field training officer to sergeant to—maybe someday—lieutenant. We'd not talked specifics, but she'd once mentioned that she aimed to be a detective.

I thought Kippy would make a great investigator.

Sue had wandered into the kitchen not long ago, licked at Kippy's hand, remembering the jar of peanut butter she'd previously given him and wondering why she'd not brought him a replacement. After scoring a pretzel, Sue walked over to Kippy's partner and looked at him as though to ask if he could borrow his sidearm. When Officer Wabiszewski refused to surrender his weapon, Sue sauntered back to his perch on the living room sofa.

Some things never change no matter where you live.

Kippy held up a forefinger. "Two winters back, Emmett and Rose Thompson, retired Wisconsin snowbirds, were heading south on I-57 to Florida for the winter months, and would have passed the rest stops at mile post 268 and 222 and 165 at Green Creek as well as several others on their trek through Illinois. The two were never seen or heard from again, but their Hyundai Santa Fe turned up at an Aurora strip mall a few days later." Kippy held up a second finger. "May of last year, Jackie Koepp was on her way from Indianapolis, Indiana, to Kansas City on I-70 for a third interview as an art director at a Kansas City ad agency. Koepp thought she had the job in the bag and took her car so she could scout out places to live. Koepp would have passed the stops at mile post 149 at Cumberland Road and mile post 27 at Silver Lake on her way to a job interview she never made. Her MINI Cooper turned up the following week in Louisville."

"But you're taking missing persons reports and connecting the dots to your assumptions."

"Not true, Wabs. Nicky Champine connected the first dot

when he crossed paths with his *visitor* on I-57, when he was abducting Ashleigh Mueller at mile post 333," Kippy said. "To your point, though, some of these dots could be bullshit—some could be coincidence—but not all fourteen."

Wabs and I were bright enough to keep quiet.

Maggie and Delta shared a secret. They both kept sneaking down into the split-level's lower level and whenever they came back up, they snuck glances at each other and looked all sheepish. I smelled their breath at one point to make sure they weren't getting into something they shouldn't be. They weren't. I figured the two were gaslighting me again as they're wont to do, but I'd go downstairs after the officers left to discover why all the clandestine behavior. Had they discovered a toy left behind by a previous tenant? A hidden dog park?

The portal to hell?

"About half of the cars disappear along with their drivers as though they'd passed through the Bermuda Triangle," Kippy continued, "but the other half of the cars turn up in other cities."

"If our guy winds up with a victim's vehicle, he wouldn't want anything to do with it," I spoke the obvious, like a kid in class hoping to score participation points. "Wouldn't he just dump it in a crappy part of town with the keys in the ignition and let nature take its course?"

"This is Chicago," Wabiszewski offered, "car parts paradise. Home of a couple dozen chop shops, which could explain the vehicles gone missing. The other ones could have been ditched after joyrides."

Vira was the only one of my troop that remained in the kitchen with us, on the floor near Kippy, an ear in the conversation and an eye on the pretzel bag, hoping for one of us to turn clumsy with drink and initiate an avalanche of her favorite salty snack.

Vira's money was likely on me.

"That's basically what I was thinking," Kippy said. "Anyway, the list goes on but let me focus on a specific traveler, a missing person by the name of Christine Dack. Dack was on her way back to Minneapolis after a friend's wedding here in Chicago last year, and she'd have passed the Egg River rest area off I-90 on her way home. Dack goes missing but her car turns up later in Milwaukee. Now the reason I bring up Christine Dack from last year is because of what happened six weeks ago."

"Denise Nieland?" I'd read ahead in Kippy's briefing.

"Absolutely. Denise Nieland was driving back home to Chicago from Madison, which would have also put her on the I-90 Egg River rest area. Now unfortunately for Christine Dack, the retention cutoff date on the video feed has long expired, nothing was reported last year and the digital recording is deleted or recorded over. But Denise Nieland was under fifty days ago, so there may still be a trace." Kippy looked at me and I knew I'd been assigned the task. "We need to get Egg River IDOTed as soon as possible."

I'd already volunteered—truth be told, I'd demanded—the IDOT assignment. The detectives as well as Kippy and Wabiszewski would rather I remain in the safe house, gathering dust, but I couldn't spend the days sitting around and rotting like old fruit. A case could be made that I'd be truly safe if I spent my time driving about aimlessly. If the killer was able to follow me from the safe house to a car wash or a Burger King, it wasn't much of a safe house to begin with.

I nodded at Kippy and asked, "Have you run any of this past Hanson?"

"A truncated version." Kippy shrugged. "The detective told me to pursue it and let him know if anything cropped up, but I think he was humoring me."

Technically, though they appreciated our help in getting Nicky Champine to open up, we weren't part of the official investigation. Untechnically, they couldn't tell Kippy or Officer Wabiszewski what to do in their free time. Even more untechnically, Hanson and Marr wanted to be kept appraised of what we were up to just to confirm we'd not be stepping on any toes in CPD's Bureau of Detectives or the investigators working the case out of Lansing PD.

In Kippy's words, they were humoring us.

"Hanson said I should be wary of forcing statistics into a pattern—kind of like what Wabs brought up—and that many of these *incidents* were likely the result of carjackings gone bad."

"But carjackers don't normally kill," Wabiszewski said, "or waste time hiding bodies."

"On a practical level, how would all this work?" I said, risking to be thought a fool. "I hide in the bushes until an opportunity presents itself—say an old man pulls in to use the facility and no one else is around 'cause it's a Tuesday morning—and I somehow subdue him and drive him back to my lair in his own vehicle."

"Drive him to your lair?" Wabiszewski said, doing nothing to hide a smirk.

"You know . . . where I do my thing. Anyway, once I've got him tethered or bludgeoned or whatever the hell the proper sequence is, I'm now stuck driving the old guy's car to Detroit and taking a long bus ride home. Either that or I drop his car in not the most savory of neighborhoods, leave the doors unlocked and the keys on the seat, and take a shorter bus ride home."

"Our perp knows he's got at least a day before the local and state police get a BOLO or ATL on the missing vehicle," Kippy said, "but from a strictly pain in the ass point of view, it'd make more sense to dump the car in the city."

"But also from a strictly pain in the ass point of view, he's left his own vehicle at the rest stop," I said. "So he's taking a cab or Uber back to the site of the abduction in order to retrieve his car."

"That would leave him highly exposed. A state trooper will ticket and tow anything that appears abandoned or looks suspicious," Kippy replied. "And maybe that triggers IDOT going to the digital recording to see what in hell happened."

"He'd be an idiot to leave his car there for however long it takes him to return and fetch it from," Wabiszewski tossed a glance my way, "*his lair.* And if he's pulled this off repeatedly, he's not an idiot."

"Aren't most of these rest areas surrounded by woods or forest?" I said. "It'd be smarter to never drive your car into the facility's parking lot to begin with, rather pull onto some back road and park among the trees. Then you can monitor the facility—maybe you've got binoculars—until an opportunity arises and jog over. Then you can retrieve your vehicle later, at your own convenience."

"But if you take an Uber or cab to a hidden spot in the trees, half the drivers will be calling the cops as soon as they pull away," Kippy said. "And those little side roads are always used by locals—folks who would notice an abandoned car in the tree line and call the police."

"Maybe he'd take a bike or motorcycle. Either would be easier to hide in the woods and he could come back for them later with a truck or van."

"So our serial killer's managed to combine two favorite hobbies," Wabiszewski said. "His enthusiasm for biking along with his need to beat travelers to death."

"I don't know," I said, throwing in the towel. "I guess you don't see a lot of bikers on the interstate highways."

"This is where the theory falls apart," Wabiszewski said. "Retrieving whatever it was that got him to the rest area—a car, a bike, a fucking pogo stick—is ripe with its own set of risks. Christ, getting rid of the victim's vehicle and then going back for your own car would take all the fun out of choking the shit out of someone."

"Unless," I said, "you're able to take your victim's car and your own vehicle at the same time."

"How's that done?"

"Tandem killers, like the ones Kippy talked about. One drives away with the abductee and the other drives away in the abductee's car." I laughed though it wasn't funny. "If our guy had whatever kind of unholy alliance he had going with Nicky Champine and his kid, maybe there's another one in the weeds."

"But, remember, Champine had only one nighttime visitor. Not two. And there was only one shooter at Gomsrud Park. If there were two, you'd be dead," Wabiszewski said. "The only way this works that isn't retarded is if the fucker's using a tow truck."

"No one would question a tow truck at a rest stop—those guys are roadside helpers." Kippy looked at her partner. "We deal with those guys every day."

"Or how about a tow bar on a motorhome?" I said. "Campers tow cars all the time."

Kippy asked me, "Aren't campers supposed to go in and park on the truck side?"

"The huge ones, but no one would care if a little camper or medium-sized RV was on the auto side. And no one would think twice about a guy hooking a car to the back of his camper or motorhome."

"He needs to get them—instantaneously—into his camper or van or truck, or to the floor or trunk of his victim's car." Kippy asked, "How do you think he subdues them?"

"A choke or sleeper hold," Wabiszewski said. "Or a disabling blow—maybe a sucker punch to the solar plexus or right hook to the jaw."

"Remember, he used some kind of pepper spray on Vira," I said. "He could use that or maybe chloroform."

"Unlike on TV, it takes about five minutes for chloroform to work as an anesthetic."

"Five minutes is a shitload of time," Wabiszewski said. "I pull into a rest stop and there's a guy between two cars holding a rag over someone's mouth, I'll kind of get the drift of where he's heading and put a stop to it."

"What about a Taser gun," Kippy asked. "You own someone for a couple minutes with a Taser."

CHAPTER 44

Everyman's new ID was in the wall.

Literally.

The birth certificate, passport, and driver's license—albeit lapsed—were in a waterproof-fireproof box behind the lavender painted drywall in Everyman's rec room. The police would have to rip his house apart piece-by-piece, screw-by-nail before they happened upon the little metal box containing his next life. Bring on the sniffer dogs. No explosives or accelerants for the bomb-sniffers, no illegal narcotics—not even a forgotten pack of cigarettes—for the drug-sniffers, and, best of all, not a dead body or rotted carcass for Mason Reid's cadaver dogs.

All would strike out.

Everyman's house was clean.

Everyman's garage was clean.

Even Everyman's backyard shed was clean.

The Pond, of course, was a completely different matter.

The Pond was anything but clean.

Everyman had been glib in his early years in Chicago, flippant, and had originally named the pond Chateau Vue sur L'eau—Castle Water View. Sure, it did boast an irrefutable irony, but as he *registered* more and more of his selective guests into Chateau Vue sur L'eau, Everyman became less playful . . . and felt the title made a mockery of all the great things he'd achieved.

Ever since he'd gone back to basics and simply referred to it as The Pond.

And The Pond would not be mocked.

It was at the point in time of the name change that Everyman began thinking of The Pond as having its own presence, its own evolved consciousness . . . of becoming a sentient being. And considering what Everyman had been feeding The Pond throughout his years in Chicago—what The Pond had unconditionally swallowed up—and considering what time and again happened along The Pond's shoreline . . . why shouldn't it?

The breeze through the trees and the bushes and across the water sounded like a rasping breath, the unexplained ripples and splashes were signals . . . The Pond was letting Everyman know—The Pond was letting him know it knew.

And that it didn't care.

The Pond—more a miniature lake—covered nearly five acres and was shrouded by 120 more of bog and dirt. The land was owned by the county, had been deemed a wetland . . . and soon forgotten. There'd be no development there any time in the foreseeable future. And in the center of The Pond, where Everyman registered his check-ins, it was nearly sixteen feet deep. In theory, the sunlight was able to penetrate the bottom, but Everyman wasn't so sure.

He'd never once donned a wet suit and dived in to check it out.

Except for the inevitable splashing, Everyman avoided the water as much as possible; he disdained even touching it. He knew the things that lay below.

There were water lilies, frogs, and the occasional turtle, but he left all that alone as well.

Also of value to Everyman, the land surrounding The Pond was too far out from town, too thick with mosquitoes, ticks, prickly pods, thistles, and mire for shit kids to slog in and do their shit-kid things—smoke pot and play doctor.

Therefore The Pond suffered no witnesses.

Having such terrain so very close had been the deciding factor in Everyman's decision to purchase the aged home. And though The Pond wasn't on his property, Everyman had made a trail, actually it was a strip of flattened grass and weeds, just big enough to cart a wheelbarrow the third of a mile necessary to reach the southern shore, in order to reach the ramshackle rowboat that lay upturned.

Underneath the rowboat sat a couple of oars.

And behind the rowboat sat a pile of thirty-seven-pound retaining wall caps.

CHAPTER 45

The throbbing in my left side kept me awake—*no pain, no gain* the doc clichéd yesterday when I called to ask if this was normal—so Vira and I jumped into the pickup and worked our way from the safe house in Park Forest to I-90 heading west. I had to keep moving—like our friend the shark—even if it were inconsequential, like lobbing a Wiffle ball against the broad side of a barn.

The powers that be knew about my upcoming field trip to IDOT, but I'd not even known about my predawn outing to Egg River until well into my third hour of insomnia, when I could no longer toss and turn and pretend to be falling back asleep. It was too early for me to make any phone calls asking for permission, and I didn't want to hear any corresponding squeaks or squeals. And the patrol car that passed the safe house on the hour, every hour, would assume I was tucked inside and sound asleep with the F-150 parked in the two-car garage.

Best to risk a tongue-lashing after the fact.

We pulled into the Egg River rest facility as the sun was peeking its noggin over the horizon. The only sign of life was a single Peterbilt with a king-sized cabover sleeper in the truck lot. Since I'd been unable to catch any z's, Evil Mason Reid wanted to pull into that section, drive up alongside the eighteen-wheeler, and lay on the horn—blast the poor SOB into consciousness—but angelic Mason Reid said no. Normal

Mace agreed, especially since I'd have to floor the F-150 and burn rubber the hell out of there lest I risk an ass-kicking by an irate trucker.

I let Vira come into the facility's lobby with me, remembered IDOT's presentation on rest stop security, and almost waved at what I assumed to be one of their hidden cameras mounted in the ceiling. I doubted anyone was watching on the other end or, if they were, that they'd take the bother of sending a state police car over to tell me to get my dog the hell out of their building. In between the double entrance doors stood a couple of vending machines hawking an assortment of pop, chips, and candy at airport-like fees. Inside, there was a map with a *You Are Here* sticker taking up real estate on the atrium's far wall; four benches sat diagonally in each corner—facing inward—for impatient travelers to sit and feign serenity while waiting for their significant others to hurry up, scrub their hands, and get the hell back out here so they could return to the road. A *Maintenance* door stood locked in a cubby just beyond the entry doors, likely containing mops and cleansers and toilet paper. Finally, a stainless-steel drinking fountain sat between the lavatories beckoning to those suffering sticker shock from the vending prices.

I left Vira to patrol the lobby, went into the men's room, took a quick leak, went to a sink and dispensed foam soap onto my hands. Although there were no cameras in the facility's restrooms, if the Peterbilt driver was psychic and had become enraged over Evil Mason's notion of a premature wake-up call and charged into the bathroom, smashed my head against the sink or bashed it into the mirror repeatedly, the next person to use the john would find what remained of my face, call 911, and IDOT would get a video of the truck driver having entered and left the lavatory around the time of my death as well as the plate number off his rig . . . and the theoretical case would quickly be closed.

Same outcome if something occurred to Christine Dack and/or Denise Nieland while they were in the women's room.

Vira and I worked our way back outside where I spotted a sign pointing in the direction of a nature walk that wound its way through the wooded area about the facility. I normally use the restroom and let the team water the grass before hopping back in the F-150, keeping any rest stops to five minutes or less, but I suppose if you're on a long haul a nature hike would be a great way to stretch the legs and run the antsiness out of the little ones. And if there weren't any cameras on the nature trail—and if very few travelers ever used the footpath to begin with—it would be a perfect spot to lay in wait or, better yet, follow someone in.

I wondered if Christine Dack or Denise Nieland had taken the Egg River nature hike.

Vira and I headed in the direction the sign pointed. About ten yards into our trek it dawned on me that the trail was wide enough for a vehicle to make it in, and it would certainly be no problem if you had four-wheel drive. Hell, that's probably what the landscapers or horticulturists or whomever is in charge of maintaining these rest stop nature trails used. And that would make perfect sense. If Christine Dack and/or Denise Nieland were attacked on these wooded trails, the perp could have dragged their bodies off the footpath, hid them behind some bushes, and then returned for them in either their own cars or his vehicle as opposed to carrying a lifeless or unconscious body out from the footpath in front of potential witnesses who would no doubt have a variety of questions and concerns.

There were multiple ways it could be done.

Vira's head popped up. I thought she'd caught hold of a scent out of the air, but then she cut off the mulch and dirt pathway and sniffed at the soil between some plants. She spun around—three-sixty—looking much like I do when I walk into a room searching for something and then immediately forget what I was looking for. Vira came to a stop and looked up at me.

"What is it, girl?"

I figured some indistinct scent had fallen on the ground—something with hardly a trace—and Vira was trying to noodle it out. If Christine Dack and/or Denise Nieland had been stabbed to death out here on the nature trail, there would have been a lot of blood, and—unless the killer bulldozed out the murder site and replaced it with fresh dirt—Vira would lead me to where it had occurred. But if Christine Dack and/or Denise Nieland had been strangled or knocked in the head . . . there wouldn't be much for Vira to go on. Cuts to the forehead can bleed quite a bit but a stunning blow, like those thrown in a boxing match, don't necessarily draw blood. And the killer would be crazy to dig a grave, however shallow, out here as that would take time and leave him exposed and vulnerable, and whatever horticulturist maintenance crew would notice the mound of dirt the next time they came out to spray or weed or drop mulch.

And in Christine Dack's case, it had been over a year since her disappearance with rain and winter and spring to cover up the tiniest of evidence.

Vira didn't sit and she didn't pat the surface. Instead, she stared back up at me, not willing to commit.

When we exited the nature trail on the opposite side of the facility, the truck driver was now up and performing stretching exercises, perhaps some yoga moves, in front of his eighteen-wheeler. I gave him a quick nod as we cut across to our side of the parking lot.

None the wiser on what—if anything—had occurred at the Egg River rest stop, Vira and I hopped into the pickup and headed back to Chicago.

CHAPTER 46

I got lost in IDOT's cube farm.

After a minute of walking in squares I asked a young guy who was farting around on an iPhone app if he could point me in the direction of Senior Director Bernt Landvik's office. He acted all put upon, as though I were ripping him out of a bathroom stall, and said, "Big office by the coffee station."

"Where's the coffee station?"

This earned me a heavy sigh and a finger point toward the far corner of the floor.

All this while he never left his chair.

Fucking Millennials.

I hooked a left at the edge of another square and there, at the end of the hallway—lo and behold—stood Bernt Landvik. And sure enough, on Landvik's left, the fabled coffee station. The senior director stared at me a second, and then raised a hand in greeting. Suddenly I got a feeling of déjà vu, as though I'd been in this IDOT office before, possibly stemming from my decision a few years back that I could never live such a life—I could never be a nine-to-five cube drone.

"I'm sorry," Landvik said, likely grateful he wouldn't have to form a search party. "I should have met you at reception."

"No worries," I said. "The guy paid to surf Facebook was very helpful."

Landvik shook my hand. "Looks like Tommy B. and I will be having another chat."

"Give him my best." Maybe I'm getting early onset asshole disease, but it had been a hell of a week. I'd started going slingless and my armpit felt as though I'd lost to an irate bull in Pamplona. I popped acetaminophen like Chiclets but got the feeling placebos would work better. And I'd just spent a painful hour navigating through downtown Chicago traffic.

Then I met Tommy B.

Landvik offered me coffee, so I sorted through the community bin, grabbed a Vanilla Bean Crème Brulee pod, and stuck it in the Keurig. After it brewed, the IDOT director ushered me into his office. I sat in one of two chairs in front of one of those rectangular straight desks that seem to be the trend. It took up much space just to house his laptop, a Dr Pepper, and my coffee. I glanced about—modestly furnished, closet, big windows, lots of natural light.

"Corner office," I said. "Nicely done."

"I'm not sure it counts if it's on the first floor. When I look outside, guys driving in traffic look back," Landvik said. "Some give me the finger."

"It is Chicago."

Landvik smiled but I got the sense that playtime was over. "So you're working with the detectives on this?" he asked.

I nodded rather than plead the fifth. This was off-the-books—something Kippy, Wabiszewski, and I were pursuing—unless IDOT made a positive ID on Denise Nieland or her Kia Sorento. In which case it would immediately become on-the-books and handed over to Detectives Hanson and Marr. Senior Director Landvik seemed like a nice enough guy, but if I bored him with details regarding some kind of half-assed tacit agreement we have with the Bureau of Detectives, it might awaken his inner bureaucrat.

"Officer Gimm called and said you'd be dropping off a file on the missing girl."

"Yes," I said. "Denise Nieland was reported missing on the

seventh of last month. Ms. Nieland was driving home from a birthday party for her sister, so driving from Madison back to Chicago would have put her on I-90 the day she left—on the sixth of last month."

"Got it," Landvik said. "Falls within the sixty-day retention limit."

"Exactly. Ms. Nieland's sister said she left at nine-thirty to miss the morning rush. She'd gassed up the night before and hoped to get home by one, or maybe two due to any construction zones." Unfortunately, as is my lot in life, I'd made a poor selection. The crème brulee turned the coffee into some kind of sugary treat you'd buy at a Dairy Queen. "But Denise Nieland was never seen again and her SUV showed up abandoned in Rockford a week later."

"Not good."

"Not good at all." I set the cup of crème brulee on the corner of his desk. Perhaps I'd drop it in the bin in Tommy B.'s cube on my way out. "Anyway, Kippy did the math and Ms. Nieland could have hit the Egg River rest area off I-90 at eleven o'clock at the soonest, so if you could check the digital recording between eleven and, say, four p.m., that would be more than thorough."

"No way did road construction push her three hours out but I'll go till four." Landvik shuffled through Kippy's folder. "Okay, you got me her recent driver's license photo, her height and weight, and the plate number on her Kia Sorento." He looked up at me. "If Denise Nieland was at Egg River, I'll let you know. We'll have her on digital."

"Is there a time I should call?"

Kippy had been clear. She wanted this front burner. It was the reason she wanted one of us to come here in person. Kippy didn't want it processed at a glacial pace by bureaucrats in the bureaucracy.

"I'd start now, but I've got a snorer at the Thompson Center all afternoon." Landvik looked at me. "I promise I'll check the Egg River digital this evening. I can set time lapse per vehicle arrivals. I may have to finish up in the morning, but would this time tomorrow be good?"

"That'd be great." We still had two weeks left in the retention cycle. "Thanks."

"You train the K-nines for the police, right?"

"I've done some of that for CPD, but I specialize in HRD dogs—human remains detection dogs."

"But you train dogs on basics, right?"

"I run an obedience school, mostly evenings and weekends."

"I could get a Labrador puppy for free from a neighbor."

"Don't even think," I said. "Just do it."

"Jim's got about a hundred in the litter and the little buggers are cute as hell." Landvik smiled and stood up. "Let me walk you out."

"Think Jim's got one for me?"

"I could bounce it off him," Landvik said as we walked past Tommy B.'s cube and entered the reception area.

Landvik was ahead of me and I dropped the cup of crème brulee into a garbage bin and followed the senior director into the foyer, and from there out to the IDOT parking lot.

"I'm always out and about and would love to have the dog with me," Landvik said, "but would hate for it to run out in traffic. I don't want any of that HRD stuff—don't want Snoopy finding corpses or anything like that—but basic commands to keep him out of the street."

"That's a piece of cake. I do private lessons as well. Take a few hours to train you on how to train the basics."

"What's that cost?" Landvik stopped next to a black BMW in a reserved spot near the front of the building.

"I usually charge anywhere between two hundred and a million dollars a session."

"Can I get it free if I talk Jim into giving you a black Lab?"

"I see how you became a senior director."

I tapped in Kippy's cell and listened to Vira bark as I approached my F-150 that I'd parked in a nonreserved spot. "I'm coming, girl," I said, though evidently not fast enough for her.

"It's Kippy." I held up the phone as I opened the door and gently pressed Vira into the passenger seat. I heard Kippy answer and held it up to Vira's ear until she settled down.

"Thanks a lot, Mace," Kippy said ten seconds later.

"Vira missed you."

"Did Landvik get the packet?"

"Yup—he'll let us know by this time tomorrow."

"Tomorrow?" I could tell by Kippy's tone she was disappointed, that she'd wanted it done yesterday.

"Landvik's a busy guy," I said in my defense. "He's got a corner office."

CHAPTER 47

"So, you're the new guy renting the old Hanegraf house?" the next-door neighbor called over the chain link.

My back was turned; I jumped out of my skin at his intro, yet somehow managed to maintain control of my bladder.

I'd been tossing the Frisbee to Vira, good exercise and it kept me from climbing the walls. My morning outing to the Egg River rest facility and the Illinois Department of Transportation had kept me in motion. And now that my shoulder was bit by bit starting to come around—a little more movement to go with the pain—farting around in the backyard helped with the cabin fever. The sister collies were content lying in the sun as spectators—their Frisbee years behind them. And when I tossed the saucer in Sue's direction, he shot me a *Yeah, right* look and then lifted a leg to water one of the deck posts.

More important, Frisbee also kept my mind off my financial woes. Sure, I'd get a few bucks from the training classes I'd set up—but wouldn't be able to teach—tossed back my way thanks to the brethren of Chicago dog handlers, several of whom had stepped up to lead the arranged sessions. I'd also need to walk through my *deadbeat* file—a list of the people I'd done work for in the past but whom, in return, had never gotten around to compensating me. I'd normally send out an invoice to those who dodged paying me on the spot, followed a month later by a second billing containing a negligible late fee, and, eventually, that would be followed up with an awkward phone call in which words were often mumbled about checks being in the mail. After that kabuki dance, if they still refused to reimburse me—into the deadbeat file they'd go.

Unfortunately, if the situation I currently found myself in dragged on much longer, my name would begin cropping up in a number of *deadbeat* files.

With a little luck I could swing the next mortgage payment. Of course I'd have to play hide-and-seek with the utility bills and other creditors. For food, maybe the kids and I could chisel the burnt drippings out of the oven. Or maybe I could let the trailer home slide into foreclosure, live in the safe house forever, and eat pineapple pizza every night.

"Hi," I said when I landed back down on terra firma. Thank God the next-door neighbor wasn't wearing a ski mask or the funeral would have been on Saturday. I hated to lie to the guy, but Detective Marr had set me up with a cover story and, after all, it was their safe house. "I'm Rick Jackson."

We shook hands after he introduced himself and said, "Sorry to scare you. I always like to meet the renters whenever I get a chance." After he complimented how well-behaved my dogs were—he and the missus *hardly* heard a thing—he said, "So what do you do, Rick?"

"I'm a database administrator." Marr had assured me there'd be a mass exodus of any overly inquisitive neighbors as soon as I brought up some mind-numbing IT job. "I'm here on contract work for a month."

"Really," the neighbor's eyes lit up. "I'm a network architect."

Evidently, this was his work-from-home day. He began talking shop and in under a minute I'd hustled the girls and Sue back inside the safe house, telling my new acquaintance I was tardy for a conference call.

Great, as if cabin fever wasn't bad enough, now I'd have to peek out the side window to see if anyone was in Mr. Network Architect's backyard before loafing on the deck or letting the kids out to play. Sue, of course, sensed something was amiss and, minutes later, stood in front of the screen door, demanding to be let outside. The safe house's deck had been perfect for him, just a single step down onto the lawn. Since his recovery, Sue had me trained as though I were a doorman, only without the tips. I shrugged and slid open the screen door. My German shepherd sauntered outside, lay down in the middle of the yard, and stared back my way.

The computer guy was next to our mutual fence, taking forever to water some kind of flower bed. The last thing I needed was to look all deer in the headlights as he waxed on about bouncing servers and building local-area networks.

"Sue," I whispered. "Get back in here."

Sue looked away, but I knew damn well he could hear me. "Sue," I said again, urgently, "Delta's got your spot on the couch. Delta took your spot."

That got his attention, all right. Sue rose and strode back inside—a middle school vice principal on his way to impose order on an unruly classroom. I slid the door shut behind Sue and followed him into the living room where he discovered his sofa to be vacant.

Sue glared at me and would have given me the finger had he known how.

"What?" I said to him. "You started it."

"A woman in one of those Knob Hill apartments—you know, the ones at the top of the hill—was out on her balcony 'cause of the sirens," Detective Hanson said over the phone, "and she spotted a guy in a John Deere cap get into a car on the far side of her building's parking lot."

I got excited. "She get a plate number?"

"Didn't occur to her at the time, and she probably wouldn't have been able to read it from the angle off her deck."

"How 'bout a description of the car?"

"She doesn't know. Said it was a gray four-door."

"But she knew it was a John Deere cap?"

"Yeah, told me her asshole ex was a John Deere dealer," the detective replied. "Anyway, it confirms what we suspected. His escape route was up the bunny hill. Pretty fucking smart, actually. LPD had the park surrounded in record time, but the shooter's getaway car was parked in a different part of Lansing and he was clear to drive away."

My excitement began to wane. "Those apartments have any security cameras?"

"Just one in the lobby, completely useless for where the guy was parked. You know Lansing better than I do, but I get the impression the top of Knob Hill isn't the swankiest part of town."

Hanson was right on that count.

He asked me, "You got anything?"

I filled him in on my trip to the IDOT office downtown, left out the Egg River excursion, and then said, "Hey, tell Marr his cover story for me here sucks. The guy next door's an IT geek. If I go outside, he'll glom onto me and know I'm full of shit."

I could hear Hanson begin to chuckle before I tapped to end the call.

CHAPTER 48

"Jake?" Bernt Landvik opened the front door of his two-story farmhouse on the outermost edge of Batavia. "It's after ten. You drive all the way out here to tell me about a hot date?"

"I wish," Saunders slipped past his boss, headed into the kitchen, and began sliding his laptop out from its sleeve. "You still got any of that Canadian swill?"

"Molson?"

"Two, please."

"How about you tell me what's up?" Saunders had a condo in the city. Although Landvik had his subordinate to his home for dinner and drinks on a handful of occasions, he had no idea what would motivate the younger man to make the forty-something-minute drive out to Kane County. "They have this new device called a phone. I think they even make some you can walk around with that you could have called me on."

"You know that woman cop, the hot babe that wants us to review the digital at the Egg River rest area? You know, at mile post 62?"

"Yeah, last month on the day that woman, Denise Nieland, disappeared," Landvik said. "Mason Reid stopped by this morning and he gave me all that information—the date and general time, a picture of Ms. Nieland, the car she was driving, and her license plate number. I told him I'd get to it tonight or first thing in the morning. Why are you involved?"

"I guess you weren't moving your ass fast enough for her and she called me."

"Called you?"

"Remember we all handed out cards at that meeting?"

"So you dove in to impress her?"

Saunders nodded. "Pretty much, but now I wish I'd left it for you because Egg River's all fucked up."

"What are you talking about?"

"Let me bring it up and I'll show you. The video recording jumps from 11:42 that morning to 1:07 that afternoon. On all of the Egg River cameras. Those eighty-five minutes are missing . . . gone . . . deleted."

"You're kidding." Landvik stared at his assistant in alarm. "That digital didn't edit itself."

"No shit."

"Let me get those Molsons." Landvik headed the long way around the kitchen island as Saunders began booting up his laptop. "You tell the lady cop?"

"No," Saunders said. "I wanted to run it by you first."

"Good move. There's got to be about six dozen or so staff members that have full or partial access, whether they actually use the system or not. We'll have to run an audit, find out who got in and tinkered before we start pushing the panic button."

Landvik stopped well short of the refrigerator, picked up the antique flat-bottom cast-iron skillet off the oven's back burner—it was more for show, he'd never used it—and swung it forehanded into the side of Jake Saunders's head. Landvik's star employee toppled off the stool and dropped hard to the floor.

There was no need for a second swing so Everyman returned the skillet to the oven top, grabbed a single Molson from the fridge, and shut down Saunders's laptop.

CHAPTER 49

I woke with a cold start.

Nights were still the hardest, no Mickie around to comfort me after a bad dream. Only this wasn't a dream. It had come to me, slowly, like mist over a lake. I knew it sounded ridiculous but it was past two in the morning—a time when your mind starts to wander toward places it shouldn't. Places where you imagine the unthinkable. Nevertheless, I found myself wide awake, terrified, and wandering into one such shadowy spot.

"I'm sorry, Vira," I said to my golden retriever, who lay diagonal from me—in the lower half of the opposite side of the bed—staring my way. Perhaps I'd woken her. Perhaps Vira never sleeps. Either way, she shot me her *What's up, Dude?* gaze.

"I'm so sorry, girl."

I'd been focused on the pain in my shoulder. I'd been focused on my failing business, on how I was going to bounce back financially after life in a safe house, after canceling a string of classes and private training sessions. How pretty soon the kids and I would be boiling rocks for soup. But most of all I'd been focused on Kippy, on updating her on the IDOT meeting on West Washington, but it went beyond that. Far beyond it. I know it sounds all gooey and syrupy and runs in the face of my he-man, macho image, but I'd kind of like to know everything about Kippy. I'd like to get lost in her minutiae. What was her favorite Halloween costume as a kid? What's her favorite breakfast cereal? Did she sleep in jammies or sweats and T-shirts like me?

I wanted to fall deep into those brown eyes and never resurface.

And that's why I didn't recognize Vira's warning growl in the IDOT parking lot this morning.

It buzzed inside my head like bees about a hive. Sure, my golden retriever had been muffled inside the pickup—the windows down an inch. Sure, I'd been distracted and crushing on Kippy . . . but Vira had done her best to tell me—she'd done her level best.

Only I wasn't listening.

And I remembered that feeling of déjà vu in the IDOT hallway as Bernt Landvik stared back at me from the coffee station across the hallway.

A feeling of déjà vu? What the hell? I'd never set foot in an IDOT office in my entire life.

But I have a distinct memory of a man dressed in black clothes and a black mask standing between pine trees and looking my way in the clearing at Gomsrud Park.

The same posture. The same exact stance and comportment.

Sure, it was a thought that would be laughed at in the light of day, but Vira had sealed the deal in the IDOT parking lot. And my head had been too far up a certain cavity for me to realize it at the time.

I reached for my phone.

CHAPTER 50

It was over.

And it was a damned shame. Right when everything was falling into place like pieces in a child's jigsaw puzzle. When IDOT had been contacted by a certain Detective Hanson at the Chicago Police Department, interested in how the video surveillance worked at the state's rest areas, Everyman was only too happy to step forward, volunteering the services of Jake Saunders and himself. He'd been mildly taken aback walking into the conference room at CPD's Headquarters Building only to find out, after all this time, the authorities had finally begun to look in the right direction.

Of course with Bernt—*call me Bernie*—Landvik acting as their liaison with the Illinois Department of Transportation, there'd be nothing for the CPD detectives to find.

Ever.

Everyman had been slightly more taken aback when he came face-to-face with the Dog Man himself as Mason Reid came strolling into the CPD conference room along with the lady cop and her partner. But Everyman was in a suit and tie and designer glasses and full of grins and casual chitchat. He'd been on his game. Quite frankly, it had been one of the better presentations he'd led in a long while.

Jake had even tossed a flattering word his way.

But that female cop, the one with all the probing questions, she just had to pressure Saunders into doing what Everyman had already committed to do, and Jake—who had never said "No" to an attractive woman in his tragically short life—had to go into the system and unearth the missing gap in the video recording at Egg River.

Goddamnit—he hadn't wanted to kill Jake Saunders. Just like he hadn't wanted to kill Eugene Knox in San Francisco all those eons ago when CEO Knox had connected one dot too many . . . when old Eugene had flown too close to the sun.

But you had to roll with the punches.

Dog Man Reid had even come to his place of work in order to hand deliver the Denise Nieland–Egg River file, which, in retrospect, he should have deep-sixed as quickly as possible, informing the investigators and that woman cop that there was nada, nothing, zip, zero, zilch to be seen, but—as twists and turns abounded—Everyman had truly been tied up in a series of afternoon meetings at the Thompson Center.

But the woman cop had to push it with Jake. She just had to push it.

He'd even had Dog Man convinced he'd be getting a fictional Labrador puppy from a fictional neighbor named Jim. Everyman didn't know any of his neighbors—Jim or otherwise—and had bought the old farmhouse on the outskirts of Batavia for, among other things, the seclusion of not having any immediate Batavians to wave to or nod at.

Everyman would have Dog Man coming to him, for Christ's sake.

It was beyond serendipitous, and Everyman imagined it being somewhat how a spider felt—spinning a web, streaming something on Netflix . . . and waiting to see what drops by.

On the bright side, perhaps he'd have some wiggle room. Perhaps he could call Mason Reid over the weekend and ask if he'd care to come to Batavia for some obedience training with Landvik's new Labrador. Good God, Reid's eyes had lit up when Bernt Landvik became a prospective client, chomping at the bit to get two hundred a pop for some private lessons as though Dog Man were some all-star tennis pro. Hell, Everyman thought, I'll even sweeten the deal and offer to buy Reid lunch and fill up his gas tank just for driving out.

Everyman noted online that Dog Man had reassigned this month's training classes to different instructors. He'd been surprised the police weren't keeping a couple of Reid's orientation sessions active as some kind of bait to lure in the Gomsrud Park shooter. Detectives Hanson and Marr probably figured there were too many people attending those events and too many ways a thing like that could head south . . . and they probably weren't willing to sacrifice Reid.

Everyman wouldn't have tried anything at one of Reid's classes anyway.

Why would he when Mason Reid was coming to him?

In the morning, Everyman would let the staff at the West Washington branch of the Illinois Department of Transportation know about Jake's father, how the poor man had suffered a massive stroke, how Jake Saunders had flown to Scottsdale to be at his side, and would likely be there as long as it took. And perhaps next week Jake could remote in for some meetings, but, until then, *please respect Jake's privacy*. He'd also email that irritating bitch of a cop that he'd found nothing on the Egg River digital—no Denise Nieland, no car with her plate number, no abduction. At nine o'clock, he'd go to his bank and, for all practical purposes, clean it out. Sure, the bank would eventually report the *cash* amount to the IRS, but he'd be long gone by then and there'd be no Bernt Landvik anywhere to be found before that meant anything to anyone. He could add that eighty-four grand to the hundred and forty grand he kept hidden in his office safe. He'd leave early tomorrow—not unusual for a Friday—and tell his secretary that he had a dentist appointment first thing Monday morning and, based on how he felt, would probably work from home.

Days would pass and by the time a serious effort was made to find Bernt Landvik, Bernt Landvik would no longer exist.

Bernt Landvik would have vanished into the ether.

Everyman knew this day would come. But Landvik'd had a long run.

Even if he stayed on at IDOT, and acted all shook up over Jake Saunders's disappearance, the detectives at CPD would dig in. Red flags would run up Detectives Hanson's and Marr's flagpoles as well as whatever pole that bitch cop danced around. Inquiries would be made about the timing of Saunders's disappearance, right after he was instructed to view footage on a certain date out of mile post 62. Others at IDOT would discover the gap in the video recording and inform investigators that Jake Saunders would likely have gone scampering to Senior Director Landvik with the news.

Eventually, a tow operator would volunteer how Bernt Landvik not only used the IDOT cars and repair vans, which made perfect sense, but, periodically, the senior director would utilize the smallest of the fleet's tow trucks.

Yes, it was over for Senior Director Bernt Landvik.

But it was just beginning for Ted Krause. Ted Krause of the buzz cut and blue eyes. Ted Krause of the beard and mustache and—hell, why not?—silver earring. Ted Krause who could certainly shed a few pounds about his midsection. Ted Krause who'd made a chunk of money when Bitcoin peaked and was bright enough to dump that "thin air" investment before it cratered.

The world was Ted Krause's oyster, and Everyman assumed Krause would have a grand old time in Reno or Albuquerque or St. Petersburg.

Ted Krause preferred warmer climates.

Ted Krause was raring to go. Up until now, Ted Krause had lived—outside of Bitcoin and a series of banking transactions—inside a box behind the drywall in Bernt Landvik's rec room.

But for right now—Everyman stared about the kitchen—he'd have to haul good-old Jake Saunders out to The Pond. What a pain in the ass to do at night. And then he'd have to ventilate his much-loved colleague, repeatedly, with a knife similar to the one he'd given the Champine boy, similar to the one he'd stuck in that old prick Weston Davies's chest. Everyman would have to do this in order to keep the gases of putrefaction from inflating his subordinate's body tissue, from making his favorite employee lighter than water, and from making Jake Saunders rise to the surface.

And Jake Saunders needed to stay put, down there, at the bottom of The Pond, hidden in the murk with the others, all those road-weary travelers he'd met at the various pit stops along the highways and byways—along his prey grounds—in Landvik's seven years as a senior director at the Illinois Department of Transportation.

Everyman looked down at his young assistant, at his dented skull, and at the blood puddled on his kitchen floor.

Christ, he'd have to use bleach.

Everyman was going to miss Jake Saunders.

And he was going to miss the Illinois Department of Transportation. He had full access to IDOT vans for repairs or replacements to be made at the various sites, full access to a string of IDOT cars from which to select for the monthly trips to the Hanley building in Springfield, and . . . best of all . . . full access to the IDOT tow trucks used by the tow and recovery operators.

One of the perks of upper management was how those down the totem pole—the tow operators—didn't come to him with any questions. If he borrowed one of the smaller tow trucks—instead of using a van on a repair run at a rest area facility—so be it. There were more than enough vehicles to go around in the back parking lot.

And if Senior Director Landvik took the tow truck home after a late-night repair—no big deal, as long as he returned it first thing in the morning. He got along great with the tow operators. Hell, Bernt—*call me Bernie*—Landvik was one of the guys; he bought the supervisors cases of their favorite beers every Christmas and on the Fourth of July.

IDOT vehicles were a symbol of trust. The general public utilizing the facilities felt quite at ease spotting an IDOT van on a dark night or an IDOT tow truck during an unoccupied weekday. Rest stop guests wouldn't be in the least bit surprised to spot an IDOT vehicle parked on the walkway by the backdoor . . . or slowly cruising the nature walks. And IDOT tow trucks reassured visitors whose cars or minivans had the misfortune of breaking down that there was help nearby.

And of course you can trust the nice man from the Illinois Department of Transportation, even offer to lend him a hand if he needs help carrying a box out of his van or help in grabbing something from out of the back storage room.

Everyman took his laptop with him on these trips, so he could block any potential viewers of any rest areas he frequented in his *off hours*. And Everyman made sure he deleted his presence off any digital recordings as soon as he'd vacated the sites.

And Everyman always brought the IDOT vehicles back cleaner than when he'd taken them out.

It was only the right thing to do.

CHAPTER 51

"It's too flimsy, Mace. We can't run to Hanson and Marr with Vira barking inside a car and you recognizing Landvik's *stance* in the IDOT hallway," Kippy said. "Body posture ain't probable cause."

I replied, "It was more an attitude or demeanor in Landvik's stance that brought me back to Gomsrud Park. And Vira's snarling was her coming down off a red alert after I left Landvik at his car and got you on the cell phone."

"I know." Kippy added, "And Hanson and Marr might give you the time of day or they might think you've got PTSD."

We sat at a table outside a busy Starbucks in Batavia—the suburb in which IDOT Senior Director Bernt Landvik lived. Kippy had a large dark; I had a small with cream. Vira had a medium water in a paper bowl—no cream—and a sliver of Kippy's blueberry scone.

"I don't have post-traumatic stress disorder."

"I know, Mace. I was shaky when you first called, but two things swayed me over. First, guess what the Illinois Department of Transportation has at their beck and call?"

"Free coffee?"

"That, too, and a fleet of motor vehicles, repair vans, and tow trucks."

I recalled our brainstorming on how our guy would move

both his and the victim's car and said, "You think Landvik's got access to all that."

"He's an executive in the Chicago branch," Kippy reminded me. "You're the one who told me he's got a corner office."

"Shit," I said. "That works."

"Driving an IDOT tow truck or repair van is like a cloak of invisibility. And if that's not good enough, Landvik gets to manipulate the digital recordings—delete any portions that involve him—and he knows it all goes bye-bye in sixty days if nothing is triggered, if no one raises a fuss."

"The fox guarding the henhouse," I said. "What was the second thing that swayed you?"

"I Google Earthed Landvik's address. He's in a private farm-house on the ass end of Batavia, where the suburb ends and the countryside and woodland and bog kicks in."

"His lair." I remembered Officer Wabiszewski giving me shit about the use of that word. "Where he does his thing."

Kippy's phone buzzed. She answered and spoke for several seconds before tapping off.

"That was Wabs. Landvik just pulled into IDOT," she said. "Time to go."

CHAPTER 52

The first thing Everyman did was grab himself a Dr Pepper—it's not just for breakfast anymore—from the refrigerator at the coffee station outside his office.

Second thing, after dropping his duffel bag and sitting behind his desk, with his office door open—Landvik always kept the door open—he texted the cell phone numbers Officer Gimm and Mason Reid had provided, sending them the following message: *Jake and I tag-teamed the Egg River digital recording. No sighting of Ms. Nieland or anyone who looked like her DMV picture. No Kia Sorento with those plate numbers. No nefarious activity. Sorry. Bernie Landvik.*

Third, Everyman dug out the cards he'd collected from that first day—when he and Jake Saunders had presented on IDOT's surveillance program at the police headquarters building on South Michigan—and sent a slightly more formal response of the same message to the email addresses of Detectives Hanson and Marr in addition to Officers Gimm and Wabiszewski.

The fourth thing Everyman did was send out a department-wide email regarding Jake Saunders's father—how he'd suffered a massive stroke—and how Jake had flown to Arizona to be with him in his time of need. Everyman further instructed that any questions in need of Jake's input or signature should be run past him instead.

All that busy work out of the way, Everyman grabbed the

duffel and headed into his office closet to access the digital safe. It was a fire-resistant twenty-four inches by twenty inches—the cost of which had been absorbed into his annual budget several years earlier—thank you, taxpayers. And though the safe did in fact contain an official document or two, a handful of work-related flash drives, and office keys for conference rooms he never used, there were only two items of interest to him in these the final days of Bernt Landvik.

Everyman tapped in the code numbers of his birth date—his true birth date, not Landvik's—and the door to the safe popped open.

First and foremost he stuffed the hundred and forty grand he'd secreted over the years—bigger paychecks without investing in a 401(k) plan he'd never see—into the duffel bag. The stacks of hundred-dollar bills fit neatly, with plenty of room for the eighty thousand from his savings account and the four extra grand from checking he'd be withdrawing from his bank about an hour from now.

This stash of cash plus the minor Bitcoin fortune would assure Ted Krause the greatest of comforts as he carefully plotted the next chapter of his life.

Everyman paused only a second before retrieving the second item of interest. He handled the weapon carefully, placed it on top of the cash and zipped the duffel shut. It was an ESEE-6P-B fixed high-carbon-steel-blade knife with a 5.75-inch cutting edge. Razor sharp, and no fucking around with stainless steel.

It could do—would do—serious damage.

Everyman started back to his desk when his iPhone began playing Wagner's *Ride of the Valkyries*. He knew immediately what that meant; it was the alert notification he'd set for the motion-activated security cameras—his *hidden* motion-activated security cameras—that he'd set up at crucial points about his rural parcel of land in Batavia, not unlike the way he'd set up the rest stop facility surveillance for the Illinois Department of Transportation.

Everyman tapped to open his video app. Of the six video squares on display, one indicated activity—two figures stood on his front porch. He tapped the screen to maximize the video square and bit at his lip.

Dog Man Reid and the lady cop were outside his front door.

CHAPTER 53

"We got the basics off DMV. His driver's license is valid. No warrants, no citations issued, no traffic violations or anything unusual," Kippy told me, pressing the doorbell on Landvik's two-story farmhouse.

"But you don't know if he's married or has kids?"

"Wabs and I didn't want to push into other databases, ones that might raise flags." Kippy now pounded on the door in addition to ringing the bell. If anyone did answer, they'd be mighty pissed off. "Landvik wasn't wearing a wedding ring if I remember right, but we want to make sure no one else is home before we start poking about."

I stood on the porch behind Kippy. Vira stared up at us from the lawn, then took off to explore the far side of his front yard. I felt nervous, on edge—like a shoplifter with store clerks closing in—and found myself sneaking peeks at the infrequent cars on the county highway that zipped past Landvik's gravel driveway, which meandered its way downward before coming to a stop at equal distance between Landvik's house and his detached garage. I don't know why I was anxious; knocking on a front door was hardly a federal offense. And in the unlikely event that someone answered, we had a better than half-assed—possibly a three-quarters-assed—cover story. Kippy and I were working on a project with the IDOT senior director and time was of the essence.

Of course we knew in advance from Officer Wabiszewski—who had close eyes on the senior director's Beamer in his reserved space in the IDOT parking lot downtown—that whoever answered the door wouldn't be Bernt Landvik.

Even though our three-quarters-of-an-ass cover story would work on a confused spouse or offspring, its shelf life had expired by the time Kippy parked her Chevy Malibu at the gravel's end. Both of us had received a text message from Senior Director Landvik informing us, in no uncertain terms, that Egg River had been a dry hole. We'd discussed this new development in Kippy's car with Vira eavesdropping from the back seat.

Kippy'd had a total of three calls in to Jake Saunders that had gone unreturned. The first had been late yesterday afternoon, followed up again later in the evening, followed up a final time as we sipped java outside the coffee shop. All three of her phone calls had flipped over to Saunders's voicemail.

"He was so eager to help when I talked to him yesterday," Kippy said. "He knew Landvik was tied up in meetings and that he'd be glad to do it . . . and now he's completely blowing us off."

I pointed at the message on my phone. "Maybe this serves as his answer."

Kippy shrugged. "It's from Landvik and Jake Saunders is not even on the text chain."

As we crawled out of the Malibu, Kippy's smartphone chimed a second time. Vira and I stood in the yard while Kippy took a moment and then said, "Landvik just sent an email with basically the same message." She stared at the screen another second. "He sent it to me and Wabs and Hanson and Marr."

I checked the email on my iPhone. "Guess I didn't make the cut."

"Neither did Jake Saunders."

Kippy finished her clash with Landvik's front door and then checked the doorknob . . . locked tight. She turned to me and said, "Let's go see what he's got in the garage."

CHAPTER 54

Everyman's first reaction was *Haven't you two fuckers checked your text messages?* But that was immediately followed by *They're at my home.*

The business cards he'd handed them contained Bernt Landvik's work address, which meant they had to have used other resources—cop resources—to locate his home address. And there's no way in hell they'd be driving to Batavia to quiz him on Egg River when a phone call would suffice. He involuntarily looked up to see if any officers were pouring into the hallway and fanning out toward his office.

Then Everyman tapped at the other surveillance cameras about his property. No cadre of squad cars lining his driveway. No Detectives Hanson and Marr directing subordinates.

And no SWAT team lying in wait.

Only the lady cop and the Dog Man.

WTF . . . as in what the fuck?

Everyman left his office, hiked up a floor, and took the hallway with the row of windows overlooking IDOT's front parking lot. Also no cadre of squad cars or SWAT teams. The employee lot was filling up—it was eight-thirty in the a.m.—and the visitor lot was nearly empty, only three cars with one backed against the curb. He spotted a figure behind the steering wheel of the backed-in vehicle—a Dodge Charger—and rushed back to his office to grab his pair of compact binoculars from the top drawer of his filing cabinet. Upon return to the second-floor hallway of windows, Everyman centered himself across from the Charger and brought the binocs up to his eyes. He worked the magnification and immediately recognized the driver—Officer Gimm's partner, the big guy with the impossible tongue-twisting Polish name.

Everyman lowered the binocs and thought for a moment. Kippy Gimm and the tongue-twister were patrol officers—glorified meter maids. And Dog Man Reid was like some minimum-wage CPD contractor or volunteer for whenever a dead body got misplaced. And hadn't it come up in conversation in their initial meeting that the two patrol officers worked the second shift?

Could it be that Nancy Drew and The Hardy Boys were freelancing? That they were dicking about into matters well over their pay grade in the hopes of . . . of what . . . discovering something?

If so, everything on his property was clean.

Unless?

Unless they checked his garage and noticed that sitting inside was Jake Saunders's Ford Escape. If they were able to dig into the Illinois DMV database—hell, in his role at IDOT he had access to the DMV database—to find his home address, they sure as hell could find out the late Jake Saunders's ride.

As if to confirm his concern, *Ride of the Valkyries* chimed again on his iPhone. Everyman brought up the video app. This time the alert came from his detached garage. He maximized the live video feed.

Officer Gimm was shining a flashlight into his side garage door.

CHAPTER 55

Kippy tried opening the side door leading into Landvik's garage while I tried yanking up the two-car garage door. Both were locked down.

Kippy looked in the window and said, "There's something parked in there."

"A tow truck?"

She didn't reply, retrieved a flashlight from the trunk of her Malibu, came back and shined it through the window. "A single vehicle on the far side. Not a tow truck, but an SUV." She continued staring into Landvik's garage and said, "I think it's a Ford Escape."

"I thought DMV only had Landvik tied to the BMW."

Kippy called her partner while Vira and I crossed Landvik's front lawn, searching for a window, any window, not draped or curtained up and obstructing a view of the interior. No such luck, the IDOT executive's home was wrapped like a Christmas present. We returned to Kippy, still manning her post along the side of Landvik's garage.

"Wabs is checking, but, yes, Landvik's only got the BMW registered."

A second later Kippy's cell phone rang and she brought it to her ear. After a moment, she said, "No shit?"

Evidently, there was no shit. Kippy hung up and said, "Jake Saunders drives a Ford Escape."

"Is that his only vehicle?"

Kippy nodded.

"What the hell is it doing here?" Batavia was a solid forty-minute drive from Chicago. And that's if the traffic's light. "Doesn't Saunders live downtown?"

Kippy nodded again and said, "According to the DMV."

"Well, what the hell?"

"I called him to see if he could view the video feed at Egg River after you let me know that Landvik was tied up for much of the day. Saunders was cheerful, agreeable, and personable. Then, later on, he's impossible to reach, isn't returning any of my calls, and his Ford Escape just so happens to be in Landvik's garage."

"So maybe Saunders sees something on the Egg River digital recording and makes the mistake of bringing it to Landvik's attention?"

"If he saw something, he should have called me," Kippy replied. "No offense, Mace, but if I trip over a video of you strangling a hitchhiker, I'm not driving over to get your version of what you did—I'm going to the cops."

"Fair enough, but I think Landvik is too bright to let video recordings like that sit around for two months at a pop."

Kippy stared around the yard and said, "Landvik tinkers with the videos, he manipulates them. Maybe he even deletes the entire day of the abduction."

"It's like that saying—*who watches the watchers.*"

"So then Jake Saunders comes along and notes a gap or a missing day—he's confused by it, probably freaking out because the request is coming from the police—and he brings it to his boss."

I added, "And now his Ford Escape is in his boss's garage."

"I've only been calling his cell phone, because that's the number on his card." Kippy tapped up Google on her phone, performed a search, found a phone number and tapped it. A moment later, she said, "Jake Saunders, please." Half a minute passed; I assumed she was being transferred. Then, she repeated, "Jake Saunders, please."

I watched as Kippy listened. Vira walked over and licked at her fingertips. Finally, Kippy said, "No, that's okay. It'll wait until he gets back."

"What's going on?"

"Jesus, Mace—the receptionist asked if I wanted to be transferred to his boss, transferred to Bernt Landvik?"

"Why?"

"Because Jake Saunders is out on personal leave until further notice."

CHAPTER 56

Everyman watched the scene from his iPhone as it unfolded before him in real time. And he didn't need subtitles to know what they were discussing. The lady cop had likely been trying to get in touch with Jake Saunders—unsuccessfully, what with cell reception being what it was at the bottom of The Pond—but they'd now discovered Saunders's SUV.

No big deal there. Nothing he couldn't talk his way out of. *Sure, Jake stopped by last night,* he could say, *he told me about his dad's turn for the worse, we had a few beers and talked about fathers and sons. Jake slept on the couch and I dropped him at the airport early this morning.*

All Everyman needed was five minutes in his rec room. Smash through the drywall, grab the waterproof-fireproof box containing his new identity—his next life—and be on his merry way. He'd let Nancy Drew and the Dog Man have their fun at his place and, as soon as they'd left, he'd head back to his Batavia farmhouse and . . . five minutes in the rec room and he'd be on his way.

But then Everyman spotted the dog—Mason Reid's golden retriever, Mason Reid's cadaver dog—the same mutt that had sniffed out Weston Davies at Gomsrud, the same mutt that had warned Reid of Everyman's presence among the pine trees, the same goddamned mutt that had gotten beyond the tear gas, that had trailed him, and watched as he scaled Knob Hill to make good his escape.

The Pond wasn't on his property. And The Pond was a third of a mile into the bog and the dirt and the weeds, but what if Reid let his dog go roaming?

Once the first diver surfaced, even the most civil libertarian of magistrates would break the sound barrier penning off a search warrant for everything.

Goddamnit.

Everyman saw red.

Blood fucking red.

If Reid and the bitch cop were in his office, he'd cut them with the ESEE-6—deep and quick. Then he'd rush into the cube farm, throwing himself at fellow staff members, at his own employees, stabbing at them until he was . . . somehow stopped. Corkscrews—long and sharp—twisted into his temples. Agony. Much worse than that night in Bridgeport when he watched as they hauled the kid out of Nicky Champine's rambler in a body bag.

Everyman dropped to his knees to keep from acting on his most basic nature. He squeezed his eyes shut, but the corkscrews continued their inward twist. And if there ever was a time for clear thinking, this was it.

Fuck it, he thought, got to his feet, and left the office.

"Hey Tommy B.," Everyman stood in the opening of his least-favorite employee's cube. Tommy's signature line on all his email was *Tommy B. Johnson* as though the Tommy B. compensated for having such a generic last name. "Can you help me load some computers into one of the vans?"

Tommy glanced up, looked as though he were contemplating Descartes's breakthrough in the fields of geometry and algebra, and finally nodded.

The two headed into Landvik's office. The arrogant nose-picking little prick, Everyman thought, spends all day rocking in his chair, feigning forward movement. Tommy B. Johnson contributed nothing—nothing of value, nothing at all—yet he was the kind of guy who'd stand up and take a bow at his own funeral. Yes, Tommy B. had proved to be completely worthless, Landvik's worst hiring decision by a country mile. And—as everyone knew, including Tommy B. himself—once hired, it was all but impossible to get rid of a government employee in the great state of Illinois.

Although . . . Everyman had some ideas.

Even though he'd utilized his position at IDOT to help supplement his *private* needs, he did take his work seriously. Not true for Tommy B.—not in the slightest—and, in a perfect world, Tommy B. would be forced to reimburse the Illinois Department of Transportation for every single penny the state had wasted on his salary and benefits since the do-nothing had been hired, up to and including extracting Tommy B.'s organs and selling them on the black market.

"The boxes are in the back," Everyman pointed Tommy toward his office closet. "We'll need to haul them down to the garage."

As Tommy B. approached the closet, Everyman closed his office door, twisted the blinds shut, grabbed a length of modular phone cable, and followed his subordinate.

"I don't see the boxes."

"Look in the corner," Everyman suggested.

Tommy bent down in incredulity, wondering what the hell his boss was talking about, and that was all the time Everyman needed. The phone cord looped around his subordinate's neck, tightening instantly, crushing Tommy B.'s larynx, asphyxiating the insignificant waste of oxygen. Everyman kneed Tommy B. in the back, dropping him to the floor. Face a boiling crimson, Tommy B. attempted to push up but Everyman shoved him down hard.

It was going quickly now, the point he'd come to know so perfectly. Everyman leaned into Tommy B., as though nibbling at the man's earlobe, and whispered, "Performance evals were a bit rushed this year, Tommy. I hope this will suffice."

When it was done, the red was gone—dissipated—along with Tommy B. Johnson's life, as though it'd never been.

Everyman felt a great release . . . and he was able to think clearly again.

He could now go kill the lady cop, the Dog Man, and the Dog Man's golden retriever.

And feed the trio to The Pond.

Everyman locked what remained of Tommy B. in his office closet. The janitors never cleaned in there anyway, not in all the years he'd been at IDOT. He'd take a second to shut down Tommy B.'s PC on his way out. It'd be as though Tommy B. had never shown up for work at all.

Damn that Tommy B.—coworkers would think, if they thought about their colleague at all—*he's always so undependable.*

Everyman slipped the ESEE-6 out from his duffel bag and into his jacket pocket, re-zipped the duffel, and placed it on his desk.

Then he called down to the garage to let them know he'd need an IDOT car—preferably the Subaru Forester—for an unexpected trip to their headquarters in Springfield.

And that he'd be leaving immediately.

CHAPTER 57

The three of us traipsed along the rear of Landvik's two-story, which, from the back appeared more like a three-story. As had been in the front, all curtains were shut and all drapes were pulled tightly together. Kippy climbed up the wooden steps of the deck and attempted to peer inside the sliding glass door, but instead shook her head. Kippy tried the door's handle, but that, too, was locked from inside.

Next, our modest search party hit Bernt Landvik's garden shed, a twelve-by-eight piece of rust on a concrete slab in a back corner of his property. It might have been shiny and new during Jimmy Carter's presidency but now appeared like the place where they hid the amputees in a bad horror movie.

I walked Vira around the shed's perimeter, watching to see if she caught hold of a scent.

No such luck.

"He's got a few stacks of those landscaping toppers," I called to Kippy. "You know, retaining wall caps."

A couple summers back, Paul Lewis had talked me into spending a series of weekends helping him construct a tiered garden and I had to lug a couple hundred of these heavy bastards into his backyard. I glanced around Bernt Landvik's yard, but saw no sign of tiered gardens or retaining walls or paved walkways. And why the heck would he only have the wall caps and no corresponding landscaping blocks?

Kippy's fortune fared better and the shed's metal doors slid open with a hair-curling screech.

We weren't able to liberate any amputees, but shrouding the shed's interior were an array of shovels and spades, hoes and rakes—none of which appeared to have seen heavy use—as well as bags of mulch and lawn fertilizer, and a gallon tank of weed killer. In the center of Landvik's shed, ironically, sat a John Deere lawn tractor, which the IDOT executive must utilize to mow his acre or four of grass.

I looked at the tractor and said, "You think he got a free green cap with the purchase?"

Kippy made no comment.

I noticed a couple of ice augers in the corner behind the tractor. "Landvik must ice fish."

Suddenly Vira began to bark. Somewhere along the line, while Kippy and I itemized Bernt Landvik's gardening supplies, my dog had slipped away. She now stood in the opposite corner of Landvik's backyard, pointing straight into the woods and marsh.

Vira turned back at us and barked once more.

My golden retriever didn't have to bark again.

I knew exactly what she was telling us.

Vira had caught the scent of death.

CHAPTER 58

Everyman pressed the Forester over eighty miles an hour on I-88 west as he raced to Batavia. The Subaru had Illinois Department of Transportation emblems on both side doors and, whether you mentioned it in polite company or not, the state police cut IDOT vehicles a great deal of slack regarding posted speed limits.

For the tenth time that day, Everyman wished he'd killed Nicky Champine that very first night or, better yet, had never gotten involved in Champine's amateur hour to begin with, but, at the time, he'd not wanted any attention drawn toward or a spotlight shined on any of IDOT's rest areas. He'd been updating the surveillance software at several of the facilities when he'd pulled into mile post 333 off I-57. He wasn't *on the hunt*—had, in fact, legitimately been carrying out his day job as Everyman took more pleasure working in the field than in piloting a desk—when he'd spotted the purse lying under a well-worn VW Cabrio. He assumed the owner had maybe struggled getting her children out and the purse had inadvertently gotten knocked below and forgotten. He'd even moved the IDOT repair van next to the VW so no one else would spot the purse and make off with it.

Ninety minutes later, when his work on the security update was complete, he'd hauled his dolly of equipment back to the van and damned if the VW Cabrio wasn't still there. Everyman packed the van, walked about the empty patch of grass containing picnic tables, checked the lobby, and then said *screw it*, got out his laptop and logged in.

Sure enough, he watched as a male abductor—all round eyed and openmouthed—grabbed a young woman in a full nelson as she returned from the ladies' room, and tossed her into the trunk of his puke-green Pontiac. It had taken the man all of five seconds. Everyman had to give the guy extra credit for speed and brutality, nevertheless, Everyman was able to maximize the video and acquire the abductor's license plate number. Five minutes later, compliments of the DMV—one of the many perks of his vocation, and the same manner in which he'd tracked Dog Man Reid per the plate number on his pickup truck—Everyman had Nicky Champine's name and home address.

That's how the entire sordid mess had begun.

And now Everyman raced to Batavia in order to finish it.

He kept one eye on I-88 and the other on his iPhone. He had two additional cameras—one on the roof of his house, one on the roof of his garage—that covered the span of his backyard. Dog Man Reid and Officer Gimm were currently fumble-fucking about his garden shed. But as they took notes on which fertilizers he used, what Everyman had anticipated came to fruition.

He glanced at the road and then watched as Reid's golden retriever slowly worked its way across his three backyard acres to the point where the woods and the wetlands began, to the point where Everyman's makeshift path began. He glanced at the road again and then watched as Dog Man and bitch cop suddenly turned toward the cadaver dog. Although at this distance he had no corresponding sound to go with the video feed, but it didn't matter. Everyman knew the golden's bark had alerted the two.

Had notified them that death lay this way.

Reid and the bitch cop began heading across his backyard lawn.

Everyman tossed his iPhone on the passenger seat and focused on the road ahead of him. He still had enough time. That goddamned dog could bark and point at The Pond all day long . . . but The Pond would not cough up its secrets that easily.

No—The Pond would demand divers or boats to drag what lay beneath.

There was plenty of time to put an end to this.

Everyman wished he'd not tossed his SIG 1911 into Lake Michigan as that would have hastened events along. He figured he'd feed the two a plausible scenario, tell them that Jake Saunders had been renting the farmhouse from him, had been doing so for the past year, and that he'd caught something on the Egg River digital—an eighty-minute gap in the period that Jake was supposed to have been reviewing. Jake had called in, something about taking an immediate leave of absence, and he'd driven out to Batavia to confront his employee. Of course, as a landlord he still had keys to the farmhouse, and if Saunders's car was in the garage, he felt obligated to go inside to check on Jake's well-being.

Everyman had to get them into the house.

There'd be no Jake at home, of course, but he'd set up his laptop and he'd show Nancy Drew and the solo Hardy boy the true feed from Egg River. They'd be fascinated—mesmerized—for a few moments as they'd note Jake's gap in the video feed.

It'd be the last thing they'd ever see.

As the Dog Man and bitch cop watched the footage, intently, not wanting to miss out on the moment they cracked the case wide open, he'd slip the ESEE-6 from his pocket and swivel—two throats in two seconds.

Everyman knew that nothing ever went off as planned, but if this did, Everyman would drop the blade as though it were a microphone, as though he were a winning contestant in a singing contest.

Then, after retrieving his new ID, Everyman would let Reid's dog inside on his way out.

CHAPTER 59

I slapped at the back of my neck as we followed Vira deep into the heart of the thicket. It was my twentieth confirmed kill in my skirmish against the unyielding swarm of mosquitoes that seemed to prefer the taste of my blood over Kippy's. It's too bad we'd taken her Malibu instead of my F-150 as I always had a can or two of Cutter insect repellent rolling about in the pickup's back seat.

Tricks of the trade.

Vira looked unfazed but she'd be on the receiving end of a serious tick check in the near future.

My hiking boots were a mess, but it didn't matter—this was my job and that's what I used them for. Kippy's newish pair of Brooks running shoes were muddied; she also didn't seem to mind. And whenever the path got overly messy or wet, someone—I'm going to put money on Bernt Landvik—had dropped a sheet or two of plywood to serve as a do-it-yourself bridge or stepway.

The undergrowth thinned as we rounded a corner and there in front of us sat Vira. She looked back from the muddy shore of an outsized and desolate-looking pond—near both an overturned rowboat and wheelbarrow—and patted her paw at the red muck beneath her feet.

What had begun as a partly sunny Friday morning had turned overcast—cloudy and gray. The pond appeared a pea soup of algae and blanketweed. And though the water appeared calm—its surface a smooth glass with scarcely a ripple—I found it to be uninviting and bleak. I knew well what Vira's pawing at the shoreline indicated.

"The missing travelers," Kippy said more to the thicket than to me. "Sometimes the cars appear later, but the travelers never do."

Vira walked a short distance—a little more than a yard—sat down, and again pawed at the mud. She stood once more, walked a few more feet, and pawed the ground. She looked back at us, walked into a slip of grass surrounding the water's edge and pawed again.

"Yes, Vira," I said. "Good girl. We know, Vira. We know."

"This is where he brought them." Kippy walked over to Vira, knelt down in the weeds, and gave our dog a hug. "Maybe they were still alive, maybe they were already dead, but this is where Landvik brought them."

I headed toward the overturned wheelbarrow and rowboat.

"Don't touch a thing, Mace," Kippy said. "It's a crime scene."

"The sheets of plywood over the muddy parts of the trail were for the wheelbarrow." I glanced around. "And he's got a bunch of those retaining wall caps out here by the boat."

"Bodies always rise, Mace," Kippy added. "The decay produces gas, they bloat up like balloons, and float to the surface."

"So he weighed them down."

"I imagine he did, but I suspect Landvik did a bit more. I think he punctured their chest cavities and their entrails with a knife in order to keep them down there . . . at the bottom," Kippy said and nodded toward the center of the pond. She turned to me. "That's why Vira kept tapping along the shoreline. He did so many, Mace. And it's in the soil."

"Jesus Christ." I looked across the patch of water. "Those augers in his shed weren't for ice fishing. They were so he could keep all this up year-round."

Kippy stood. "Let's get the hell out of here."

I didn't argue.

Kippy did five minutes with Detective Hanson on the trail back, making the detective realize what we'd found was a game-changer. He and Marr planned to dive straight into a car, siren it to Batavia, and work their magic to get a diver onsite as soon as possible. She did another minute with her partner, telling Officer Wabiszewski to keep his eyes trained on Landvik's BMW.

A few minutes after that we were at the corner of Landvik's property. We cut diagonally across his backyard, rounded the side of his house, and watched as an SUV with IDOT plates pulled down the gravel driveway and parked next to Kippy's Malibu.

Bernt Landvik stepped from the vehicle.

CHAPTER 60

Vira snarled. I stooped down, put a hand on the back of her neck, and connected the leash to her collar. "Shh, girl. We know."

Bernt Landvik stood on the cement walkway leading up to the foot of his porch. He held a laptop sleeve under one arm and keys in his other hand. Nonthreatening body language, though he did look surprised to see us.

"Is Jake home?" he said, turned, and began stepping toward his porch.

"Stop right there," Kippy said, cop's voice, no bullshit. She popped the Velcro on her olive green waist pack and slipped a hand inside.

Landvik turned back. "What the hell's going on?"

"Hanson and Marr are on their way," Kippy said. "And we're all going to wait right here until they arrive."

"Why?" Landvik looked confused, startled at the thinly veiled hostility. "What have you done with Jake?"

"Why would Saunders be here?" Kippy replied.

"Because it's his house," Landvik said matter-of-factly. "Jake's been renting it from me for over a year."

"Has he now?" Kippy's voice dripped sarcasm.

"Jake called in this morning to request an emergency leave of absence. He said his father was ill and he's flying out in the afternoon." Landvik tread backward toward the porch.

"Not another step," Kippy said, gun out now, pointed at center mass. Kippy's off-duty was a subcompact—a *Baby Glock*, she'd informed me after I riddled her with questions about her trendsetting fanny pack at the coffee shop.

Landvik's jaw dropped. He glanced from me to my visibly seething golden retriever and back to Kippy. "You're going to shoot me because I came here to ask Jake a question?"

"Not another step," Kippy repeated.

"I've got cameras everywhere, like we do at the rest stops." Landvik shrugged. "It'll be the world's shortest trial before you get life in prison."

That answered the question I'd been wondering; why would Landvik drive all the way downtown for work, and then turn around and race back in a different car?

Because we'd triggered the cameras.

"Look, I know why you're here," Landvik said. "And thank God the real detectives are on their way. They need to see the video feed. And so should you."

"What video?" I asked.

"Egg River." Landvik looked about the yard and said, "Jake's dealing with a family emergency so I spot-checked his section of the video feed right after I sent out those texts this morning. And guess what? There's a jump in time, more than a missing hour of footage at the Egg River facility. I damn near had a heart attack. No way could Jake miss something like that, so I came out to talk to him about it and find you guys here . . . and now you're pointing a gun at my chest."

"Get on your stomach with your hands on the back of your head," Kippy ordered.

"Sorry, dear, but I need to get inside and find out if Jake's okay." Landvik looked up at the decorative base of his porch light and said, "Officer Kippy Gimm has pulled a gun on me. She's threatened to shoot me twice so far," he glanced our way, "no, make that three times. As you can see I'm unarmed. Officer Gimm is on my rental property—she has not been invited, and she's here without a warrant or supervision." Landvik turned to Kippy. "The system has superb audio; at your hearing it'll be like a voice reaching out from the grave."

"Cute," Kippy replied. "I imagine it'll also show Jake Saunders coming over last night but never leaving."

Landvik said nothing.

The Mexican standoff continued. Vira snarled from the grass, her eyes never leaving the man from the Illinois Department of Transportation.

"Toss the keys on the porch and stand against the side railing," Kippy said finally. "Mr. Reid will be opening the door."

"As you wish." Landvik sighed and flipped the keys onto the porch deck.

He shuffled backward against the handrail—a right foot on the first step, his left on the cement walkway—looking awkward with hands midway in the air and a laptop under an armpit. Kippy matched him move-for-move, a line dance of Landvik backing up while Kippy swung around, Baby Glock continually aimed at the IDOT executive's center mass. There'd be no chance of Kippy missing at this close a range, yet she was far enough back from Landvik that he couldn't strike out.

Vira and I detoured around Kippy's back as she kept her focus centered on Landvik. We arrived at the steps from her left side. Vira growled at Landvik. I clutched her leash tight as we took the three steps up to the porch deck.

"Stay, Vira," I said, wrapping her leash once around the handrail.

I kept my eyes on Landvik as I knelt to pick up the keys, then turned to the door, and rang the bell a string of times as if Jake Saunders had just gotten out of the bathtub and dried himself off since Kippy had last manhandled the front entrance.

Then I began sorting through the key chain.

"It's the one that's not a car key," Landvik offered.

Kippy asked him, "Any chance of you shutting up?"

"I don't know," he replied. "Turns out I'm a Chatty Cathy when someone has a gun pointed my way."

I popped the key in the dead bolt and gave it a twist, then did the same thing in the doorknob, swung the door inward several inches and peeked inside. The entryway had a staircase heading upstairs, but otherwise took a left into a fair-sized living room. No lights were on, no curtains open—the house was dark.

"Stay here," I said, not wanting to leave Kippy, but I hadn't tied off Vira's leash and knew she'd have Kippy's back if Landvik so much as blinked twice.

Plus, I knew I wouldn't be long.

"Jake," I said aloud, stepping into the house and borrowing Kippy's no-nonsense cop voice. "Jake Saunders, are you in the house?" I looked up the staircase and called, "Jake Saunders, the police are here and have arrested Bernt Landvik."

I heard a snort from behind, but ignored Landvik. Instead, I listened to the house for any telling creaks or steps or cries for help.

The house was dead.

I stepped into the murk of the living room before realizing I'd forgotten to flick on the light switch in the entryway. I crossed over into the dining room where a dejected wooden table and six lonely chairs lay in wait for a dinner party that would likely never arrive. I crossed over to the wall behind the dining table and fumbled with some cords before finding a thin chain that slid open the curtains, allowing natural light to flow in through the sliding glass door.

I stared out onto Bernt Landvik's second-story deck and off to the far corner of the man's property where the pathway to his pond commenced its many twists and turns. I then glanced about the main floor and realized why the dining room had seemed so abandoned. Opposite the table was a full-sized kitchen containing a spacious island and enough stools to seat a dozen—likely a remodel had been done somewhere along the ownership line.

Unlike Nicky Champine's rambler, Landvik's farmhouse was relatively modern . . . and amazingly tidy. There were no dishes stacked in the sink, no mail—opened or unopened—lying about, no forgotten mugs of coffee or empty cans of Dr Pepper waiting to be cleaned or tossed. His kitchen countertops glittered as though recently wiped. I even caught a whiff of cleansers.

Bernt Landvik ran a tight ship, perhaps obsessively so.

I looked at my watch as I passed back through the living room. I figured that Detectives Hanson and Marr would be at least ten minutes out, maybe more, hopefully less.

"There's nobody here," I told Kippy upon my return to the front porch.

CHAPTER 61

The bitch cop was hardcore—kill or be killed type. If he twitched funny or took a step in her direction, he'd be a dead man. The golden retriever was the secondary threat, with its incessant snarl in his direction—guttural—wishing her master hadn't forbidden her from attacking, from ripping him to shreds. Everyman was happy she stayed put at the top of the porch steps. Everyman was unhappy that the Dog Man had only looped the leash around the handrail instead of tying it off.

As for the Dog Man, Mason Reid was the wild card. Dog Man Reid had certainly proved brighter and more daring than his lot in life would suggest. Nevertheless, Dog Man was no soldier, no cop . . . and no killer. He had no weapon and, without his dogs, Reid would be dead long before he knew what hit him.

Everyman thought he had them beat until they rounded the corner of his farmhouse. It sure would have been nice to have his SIG 1911 on hand, but his new plan—Plan A—was to get the rifle from the cabinet in the basement and then lay in wait for the three of them as they strode out from the wetlands. He'd let them cross halfway through his backyard before putting a round through the center of the bitch cop's forehead—payback for all the trouble she'd caused him. Then he'd take out the golden retriever and, in conclusion, he'd shoot Mason Reid in the face. After that he'd get his new ID packet from the rec room wall, hit a nearby branch of Bernt Landvik's bank for the saving and checking withdrawals, and then take the IDOT Subaru a hundred miles in whatever direction before dumping it.

But as he gunned the Forester down the county road leading to his gravel driveway, he'd peeked at his iPhone and saw the three of them stepping out from the woods.

Fuck.

Plan B—his original plan—was to bullshit his way into the farmhouse. Everyman knew the layout of the rooms; their individual twists and turns . . . he knew their blind spots, he knew where weapons lay. If he could get the two of them into the house—optimistically without the mutt—he'd kill them quickly. He had to, what with a cavalry of detectives and divers and the lady cop's muscle-bound partner on their way, he wouldn't have a moment to spare.

He knew he should be terrified, but instead Everyman felt . . . exhilarated.

"My arm's fallen asleep," Everyman told the bitch cop. "I fear I may drop my laptop."

"Tough shit," Officer Gimm replied.

Everyman looked forward to killing her.

CHAPTER 62

"You didn't check the entire house," Landvik said. "Jake may have hurt himself in one of the upstairs rooms?"

"He never shuts up," Kippy said to me. "Plus, I'm an idiot."

"Why?"

"As soon as we get him into a chair, you call 911," she replied. "Get Batavia PD out here ASAP, no more screwing around."

"Excellent idea," Landvik said and smiled. "Chief Eullen and I go way back."

"Let's have you back up into the living room, Mace," Kippy instructed. "Stay out of his reach, but be ready to kick him in the nuts if he tries anything."

"That's hardly sporting," Landvik replied.

I backed up until I was a few steps from the dining room table and watched as Kippy marched Landvik inside the home he claimed was now rented by Jake Saunders. I realized a mistake had been made as soon as the screen door slammed shut behind Kippy.

Vira had been stranded outside.

"I'm going to put the laptop on the table and then I'm going to sit down," Landvik said as he crossed the living room toward the dining room table. "Okay?"

Kippy made no comment but her Baby Glock spoke volumes as it tracked his every movement.

Bernt Landvik studied Kippy as he slowly pulled the laptop

sleeve from under his armpit and placed it on the dining room table. He shook his arm as though to wake it from hibernation and then, like a professor about to begin the morning lecture, began unzipping the sleeve.

"Mace," Kippy shouted.

Immediately I knew what she meant.

Danger—do not let Landvik reach into the case.

The second mistake was on me . . . because that's when I crossed between them, stretching forward to take hold of the laptop case. I was only stuck between the two of them for an instant—blocking Kippy's line of sight—but it was all Landvik needed, all Landvik had been waiting for.

He threw himself into the kitchen.

CHAPTER 63

Everyman kept a poker face as his wish came true. They'd left Dog Man Reid's pissed-off golden retriever on the ineffectual side of the screen door. And unless the damned mutt evolved opposable thumbs in the next few minutes, there was only one real threat left . . . the bitch with the gun. He'd have to work fast because at any second Reid would scurry back to the front door, let his dog in, and restore the imbalance of power.

Businesslike, Everyman walked to the dining room table. At the table he made a big production out of laying down the laptop, shaking the cobwebs out of his left arm—a pinched nerve or something—and then began unzipping the laptop's case as though it were the most natural thing for him to do, just another day at the office. He deserved an Oscar nomination for his performance, at least a Golden Globe.

As theater people say, Everyman was "in the moment."

He'd already glanced in the kitchen and there it was, as though it were waiting for him, the handle of the cast-iron skillet—the 12.5-inch flat-bottom cast-iron skillet that weighed damn near ten pounds—jutted out over the oven, almost begging to be used. And use it he would. He'd scrubbed it with bleach the night before, even tossed it in the dishwasher for good measure.

The skillet had certainly done the trick with Jake Saunders. The lady cop would expect Bernt Landvik to run and come rushing after him. But running was the last thing on Everyman's mind.

As he began unzipping the laptop sleeve, the cop went ballistic, as expected, and, as expected, Dog Man Reid reached for the laptop case, his body crossing in front of Officer Gimm . . . and Everyman dived into the kitchen . . . he dived for the cast-iron skillet.

CHAPTER 64

Kippy lunged for the corner, spinning around the kitchen wall blocking her from Landvik. He grabbed at a skillet off the oven, swung it in a blur of motion, forehanding it like a tennis pro. Her Baby Glock swept across the kitchen, beginning to center on Landvik . . . but Kippy was too late.

And Bernt Landvik won.

The flat bottom of the skillet smashed Kippy's two-handed grip into the refrigerator with a bone-crunching thud. The Glock dropped to the floor and Landvik was on her, kicking the pistol into the dining room, jabbing her hard in the chest with a fist, sending her ass over teakettle.

I stepped in front of the man, threw a right hook that rolled off his forehead, a left fist that scraped his cheek. Something snapped inside me and this fucker was going to pay for what he'd just done to Kippy. Shards of pain shot through my left side as though my recent wound had been poked with a cattle prod, but I'd worry about that later. My shoulder blocked Landvik from leveraging the skillet, which he surrendered to the floor. I didn't know much about boxing, but had grown up with two brothers—had gone at it with each of them while growing up—and that had to count for something.

I threw all I had into an uppercut that skimmed against Landvik's ear. The man knew defensive moves and parries, but he dropped his right hand and I charged with everything I had. A left smashed into his ribs.

Landvik grimaced and I knew that one struck home.

Somewhere in the background was Vira yowling, wild and fierce on the porch, unable to get into the mix. I threw another right that glanced off Landvik's chin . . . but all of a sudden he was walking past me, heading into the dining room, heading toward Kippy.

I felt I'd somehow been dismissed—unceremoniously dropped from the high school team—but soon discovered I had trouble moving.

For some reason I'd been short-circuited.

CHAPTER 65

Everyman went into Muhammad Ali's classic rope-a-dope, falling back and dropping the skillet, giving Mason Reid the apparent upper hand, drawing him in, making him pounce closer until Reid was on him like wallpaper. Everyman saw the confidence grow in the younger man's eyes. Dog Man Reid was, after all, taller and heavier, and what Reid's blows lacked in form, they made up for in power.

Everyman rolled off some punches and took a solid hit to the ribs—it hurt—as he slipped the ESEE-6 out of his jacket pocket. Then, like the master surgeon he could have been, Everyman slid the knife into Reid's lower abdomen, below the Dog Man's navel—saw the disconnect flicker through Reid's eyes—and then stepped around him as though Reid were nothing more than an aged pedestrian on a crowded street corner.

Everyman left the ESEE-6 protruding out of Dog Man's gut.

He would come back for Reid—if there was anything left for him to come back to—but for now he had a cop to kill. And Everyman needed to move fast since Officer Gimm had recovered from her fall and even though one of her hands was red with a couple fingers misshapen, jutting sideways at impossible angles, she was going for the gun.

CHAPTER 66

I staggered backward into the dining room, had trouble thinking, and wondered what the hell was going on. Why wasn't my body functioning properly? If I'd been knocked out, why wasn't I on the floor? I then glanced down and spotted the brutal-looking handle of a brutal-looking knife sticking out of my stomach. I was stunned, at a loss, had no idea how that had occurred or what it was doing there . . . or why my blood appeared to be trickling down my legs and onto the floor.

Kippy had retrieved the handgun, a difficult task since her left hand was crimson, two of her fingers crooked in unworkable positions. She was rising, but Landvik was on her.

I heard Vira, now somehow on the back deck—going apeshit, calling for me—throwing herself against the sliding glass door. She must have rocketed about the house, leapt up the wooden steps, and here she was, trying to break in. Our roles suddenly reversed, Vira now issuing commands.

And though I could barely remember my name, I read my golden loud and clear.

Get . . . Me . . . In . . .

I stumbled toward her, hitting the doorframe with a shoulder, listening to Vira's upheaval as though she were miles away instead of inches. I slipped the latch and shoved. Didn't budge, not an inch. No sawed-off hockey stick in the door track like I have, but spotted a foot bolt—like what my parents have—built into the bottom rail. Step down on bolt to lock, press side knob inward to pop free. Convenient as hell—easy-peasy for those on the run—but today it was Everest in a blizzard.

I stepped forward on limbs of rubber and pressed the tip of my boot against the release. The security bolt popped open but my legs gave out and I began to tumble. I grabbed at the handle with both hands, and let my falling weight slide open Landvik's heavy glass door.

I was on my knees and then a sideways drop onto my ass, now watching Kippy battle Landvik—up-close, heated, a head-butt and elbows—but she was losing. I pawed at the screen door with my left hand, trying to glide it open, but it was a bridge too far. I had nothing left to give, and my fist dropped to the floor. A screen door stood between us—not much thicker than paper but the consequences could be no clearer. Vira smashed against it, and then smashed herself against it again. The screen thrust inward, a slash in the lower half, maybe six inches, and I knew she'd brought her teeth into play. My golden retriever backed up against the deck railing and threw herself forward.

I turned to Kippy. Landvik had wrestled the gun from her broken hands, and he was swinging it toward Kippy's face. She held tight to his wrist, a couple fingers still pointing in absurd directions, but it was a lost cause. The Baby Glock was inches from her face and closing fast.

Then a ripping sound as the screen split open—a violent emancipation—and Vira burst into the household. She shot across the dining room, suddenly hanging from Landvik's wrist—his gun hand. My golden had gone full pit bull—sixty pounds of clawing and scraping and twisting and wriggling—a tornado that bites.

It was no match.

The Glock fell to the floor a second time and Kippy went for it.

Landvik shook Vira loose, blood flowing off his arm. He kicked at Vira, realized Kippy now had the gun, spun about and shot for the screen door that Vira had just broken through.

With Vira on his ass, Landvik hurdled the deck rail, dropped ten feet to the ground and tore off at a sprint across his yard. He was heading toward the corner of his lot, heading toward his hidden pathway—his death trail.

Vira leapt down the deck stairs, now hot on his heels.

I started to sag, but bobbed back up as Kippy followed Landvik through the screen, stopped at the rail, aimed the Baby Glock with her right hand only—steadied on the forearm of her wounded limb—and shrieked, "Vira!"

I'd turned my head sideways and watched through the deck slats as my golden screeched to a halt. A split second later Kippy shot, and then shot again and again. I have no idea which shot hit Bernt Landvik, but there was a sparkle of pink mist. Landvik sputtered a step but kept on running, so I figured a glancing blow.

Vira was back on his heels . . . barking and biting at him, barking and biting.

I blinked and Kippy was next to me. Her eyes moist and telling me to *stay with her*, to *stay with her*. I blinked again and there was Hanson and Marr, looking concerned, and a team of paramedics setting down their gear.

And then everything went dark.

CHAPTER 67

Everyman raced through the brambles and dirt and muck, sometimes successfully scuttling across plywood that had been laid down, more often misunderstanding their worth.

That's how he lost both of his dress shoes to the mud.

He touched the side of his head, where something he didn't understand had occurred. His fingers slid in the blood along the exposed bone . . . and something else, but he could make no sense of it.

He was no longer Everyman or Bernt Landvik or whatever other names he'd lived under these past decades, but a simple organism scampering away on the most basic of instincts—flight—somehow intuiting he was the prey in this particular scenario.

A creature was behind him. And gaining. He could hear it growl and snarl, and if he slowed for even a second, he felt the teeth—nipping at his calves and thighs and arms.

If Everyman were still with him, he'd know that he was being guided someplace from behind, that he was being shepherded to a destination.

But Everyman was gone.

Everyman was dead.

And he didn't dare turn around.

He didn't dare.

And so he ran into The Pond. And he kept running until the

muddy bottom caused him to stumble and trip to his knees. He sucked in air and stared forward into the gloom.

He had a final thought or, to be more accurate, a final intuition.

He knew this place.

He thought it might be home.

And then he fell forward and sunk beneath the surface.

CHAPTER 68

Vira sat on a thin strip of grass along the shoreline, away from the red muck.

It didn't take long for the man she'd chased there to sink to his knees in the shallows, waist deep in the weeds and algae.

Not long after that the man slumped forward into the green waters.

Not long after that the bubbles stopped.

Not long after that Vira turned and headed back to the farmhouse.

CHAPTER 69

TWO WEEKS LATER

I was rushed to Northwestern Medicine Delnor Hospital in Geneva, where I had emergency surgery to stop the bleeding and fix the damage done to my large intestine. The doctors informed me later that I'd lost nearly twenty percent of my total blood volume. It would have been more had I not received first aid at the scene—thank you, Officer Kippy Gimm. My second day at Northwestern Medicine, additional surgery was required to remove an inflamed appendix.

I've taken to referring to the web of scars about my abdomen as *the Caesarean*.

Kippy had two dislocated fingers treated at the hospital, one of which she'd popped back into place herself in Bernt Landvik's dining room as she scuttled between making phone calls while applying pressure with kitchen towels to yours truly. Her left hand had taken the brunt of Landvik's cast-iron skillet. Kippy had a couple dozen stitches to show for it as well as an updated tetanus shot.

I somehow managed to keep my mouth shut for a change, but did find myself thinking that even Kippy's bandaged paw looked kind of cute.

That first night she stopped by to see me and sit in my room a spell. I have no memory of Kippy's visit but she claims that, though the TV was off and the remote control lay on a nearby tray, I had an intense concern over the whereabouts of the clicker—which I slurred on about nonstop—up to and including accusing her of having taken it.

I thought she might have been confusing me with Sue.

The next day, a few hours after my appendectomy, Kippy stopped by again and we had a vaguely more coherent chat.

Kippy had initially been damned with faint praise by the powers that be at the Albany Park District Precinct. Her captain felt she should have had Landvik on the ground, in cuffs, as soon as he stepped out from the IDOT vehicle, but—in her defense—Kippy was off duty, on the suspect's property on *unofficial* business, had no warrant or solid proof at that point in time that a crime had been committed. She'd also had no backup except the idiot dog trainer who crossed in front of her and gave Bernt Landvik a final chance to kill.

Plus, Kippy was right to stay out of Landvik's reach. Her captain was wrong. I suspect if she'd attempted to place Landvik in handcuffs, she'd have been the one sporting the wrong side of the commando knife instead of me.

Fortunately, Detectives Hanson and Marr provided Kippy with their highest accolades in both police reports and press interviews. And they'd personally informed her Albany Park captain that—yes—Officer Gimm had been working with them in her downtime and was keeping them apprised every step of the way regarding her theory on how this rash of disappearances was somehow related to the rest stop facilities along the Illinois interstate highways.

Soon after—when they began hauling body after body out of Bernt Landvik's pond—the damnation via faint praise came to an abrupt halt.

If I ran the circus, she'd be first in line for a promotion. Hopefully, there are some great minds at CPD that think alike.

Both Hanson and Marr stopped by a half week into my eight-day holiday at Northwestern Medicine Delnor. Detective Hanson, of course, brought with him a Canadian bacon and pineapple pizza. After two days of a liquid diet and two more of what the hospital deemed I should be eating, I wolfed down the single slice the floor nurse allowed me to consume and swore to the CPD detective I'd never badmouth Hawaiians again.

"You should have seen the look on the diver's face after he swam back to shore," Marr told me. "White as hell—he said it was a graveyard down there."

Not long after, the nurse chased them away so I could get some rest. Hanson picked up the half-filled pizza box and said, "Your girlfriend put one in the side of Landvik's head."

"She's not my girlfriend."

"Like I keep telling you, that's a damn shame." Hanson stared off into space and said, "Her bullet took out more than a piece of Landvik's skull. The medical examiner can't figure out how he made it to the pond."

"Of course he did have Vira on his ass."

"Vira the vigilante," the detective said and chuckled. "She's playful, gentle around children, but if she finds out you've hurt someone . . . you'd best be on the next train out of town." Hanson looked at me. "You ever going to go back to training dogs, Reid? And leave the serial killers for us?"

I lay in my hospital bed those eight days and nights, staring up at the ceiling tile, and wondering why Landvik let me live, why he didn't kill me outright. It would have taken him an eighth of a second to yank his commando knife upward. Then I'd have never made it to the sliding glass door, much less open it for Vira to get in. And it wouldn't have slowed him down one iota on his way to deal with Kippy Gimm.

But I suspect I knew why.

Bernt Landvik or whoever the hell he really was—CPD was still trying to piece his true identity together—wanted me to witness him blowing Kippy's brains out. Then he wanted me to witness him shooting Vira.

Then, and only then, he'd come over and finish me off or leave me to bleed out.

Once again I owed Kippy and her partner the highest debt of gratitude for taking care of the girls and Sue while I was laid up at Northwestern Medicine Delnor. They were able to caravan the gang from the safe house in Park Forest back to my trailer home in Lansing. They were then able to hook up with Paul Lewis and his team as well as with Dick Weech—my always-reliable neighbor from down the street—to figure out times for feeding and walks and time in the yard and tucking them in at night.

When I was finally able to return home, the kids mobbed me as though I were a rock star on tour. I wasn't able to roughhouse, but I rubbed heads and tossed Milk-Bones. I even showed Sue my scars. He nodded in what I took to be genuine approval.

I then sat on the floor with an arm around my golden retriever a long while before saying, "There aren't enough Milk-Bones or pretzels in the world for me to thank you, Vira."

She looked at me as though it were no big deal, gave my elbow a poke with a wet nose, and headed off to see what trouble Maggie and Delta were getting into.

Hard to believe I'd made it through nearly three decades of life only to be shot and stabbed over the course of the same month.

But I'm a cup-half-full kind of guy . . . I got to meet Kippy Gimm.

And today was a special day.

Kippy was coming over to take the girls out for a walk as Sue—though in much improved condition himself—continued his boycott of walks and other mundane activity. I'm not positive, but I got the impression Sue wanted me to score him a subscription to *TV Guide*.

It was the first time Kippy had been over since I'd been home.

It would be great to see her again.

It was always great to see Kippy Gimm.

Perhaps we could compare scars.

Sue wasn't the only one to observe my *Kippy's coming over* routine this go-round. The four musketeers followed me about the house as I changed from a dress shirt to a casual shirt and then back into the original dress shirt, as I kept ducking into the bathroom to run a hand through my hair and put on more deodorant, as I made sure every dirty dish was in the dishwasher and all countertops were wiped clean, as I doused the kitchen and bathroom with Lysol.

The dogs knew something was up and when Kippy's Malibu finally pulled into my lot, the three girls got excited as they knew a walk was in their imminent future. Meanwhile, Sue sat at the top of the doorway steps, his back arched, and an *I told you so* glint in his eyes.

"I brought a frozen pizza," Kippy said as she stepped out of her car and held up a bag.

"Perfect."

"It's a Hawaiian."

"Why not," I said.

"I'm just messing with you," she replied. "Is sausage and black olive, okay? I don't do pepperoni."

"I love sausage."

I watched as Kippy petted, scratched, and spent time with each of the kids, both individually and jointly, even Sue—who discovered unconditional love in his heart for Kip as soon as she spooned a wad of peanut butter the size of the Sears Tower into his dinner bowl.

I tossed the pizza on the table and walked Kippy and the girls back outside.

"Hey," I said.

"What?"

There was a lump in my throat, but I soldiered on. "Vira was kind of wondering if you—you know—were still off guys?"

"I'm sure *she* was," Kippy replied. "It's been a crazy month, Mace, and the dust has yet to settle. To be honest, I don't know where I'm at." She held up the leashes for Delta, Maggie, and Vira—all three chomping at the bit to get the show on the road. "But I know one thing for certain—I'm game for a walk." She smiled and said, "Would you care to come along?"

I stared at Kippy's smile a moment longer and said, "I'll go get my leash."

Cindy Archer-Burton

JEFFREY B. BURTON is the author of *The Chessman* and *The Eulogist*. He is an active member of Mystery Writers of America, International Thriller Writers, and the Horror Writers Association, and lives in Saint Paul, Minnesota, with his family.